THE NEW BOY

'Why don't you like Donovan?' asked Amy.

'I just don't ' said Cynthia.

'But why?'

'He's a nuisance. He makes trouble. And he don't look you in the face.'

'You liked him first,' said Amy. 'And the gang.'

'I changed my mind.'

'I think he's coming,' said Amy.

'You've gone all red,' said Cynthia.

Donovan swaggered up. 'I got a lot more kids for the gang,' he said. 'Tomorrow afternoon, right?' His tone was very offhand.

'You didn't ought to let him speak to you like that,' said Cynthia.

'I don't mind' said Amy miserably.

'You only say that because you love him.'

Also available in Red Fox by Ruth Thomas

The Runaways
The Class that Went Wild
The Secret
Guilty!
Hideaway

THE NEW BOY

Ruth Thomas

RED FOX

A Red Fox Book
Published by Random House Children's Books
20 Vauxhall Bridge Road, London SW1V 2SA

A division of Random House UK Ltd
London Melbourne Sydney Auckland
Johannesburg and agencies throughout the world

First published by Hutchinson Children's Books 1989
Red Fox edition 1990

5 7 9 10 8 6 4

© Ruth Thomas 1989

This book is sold subject to the condition that it shall not,
by way of trade or otherwise, be lent, resold, hired out, or
otherwise circulated without the publisher's prior consent in
any form of binding or cover other than that in which it is
published and without a similar condition including this
condition being imposed on the subsequent purchaser.

The right of Ruth Thomas to be identified as the author of
this work has been asserted by him in accordance with the
Copyright, Designs and Patents Act, 1988.

Printed and bound in Great Britain by
Cox & Wyman Ltd, Reading, Berkshire

RANDOM HOUSE UK Limited Reg. No. 954009

Papers used by Random House UK Limited
are natural, recyclable products made from wood grown in
sustainable forests. The manufacturing processes conform to
the environmental regulations of the country of origin.

ISBN 0 09 973410 9

To the children and staff of
Princess Frederica School

1

Thief

Amy turned her head, briefly, to peep at the new boy. He really was very good-looking, she thought. Neither black nor white, but something in between; curly black hair, skin the colour of milky coffee, and dark, secretive eyes. Amy glanced again, and then her cheeks flushed scarlet because Donovan was looking at her, she thought, and it was embarrassing to be caught showing interest.

At least Cynthia hadn't seen, thank goodness. In the other half of their double desk, Cynthia was very busy fuss-potting as usual. The black head, short tight braids sticking up all over, was propping up her desk lid, and she was complaining quite loudly. 'Where's my felt-tips? I can't find my felt-tips.'

'But you don't need them now Cynthia,' said Miss Elliot. '*Please*. I mean, you're supposed to be listening.'

'All right, Miss Elliot,' said Cynthia. 'Sorry, Miss Elliot. I can't find them though. Somebody thiefed them.'

'Oh Cynthia, I'm *sure* not,' said Miss Elliot, in her rusty-saw voice. And then the nice smile trembled, and the eyes behind the big glasses began to blink, as they always did when Miss Elliot was specially worried or nervous. 'They'll turn up, they'll turn up,' she insisted, and the funny little voice went squeaking on, in a troubled sort of way, about adjectives or something.

1

Amy frowned disapprovingly at Cynthia for interrupting Miss Elliot, and then her mind slid away and
away into a fantasy, which had nothing to do with
adjectives but was all about Miss Elliot asking *her*,
Amy Baker, to look after the new boy. In reality Miss
Elliot had asked Kevin Riley to do it, and that was
why Donovan was sharing a desk with Kevin now.
This couldn't be very nice for Donovan, since Kevin
had a perpetually runny nose, and was a bit smelly as
well. Being a kind class (as eleven-year olds go), 4E
were not actually nasty to Kevin for being smelly;
they just tended to leave him out of things. Miss
Elliot thought she was being cunning, of course,
putting the new boy with Kevin Riley. She thought
she was arranging for Kevin to have a friend at last,
but anyone could have told her *that* wasn't going to
work. No one ever stayed with Kevin once they had
found someone better.

Amy wondered and wondered about Donovan.
How quiet he was! He had hardly said a word in four
days; just 'yes Miss' and 'no Miss' quite politely
when Miss Elliot spoke to him. Otherwise he just sat
there, brooding and tense, watching the rest of the
class with narrowed eyes. . . .

'Take out your pencils and your writing books,'
said Miss Elliot. Amy was still in a trance, staring
into space, so Cynthia gave her a nudge. 'Come on
Amy, Miss is saying—'. There was a lot of shuffling,
and banging of desk lids. Amy smiled dreamily, and
prepared to open hers.

'My 50p's missing! It's missing, it's not there!'
Everyone turned to look at Bharat, who was calling
out.

'Where's my crisps?' said Andrew.

2

'I had a apple – it's gone!' That was Hansa.

'And my felt-tips you know,' said Cynthia. 'Don't forget my felt-tips. I told you, didn't I, Miss Elliot? I did tell you. There's a thief around.'

Miss Elliot was very upset. 'Oh no!' she kept saying. 'Oh *no*! He *promised* – I mean, it just can't be.' Her eyes blinked and she looked all flustered. 'I don't know what to do,' she said. 'I don't know what to do.'

Miss Elliot was very young, and very new to teaching. She was a little person, not quite as tall as some of the children in her class. And she was very, very untidy; always in a muddle over something or other. She often had her cardigan on inside out, for instance, and Class 4E had to tell her about it. Or she mislaid important papers and Class 4E had to find them for her. They looked after her well because she was their teacher, and their responsibility, and they loved her very much.

'You should tell everyone to empty their pockets Miss Elliot,' said Cynthia, who always had plenty of ideas about what other people ought to do. 'That's the best, you know, and take their shoes off.'

'Wait a minute.' Miss Elliot hesitated. 'Let's . . . no, wait a minute . . . let's . . . *I* know, let's see if the things have got into the wrong desk by mistake. Everyone look now.'

By *mistake*? This was just one of Miss Elliot's unclever ideas – a trick, so they wouldn't think they were being searched. Who did Miss Elliot think she was fooling?

Amiably, to please their teacher, Class 4E opened their desks anyway, and scrabbled through the contents. Amy lifted her desk lid to be the same as the rest – and shut it again in horror! She went very red, and then pale, until the freckles stood out on a dead-white face, framed by silky, flame-coloured curls.

'Look properly everybody,' said Cynthia. '*You* didn't look properly,' she told Amy.

'Yes I did,' said Amy, faintly.

'No you never – let me.'

'NO' Amy leaned both arms on her desk, and wouldn't look at Cynthia.

'You're hiding something,' said Cynthia.

'No I'm not.'

'Yes you are. You look all guilty. You got something in that desk you don't want anybody to see.'

'I haven't,' said Amy.

'Is it love letters?'

'Course it isn't.'

'I bet it is,' said Cynthia. 'Miss Elliot – Amy got love letters in her desk!'

Miss Elliot did not seem to be interested in Amy's love letters. She was twitching around at the back of the class, hovering near Kevin Riley for some reason. Her blouse and skirt had parted company at the waist, and the straggly hairstyle was all messy, where Miss Elliot had ruffled and pulled at it.

'Shut up,' said Amy, to Cynthia. Cynthia was Amy's best friend, but she could be really annoying at times. 'Leave me alone,' said Amy fiercely.

'Temper, temper,' teased Cynthia. 'Come on, you lot,' she invited the other girls in her group. 'Let's all have a look at Amy's love letters.'

Faces loomed from all directions, all giggling, all black. An octopus of arms, with clutching hands on the ends of them, invaded Amy's space and in spite of her struggles prised open the desk. On top of the neat

4

pile of books was – an apple, a packet of potato crisps, and Cynthia's felt-tipped pens.

There was a shocked, bewildered silence. Even Cynthia, for once, had nothing to say. 'I didn't think you was a thief, Amy,' said a girl called Gloria, at last.

'I'm not. Somebody must have put them there. They must.'

'Oh yeah—'

'*You* done it,' said Lorraine. She was a big, cheerful, good-natured girl, but her eyes had gone quite hard. 'We found the thief, Miss Elliot. It's Amy.

Miss Elliot scurried back to the front of the class, looking more upset than ever. The big glasses had slipped down her nose and she pushed them back, ramming them agitatedly against her forehead. There would be a big red mark on her forehead tomorrow.

'Somebody put them there,' said Amy, desperately.

'Of course,' said Miss Elliot. 'Of course they did. Oh come on girls, you *can't* think it was Amy. I mean you know Amy. You can't think that.'

'I think it was her,' said Lorraine. 'She knew those things was in her desk, she was hiding them.'

'I was scared,' said Amy.

'I bet,' said Lorraine.

'Listen—' Miss Elliot begged.

'You took them, Amy,' said Gloria. 'You know you did.' Gloria was the beauty of the class, slender and willowy, with the face of a dark brown angel.

'I didn't,' said Amy. 'I never took them, I never.'

'Yes you did, you was hiding them. She was hiding them, Miss Elliot. She wouldn't let us look.'

5

'Listen—' said Miss Elliot.

'That's right, that's right,' said Maxine. 'She wouldn't let us look.' Maxine wasn't very bright. To be strictly accurate she was a bit of a dunce, but even a dunce could see Amy Baker was guilty. 'She done it, Miss Elliot, she did!'

'Nobody believes me,' said Amy, in despair. She didn't cry, because she hardly ever cried, but she felt cold inside, and shrunk, as though all her feelings had curled themselves up into a tight little ball.

'*Please listen to me,*' said Miss Elliot, looking really distressed. 'Listen everybody . . . no, shush, shush, *listen* to me. . . . Who saw anyone near Amy's desk?'

Nobody.

'Coming into school then? Dinnertime perhaps? . . . Think, everybody, *please*. Please think. . . . Kevin, did you notice anybody?'

'No miss.' He was looking unhappy, but that was nothing new. His face was pale and mournful always, the mouth permanently gaping open because of his blocked nose.

'I'll have my felt-tips anyway,' said Cynthia, in a hurt voice. She snatched them back, and held up the other things. 'Whose apple? Whose crisps?' The owners claimed them.

'What about my 50p?' called out Bharat.

'Give him his 50p,' said Lorraine. 'Go on, Amy, give it to him.'

'I haven't got it,' said Amy. She heard herself saying that, but her own voice seemed to be coming from far away, because she herself was all shut up inside.

'Yes you have,' said Cynthia miserably. 'Don't make out.'

6

'I know what,' said Miss Elliot, 'we'll ask Mr Bassett to come!'

Oh yes, yes, thought Amy, in sudden relief. Mr Bassett would sort it out. Mr Bassett could sort *anything* out.

'Will you go, Gloria?' said Miss Elliot – but Gloria was tidying her desk all of a sudden, and seemed quite unable to hear Miss Elliot.

'Lorraine?' said Miss Elliot – but Lorraine was studying something very important on the floor.

'Mr Bassett's gone out anyway,' said Andrew.

Amy's hopes ebbed away. What did Mr Bassett want to go out for? He was always going out. It wasn't fair for the headmaster to go out all the time, to meetings and things. He ought to stay in school, so he could sort things out when people got into trouble for things they didn't do.

'Look,' said Miss Elliot, trying once more. 'Listen everyone. I mean *listen*. I mean, it would be nice if someone would *own up*. . . . Someone *very brave*. . . . No?'

'We don't need anyone to own up,' said Gloria. 'We found the thief already.'

'You're jumping to conclusions though,' said Miss Elliot. 'I mean, you shouldn't jump to conclusions so quickly. I mean . . .' She stopped and swallowed. It was as though she knew something she wasn't allowed to say.

'Why not?' said Lorraine, then squirmed uncomfortably, realizing she had been rude. 'Sorry, Miss Elliot, sorry.'

'Look – why don't we just get on with our work?' said Miss Elliot. 'Why don't we just forget all about it for now? Please everyone, please.'

As though they could. But to keep Miss Elliot happy they found pencils and settled down, after a fashion, to an English exercise about adjectives. And Miss Elliot began floundering about in the mounds of papers on her desk, twitching and blinking and sighing, and spoiling her forehead with her glasses.

Amy could not do the exercise. Her eyes would not even focus properly on the page. Her world had been so safe and happy, right up to this afternoon. So where had this nasty crack come from? How could her safe world get cracked up like this? Who had put those things in her desk, and why? And what was going to happen next?

The other girls were whispering about Amy while they did the exercise about adjectives. Cynthia, Lorraine, Gloria, Andrea and Maxine – all in a huddle with their heads together, across the group of desks. Amy knew they were whispering about her, and she pretended not to notice, but presently a folded piece of paper was pushed in front of her, and it was a note in printed letters. The note said 'WE WANT TO BE STILL YOUR FREND BUT YOU GOT TO GIVE BACK BARRETS MONEY. IF YOU DONT GIVE IT BACK WE WONT SPEAK TO YOU. SINED ALL THIS TABLE.'

But she couldn't give it back because she didn't have it. Withdrawn into herself, like a snail in its shell, Amy felt she wanted to die. Playtime was coming, and with it the ultimate horror, the ultimate disgrace. To be seen standing in the playground alone – conspicuous – without any friends! Let it rain, Amy prayed. Oh *please* let it rain so we don't have to go out. But the sky remained blue, and the early summer sunshine continued to slant heartlessly through the tall classroom windows. 'I've got a headache, Miss Elliot,' Amy pleaded, when the bell went.

Miss Elliot blinked, pushing aside the mounds of papers on her desk. 'Oh dear – yes, that – oh please let it drop,' she begged the other girls, understanding quite well why Amy didn't want to go out to play. 'Till Monday – leave it till Monday. Come on, *please*.'

'Why?' said Gloria. 'Amy got caught, didn't she?'

'But *she* didn't take – you'll see – Mr Bassett will know how to explain it – I mean you'll see . . . I mean, I'm *sure*.'

What was Miss Elliot on about? How could she be sure? She was just thinking muddled, as usual. Miss Elliot was a dear darling love but she was silly. 'You're my *best* teacher,' Lorraine declared fervently, as she did most days of the week. She gave Miss Elliot an affectionate hug, but didn't say anything about being friends with Amy again.

'You're *my* best teacher as well,' said Andrea, giggling because she was a bit simple, and kissing Miss Elliot on the cheek as she passed. All the group lavished kisses on Miss Elliot, all pointedly ignored Amy Baker.

'All right, Amy, you can stay in,' said Miss Elliot, her rusty-saw voice full of anguish. 'Mr Bassett will sort it out, you know. I mean – he will!' Silently and humbly, Miss Elliot begged Amy's forgiveness for not being clever enough to sort it out herself.

Amy was halfway down George Street when she remembered she hadn't collected Simon from the Infants. This frequently happened when Amy was in one of her dreams, but usually there was Cynthia to thump her on the back and say 'Wake up – what's missing?' Today there was no Cynthia; Amy was going home alone.

She must turn round, and go back, and run the gauntlet of the straggling groups of children along the pavement *again*. No one was speaking to her, but everyone must be looking. Amy kept her eyes down as she pushed past. A more observant child would have recognized her classmates by their shoes: Lorraine's plimsoles, Maxine's button-ups, Gloria's high heels. Only Donovan Grant, the new boy, could she positively identify from the scuffed toes kicking a stone against the wall.

Simon was fretful, cross at being kept waiting. He was only four and a half, and it was a long day for him anyway. 'Don't hold my hand so tight,' he whined.

'Come on then,' said Amy, dragging her brother along the pavement. Most of the children had gone by now, but Donovan was still there, still kicking his stone against the wall. He looked at her sideways, and Amy dropped her eyes. I suppose Donovan thinks I'm a thief as well, she thought. It's not fair, it's not fair!

'You're *hurting* me,' said Simon. He struggled and pulled, and stamped on Amy's feet to make her let go.

'All right, I won't hold it at all,' said Amy, losing patience. 'You keep on the pavement though.' She went into a dream about the real thief owning up. ('I was jealous of you Amy,' said the real thief, who had no clear face at that point. 'I put the things in your desk to get you in trouble, because I was jealous of you, because you're the beautifullest girl in the class. You're even beautifuller than Gloria, and you write good stories that Miss Elliot says she wishes she wrote herself.') 'That's all right,' said Amy nobly to

10

the thief. 'I forgive you.' And all the girls crowded round wanting to be her friend. And Donovan was watching, with his dark secret eyes. And then . . .)

There was a sudden scuffle behind her. A screech of car brakes in the city street, screams coming from somewhere, and a voice which called 'Hey you! Whatsyourname! Amy!'

It was Donovan. And he was holding Simon by the hand. And Simon was very white around the gills; shamefaced, as well.

For the second time that day, Amy was paralysed with horror. Of course she should have taken better care of Simon. Of course she knew Simon had a habit of wandering off the pavement. 'You nuisance!' she scolded him. 'What did I tell you? What did I tell you?'

Tired and confused and frightened, Simon began to bawl. Amy hugged him. She loved him dearly, when he wasn't being too maddening.

'You shouldn't go on at him, he's only a little baby,' said Donovan. He had an abrupt way of speaking, and his shirt, though clean, was rough and creased as though no one had bothered to iron it. It had two buttons missing as well.

'All right then,' said Amy, anxious to please.

'It's lucky I caught him in time,' said Donovan. 'You better hold his hand.'

'All right, I will.'

She looked gratefully, wonderingly at Donovan, and Donovan turned his head, avoiding her eyes. 'Don't let him go on the road again. Right?'

'No I won't, I won't.'

'I mean it, you know. . . . Shall I walk along with you a bit? Make sure?'

11

'If you like.' Amy's head swam. It was amazing, the way things changed sometimes. One minute horrible, the next minute lovely. Uninvited, Simon pushed his other hand into Donovan's, and the three of them walked along like that; Donovan and Amy with Simon between them, swinging on their hands.

'Don't do that Simon,' said Amy, for something to say.

'Ah – let him,' said Donovan. 'He's enjoying it, right?'

'We're nearly at my house,' said Amy. She felt shy and awkward and embarrassed. What was supposed to happen now?

'Can I come in?' said Donovan. 'Can I come to tea?'

Amy was quite overwhelmed. She tried to say he would be ever so welcome, but only managed 'What about your mum?'

'What about her?'

'My mum doesn't like it if I stay out long.'

'I don't live with my mum,' said Donovan. 'I live with my gran, right?'

'What about your gran then?'

'She don't mind what I do. Anyway she won't be in till six o'clock.'

'Oh.'

They crossed the hall, which smelled of cabbage and onions and old, unventilated house. A sour-looking crone, brandishing a stick, glared at them from an open doorway.

'What you staring at then?' said Donovan to the bad-tempered old thing, who muttered and thumped her stick.

'*Don't*,' said Amy anxiously. 'That's Downstairs. She's a terrible person.'

12

On the upper floor, Mum was laying the ironing in piles, all over the seats. 'Hello, who's this?'

'It's Donovan,' said Amy, proudly.

'No Cynthia today? . . . You wouldn't like to go to the shops for me, Amy, would you? Would you believe it, I forgot the bacon *again*, your dad'll kill me,' said Mum with a beaming face. 'Nah, it's all right though, I'll go myself, do me good. Seeing you got company. . . . You two go and watch the telly and keep an eye on Simon for me. . . . What happened to Cynthia then? . . . Cheerio, won't be long at the shops. There's a bottle of Coke, I think, and some biscuits if you're hungry. Don't let Simon stuff his face and spoil his tea. . . . Move the ironing off the chairs and you needn't laugh at your dad's pink shirts. Everything come out pink this time. Goodness knows what happened, something must have run. . . . Cynthia gone home on her own today? . . . Anyway he'll have to go to work in pink shirts next week. *Pink shirts*, he will look fetching! Like a bridesmaid, he'll *kill* me!' Mum's laughter bubbled and gurgled all the way down the stairs.

Amy was embarrassed about the ironing being all over the chairs in the front room. Normally she would not have noticed – would quite likely have seated herself on one of the piles without realizing it was there – but today was different. Today it was important to make a good impression.

'Your mum talks too much,' said Donovan.

'Oh,' said Amy. She was mortified to have a mum who talked too much.

'Amy, Amy, put the telly on,' nagged Simon, who was not allowed to touch the set himself. 'Amy, Amy,' he tugged at her skirts.

13

'All right, you little pest, wait a minute,' said Amy, who was still moving piles of pink ironing from the couch.

'Don't snap at him,' said Donovan, 'he's only little. Shall I do it?'

'If you like,' said Amy, mortified that she had made a bad impression. She hadn't meant to snap at Simon, it was only because she was embarrassed about the ironing.

The programme was for young children, and very babyish. 'Do we have to watch this stuff?' said Donovan.

'*Course* we don't,' said Amy, falling over herself with anxiety to please. 'What do you want to do then?'

'We could explore.'

'There isn't nowhere to explore.'

'I seen somewhere.'

'Where? Show me.'

'Out in the passage, right? Come and look.'

Amy followed Donovan and saw where he pointed. 'That's just the loft.'

'I know. There's interesting things in lofts. All sorts of junk and interesting things. Shall we see?'

'I don't know.' Amy was not at all adventurous herself. She had never been in the loft in her life. 'We don't go in our loft, hardly.'

'How do you get up?' said Donovan.

'I don't know.'

'You don't know much, do you?'

Amy swallowed. It was true – she didn't notice much of what went on around her. 'There's some steps in the cupboard,' she said, glad to be able to show she knew that much, at least.

'Which cupboard? This cupboard? *They're* no good, they ain't high enough. . . . Oh I see, I see, you got to stand on the shelves.'

The cupboard was directly under the trapdoor which led to the loft, and the shelves were cluttered and messy. Mum was going to sort them out one day, but meanwhile they were cluttered and messy. Amy was embarrassed again, and confused, and everything was moving too fast. Donovan had the trapdoor open already, and was hauling himself up, his feet neatly finding spaces among the jumble of odds and ends on the shelves. 'Come on then!'

'Me?'

'Yes, you! What's the matter, you crippled or something?'

'I'm scared.'

'Come *on*.'

Amy climbed the steps and took the hand Donovan held out to her. It was like something not really happening. Whatever was she doing, climbing into the loft with this boy? She was not a climbing sort of person, she never climbed anywhere. Her feet kicked out, knocking tins and bottles off the cupboard shelves. 'Look at all that mess,' said Amy, quite distressed.

'Don't matter for now,' said Donovan. His grip on her hand was so hard it hurt, and her knee scraped painfully against the trapdoor frame, as she was hauled into the dark unknown.

It was hard to see anything at first – only a tiny chink of light where a slate was missing off the roof. 'Careful,' said Donovan. 'Don't stand upright, you'll knock your head.'

There was a great wooden beam, low across the

opening. There was no floor in the loft, only rows of joists with spaces in between. 'Careful,' said Donovan. 'Don't put your feet in the spaces, you'll make a hole in the ceiling.'

Amy was terrified. She could hear the television chuntering away in the room beneath, and she imagined Simon looking up and seeing a leg with a wavering foot on the end of it, sticking through the ceiling. She imagined his screams, and her screams. 'It's all dirty too,' she said, recoiling. Amy hated to be dirty.

'Don't matter about the dirt,' said Donovan. 'It's a good place. It's secret. Didn't you never think you could have a secret place up here?'

'No.' Amy was quite ashamed that she had never thought of having a secret place in the loft.

'You said nobody comes up here, hardly. We could get some boards and make a floor, right? We could find some old chairs and things and make a camp, right? Then we could get some other kids in and have a gang. . . . Be good, eh? Who's the boss of the boys in our class?'

'I dunno,' said Amy. 'I don't think there is one.'

'Oh, good. I can be the boss of the gang then, and you can be the second boss.'

'I don't think I want to be a boss,' said Amy.

'All right,' said Donovan, sounding pleased, 'I'll be the second boss as well. . . . Why are you the only white girl in our class?'

'Am I?'

'Yeah you are – you mean to say you never noticed?'

'I didn't think about it,' said Amy.

'Anyway, they're all boring except for you,' said

16

Donovan. 'You write good stories, don't you? It was good when Miss made you read out your story. About the teacher who was really a Martian, and he had a extra pair of arms under his pullover. I liked that . . . . I like your hair too. You got nice hair.'

Amy was overcome with confusion. 'It's horrible hair,' she declared. 'I *hate* my hair.' That wasn't true at all; why had she said it? 'I suppose it's not bad,' she amended, afraid Donovan might change his mind about liking her hair if she said it was horrible. But Donovan was already crawling across the joists to where the roof was highest; he had lost interest in Amy and her hair. 'You can stand up here,' he called. 'We *could* have a camp, we *could*.'

Amy started to follow and stopped: she was still very nervous of slipping and putting her foot through the ceiling. She felt around with her hands and found various mysterious mounds and bundles, all covered with a thick layer of dust and grime. She tugged at damp bits of carpet, and plunged her arms into filthy cardboard boxes, leaning across the nearer ones to get to those further away. Clouds of dust rose from everything she touched. 'There might be stuff we could use here,' she said, desperately anxious that Donovan shouldn't decide she was boring after all. . . .

Mum's voice from below, rising shrilly into the gloom, did not sound pleased. 'What's going on then? What you doing up there?'

'Nothing,' said Amy, suddenly worried she was going to be in trouble.

'Funny sort of nothing I can see all over the floor here! You come on down, Miss, and explain yourself!'

Coming down was more frightening than going up. Amy's flailing legs knocked a cascade of household oddments from the shelves. 'Do you mind!' said Mum. Donovan came down after Amy. 'You look like a pair of chimley sweeps the both of you,' said Mum. 'You want to see yourselves! Whatever got into you, Amy? I can't believe it! Last thing I expected to see in my life, and that's the honest truth!'

Donovan looked away, uneasy and evasive now that Mum was back. 'I suppose you put her up to it,' Mum said to him. 'How d'you get her to climb them steps though? Fuss enough getting her to climb into bed one time! . . . All right, all right, I'm not cross. Do her good I daresay. . . . Do Miss Finicky-drawers good! . . . Is Donald staying to tea?'

'It's Donovan,' said Amy.

'Oh yeah, so it is. . . . You staying to tea then, Donovan?'

'No,' said Donovan. 'I got to go.' He shifted his weight from foot to foot, and turned his head again.

Amy was puzzled. 'But you said.'

'I changed my mind,' said Donovan. All of a sudden he couldn't get away fast enough. 'I changed my mind, right?'

'Donovan changed his mind.' said Amy. He had a right to, didn't he? Anyone could change their mind if they wanted to.

'I like Donovan,' said Simon. 'I like him more better than Amy.'

'You wait!' said Amy happily. 'You wait saying that, Simon Baker! You just wait till you hear the story I'm going to tell you when we're in bed. I'm going to put *you* in it. I'm going to have a witch with red eyes that come out on stalks so she can see round the corner. And she's going to make your nose grow. She's going to make it grow longer and longer, and all curly and twisty like a pig's tail. And. . . .'

'Go on,' shrieked Simon, in delicious terror. 'What else will happen to my nose? What else will happen to my nose?'

'You got to wait and see,' said Amy, hugging the joy inside her. Donovan *liked* her. He liked her hair, and how she wasn't boring. And he couldn't have believed all that about her stealing those things in school. And he saved Simon from going under the car. And they were going to make a secret place in the loft, perhaps. Oh Donovan Grant was lovely, he was lovely.

'I could have swore I put two pound coins by the telly,' said Mum in a puzzled voice. 'Now I can't find them anywhere!'

2

A dangerous escapade

Amy slept badly, a troubled sleep full of nightmares.
All through the night there were faces coming at her,
fingers pointing, voices screaming 'THIEF!' The faces
surged and receded, surged and receded; they were
Cynthia and Gloria and Lorraine, then all the class,
then dear Miss Elliot joining in as well. Then
Donovan, and that was *too* much. Amy woke, distraught, and lay awake a long time in the bunk bed she
shared with Simon, worrying about Monday, and
about being in the playground without any friends.

Then there was a banging on the front door, very
early in the morning, and Downstairs thumping with
her stick and screeching, couldn't they have any
peace in this house? Downstairs didn't like anybody
to have visitors, ever. And it was *Donovan*, standing
on the doorstep, looking sideways. Behind him, on
the pavement, was a rickety old pram, and on the
pram a pile of wooden planks. 'I found them,' said
Donovan, his eyes still avoiding hers. 'They're for our
camp, right?' Whatever had been troubling him
yesterday was apparently forgotten today.

Amy and Mum went to the bedroom to talk it over
with Dad. 'Amy wants to know if her and Darren can
make a camp in the loft,' said Mum, digging Dad in
the ribs. 'Go on, let them!'

'It's Donovan, actually,' said Amy, hurrying back
to the passage where he was waiting.

20

'Her and Donovan,' said Mum. 'They want to have a gang.'

'Oh, ah,' said Dad, who was trying to have a lie-in, seeing he was on late shift that day, and didn't need to get up.

'He's a nice boy,' said Mum. 'I think he's quite a nice boy.'

'Funny thing for Amy to want to do though,' said Dad. 'Don't sound like her at all.'

'Well, do her good,' said Mum. 'Put some go in her. Get her nose out of those everlasting story books. I like a good read myself, but she doesn't know when to stop! Get her a few more mates too. It's Cynthia, Cynthia, Cynthia all the time, nothing but *Cynthia*'.

'I like Cynthia,' said Dad. 'Anybody says anything against Cynthia got me to deal with.'

'I'm not saying anything against her. . . . Only what a gossip she is, and that's all I ever see her do! Jaw, jaw, jaw, wonder her tongue don't drop off! . . . Shut up, you, I know what you're thinking. I know I'm a chatterbox and I'll say it for you and save you the bother, but we're talking about Amy, not me, and you know as well as I do, Amy doesn't have enough friends and she doesn't have enough fun. Fun,' Mum repeated, digging Dad in the ribs again. 'I said, she doesn't have enough fun.'

'Are you going on like this all morning?' said Dad.

'Say yes then,' Mum nagged.

'All right,' said Dad, to get a bit of peace, and he turned over and went to sleep.

'Your dad says you can do it,' said Mum, with a beaming face, shuffling into the passage on slippered feet.

'*I* wanna come,' whined Simon.

21

'Shut up,' said Amy, terrified that Simon was going to spoil everything.

'Don't be nasty to him,' said Donovan. 'He's only little, he don't understand.'

'That's right,' agreed Mum, 'You tell her!'

'You be a good boy Simon,' said Donovan. 'You stay down here, right? And I'll buy you something to make up for it. Right?'

'A toy car?' said Simon hopefully.

'If you like,' said Donovan.

'They cost a lot of money,' said Amy.

'*I* got money,' said Donovan.

Mum was impressed. 'He's such a kind boy,' she told Dad, later on. 'Really generous!'

'I don't *always* go on at Simon,' said Amy in the loft, anxious that Donovan might be thinking she was a boring person after all, always going on at her little brother.

'Yeah, well, don't do it, right?'

'I won't do it any more,' said Amy humbly.

'I don't like to see people going on at little kids,' said Donovan.

'Have you got a little brother or sister then?'

'No.'

'Haven't you got a mum?' said Amy.

'Yes.'

'Have you got a dad?'

'Yes,' said Donovan. 'What d'you want to know for?'

'Well you live with your gran,' said Amy. 'Like you said.'

'Sometimes I live with my mum, sometimes I live with my gran, right? All depends.'

22

'All depends what?'

'If either of them wants me, innit?' said Donovan, his head turned away.

'Oh!' Amy couldn't imagine not being wanted. She couldn't grasp that idea at all.

'I don't care. Don't matter to me,' said Donovan.

'Oh.'

'I do what I like. It's good.'

'Oh . . . What school did you go to before then?'

'Norfolk Street.'

'Where's your gran's house then?'

'Kendell Road.'

'That's just *by* Norfolk Street. It's on the way to the park. Why did you change when you live just by it?'

''Cos I wanted to.'

'Really, just 'cos you wanted to?'

'You deaf or something? I changed 'cos I wanted to, right? It's a *horrible* school. Norfolk Street is a *horrible* school.'

'No, but – I do think it's a bit funny, you know, changing schools just for one term. I mean – we're fourth years, we're all going to change in September. I think it's funny, Donovan, why did you do that?'

'Stop keep on asking me a lot of questions!' The words were shouted, the voice thick with sudden rage. 'I said Norfolk Street is a horrible school and it is! Now shut up about why I changed.'

'All right up there?' called Dad, from the landing below, but no one answered him. Donovan was rocking on his haunches, the fist of one hand pounding into the palm of the other, his face all twisted up as though he were in pain. 'Have you got a stomachache?' said Amy, concerned, and a little bit frightened.

23

Donovan swallowed hard and shook his head.

'What's the matter then?'

'Banged my head, didn't I?'

'Oh,' said Amy, relieved that that was all it was.

'All right?' Dad repeated, his head poking through the trapdoor.

'Donovan banged his head,' said Amy.

'I'm not surprised,' said Dad. 'Can't see a dicky bird in here. Wait a minute.' He came back with a torch and some lengths of wire. 'Fix up a light for you.'

'We made the floor, see,' said Donovan. 'With the boards I brought.'

'Like a craftsman!' said Dad. 'You weren't at the back of the queue when the brains were given out, were you?'

Dad seemed to enjoy fiddling about with tools and wire. And when at last a glaring electric light bulb, with its very own switch, hung over the boarded area, Dad was *very* pleased with himself. 'It's a good light,' said Donovan, seeing that Dad had praised his floor.

'Don't you never smile, son?' said Dad.

Donovan smiled stiffly, not looking at Dad.

'Oh you do,' said Dad – but the smile was clearly not real, and Amy saw Dad give Donovan a funny look. Amy thought it was unreasonable of Dad to give Donovan a funny look just for not smiling properly. Donovan was probably shy. He would smile the same as everyone else when he got used to people, probably. Amy gave him a shy smile of her own to start him off, but he only looked the other way. That was it then – he was shy! That was why he shouted at her just now, probably.

'Look what I found, look what I found!' Donovan

called. He sounded pleased and eager, and Amy thought perhaps he hadn't really shouted at her at all before. Perhaps she just imagined it. That was right, she imagined it! 'Old curtains, see?' said Donovan. 'We can make walls for our camp. We can hang them up, see, and make walls! Be good, eh?'

Oh Donovan was lovely, he was *lovely*.

At twelve o'clock Mum shouted through the trapdoor to ask, wasn't Donald going home? Wasn't his mum expecting him for dinner?

'Nah,' said Donovan. 'Don't have dinner, Satur-days.'

'No dinner?'

'Nah – my gran goes down the market Saturdays. Has a cup of tea with her mates. She can't be bothered to make dinner.'

'But you'll be hungry,' said Amy, not under-standing at all.

'I don't care,' said Donovan. 'It don't bother me. . . . How about if I have dinner with you then?'

Amy was thrilled.

After dinner Donovan and Amy took Simon to the High Street.

'Aren't you going round Cynthia's?' said Mum. 'What's wrong then, you two fell out? . . . All right, I only asked!'

In the High Street, Donovan bought Simon a shiny new car. It cost over a pound. Donovan had two pounds and a 50p piece in his pocket. 'I like Donovan the best in the world,' said Simon.

On Sunday morning, very early, there was a pound-ing and banging again. 'It's supposed to be a day of rest!' screeched Downstairs, thumping on the ceiling with her stick. 'And your visitors supposed to ring the bell!'

'Shut up, misery-guts!' said Mum, with a wide grin. Downstairs was a sitting tenant and couldn't be asked to go, but Mum was quite brave about answering her back, particularly when Downstairs was too far away to hear.

Donovan was on the doorstep, wearing the same rough-dried shirt with the missing buttons. He had found a small chair, with broken springs, on a skip down the road. The chair was far from clean.

'You're not bringing that filthy old rubbish through my hall,' said Downstairs, scolding them from her doorway, and thumping her stick.

'Don't take no notice of her. Silly old cow,' said Donovan.

'It's not your hall, it's ours,' said Amy, to Downstairs. 'And it's not your filthy old rubbish either. It's *our* filthy old rubbish, so there!' What had got into her? She had never dared to speak like that before.

'Your mum wants to learn you some manners,' said Downstairs.

'I'm not scared of you,' said Amy untruthfully.

They struggled to get the chair into the loft. Dad kept giving Donovan funny looks; Amy felt uncomfortable with Dad giving Donovan funny looks just because he was too shy to smile properly. She was glad when Donovan said 'Let's go out now, and look for some more chairs.'

Donovan and Amy pushed the old pram up the sunny street. Amy kept looking at Donovan to see if he was smiling yet, but he wasn't. She wanted to ask him about something that was so important she was

26

afraid to say it. 'Donovan,' she said at last, in a small timid voice, 'you know Friday.'

'What about Friday?' said Donovan.

'I don't mean Friday in school,' said Amy hastily. 'I don't mean that. I mean Friday after school when Simon went off the pavement and you were there. I mean Friday then.'

'So?'

'But Kendell Road's the other way, over the railway. How come you were there, behind us?'

'I was following you, wasn't I? said Donovan.

'*What?*'

'You heard.'

'What were you following me for?' said Amy, trying to pretend she couldn't guess.

'You know.'

'No I don't. Tell me.' Her heart was pounding; she was afraid to push him really. 'Go on, you tell me.'

'I wanted to see where you live, right?' Donovan was looking the other way, punishing someone's hedge with his fist, ripping off large pieces and throwing them on the ground, to cover his awkwardness.

'*Oh!*' Amy thought she was going to burst. She thought she was going to burst with happiness. All in a rush, without meaning to, she said, 'You know in school, those things, I never took them, I never did!'

'I know,' said Donovan.

'You *know?*'

'I know you never took them.'

'How do you know?'

'I just know, right?'

'But *how?*'

'Don't ask stupid questions.'

'It's not stupid,' said Amy, puzzled.

'Yes it is, it's stupid. You're really stupid some-times, Amy Baker, do you know that, you're really stupid! And you ask stupid questions that get on people's nerves.'

Happiness drained away. Suddenly the bright morning sun only mocked. Hurt and bewildered, Amy trailed silently behind Donovan. What had happened now? She didn't understand it at all. It must be her fault; she must have done something wrong.

Donovan began to run with the pram and Amy called after him, 'Wait for me! Please Donovan, wait!' But Donovan ran faster, running and leaping with the pram, zig-zagging wildly along the pave-ment, crashing into walls and parked cars. 'Oh *wait*,' begged Amy.

There was a stitch in her side, and she couldn't catch up. She strained to grasp at her joy again, before it disappeared for ever round the corner, with Donovan and the pram. But round the corner, surprisingly, Donovan was waiting for her. 'You run too slow,' he said.

'Sorry,' said Amy humbly.

Donovan began to run again, purposely crashing the pram as he went. 'Oh careful!' Amy begged. 'Look, you scratched it, you scratched that car!' Her dad had a car, and she knew how upset he always got about dents and scratches – and Dad's car was only an old banger, always breaking down. 'You scratched that car, Donovan, and it's a *new* one!'

'Don't matter,' said Donovan. He wet one finger and rubbed it over the scratch, which was near the door handle. He tried the door, but it was securely locked.

'What you do that for?' said Amy uneasily.

'Nothing.'

Donovan gave the pram a push, and it went careering along the pavement by itself. With hands thus freed, Donovan tried the handles of the next car, and the next, and the one after that. 'What are you doing?' said Amy.

'Nothing. Just testing, right?' Donovan was all excited, tight like a wound-up spring.

'Leave them though,' said Amy fearfully. 'Somebody might see.'

'There's nobody here.' It was true. They were in a quiet street, several blocks from home, and not a person in sight.

'Looking out the windows then.' Something terrible was going to happen. She didn't know what, but the sense of disaster was all around, hanging in the air like a bad smell.

'They can't be bothered to look out the windows,' said Donovan. 'They're all in bed having their Sunday kip.'

'Leave them anyway, Donovan. You didn't ought to touch other people's things.' She shouldn't have said that. She knew immediately by the thundercloud on Donovan's face that she had made another mistake.

'Don't tell me what to do, right?' Donovan caught the pram, as it rolled back down the slight slope. 'You take it,' he said abruptly. Amy held the pram because Donovan said so, and watched with helpless dismay as he tried the doors of one car after another, along the road. Her dismay turned to panic when she saw, ahead of her, that Donovan actually had one of the car doors open. The car was bright red and shiny, as though its owner had just finished polishing it.

Donovan was smiling at last, and there was nothing very nice about Donovan's smile. Amy stood still.

'Come on,' said Donovan.

'What for?'

'Come *on*. . . . He left the keys, didn't he!'

'What?'

'You heard. Come *on*.'

Against her will, Amy's legs carried her forward. She was cold with apprehension, but she could not say no.

'Get in.'

'What?'

'Get in, I said.'

Amy got into the bright red car. The abandoned pram rolled backwards, and came to rest against someone's garden wall. Donovan was already in the driving seat, fiddling with the ignition key. What they were doing was madness. If the keys were in the car, the owner was not going to be more than a second or two away. Any moment now he would come out of his house, Amy thought, and catch them. The engine roared. 'You're not going to *drive* it, are you?' said Amy, horrified.

Donovan did not answer. His face was strangely alight; he was riding high on a wave of excitement that lifted him far beyond the reach of her words. With a great kangaroo leap, the car shot forwards.

Amy screamed. She thought they were going to crash into the car in front, but Donovan knew what he was doing. He wrenched the wheel round, and although they nearly crashed into the cars on the other side of the road, he managed to turn just in time. There were shouts from behind. Too late; the car was weaving along the street now, quite fast, and approaching the corner. 'Stop!' begged Amy, but Donovan did not hear her.

Donovan turned the corner. He forgot to slow down, or perhaps he didn't know how, and there was a sickening jolt as the nearside wheel mounted the kerb. Amy fell sideways, and Donovan thrust her back with his elbow. 'Keep over, stupid!' Donovan's elbow was sharply painful in Amy's ribs. She had a sudden silly thought that they ought to be wearing seat belts, and the thought was almost as worrying as the fact that Donovan was driving. She clung to the door handle, in case the car went on the pavement again.

They were gathering speed now – faster, faster, faster, still swerving all over the road. The engine was making a horrible noise. 'Look out!' Amy screamed. They had nearly hit an oncoming car, which scolded them with its horn, but didn't stop. No one had noticed that there was only an eleven-year-old boy at their wheel.

They were careering towards the traffic lights at the High Street. Green, green, green. Let them change, Amy prayed. Then Donovan will have to stop. Amber, then red! But Donovan did not brake; instead he rammed his foot harder, harder on the accelerator. The engine sounded terrible, but Amy felt they were going faster still, and again she screamed. She screamed and screamed as they shot the lights; and only because it was Sunday morning, with little traffic on the roads, did they get away with that!

'We going to have a accident, we going to have a accident! Don't make us have a accident!' Amy implored. Donovan made a right turn, much too fast and cutting the corner. There was a large van coming towards them, and they were on the wrong side of the road. Amy screamed once more. Donovan swerved to the left, but swerved too far. With another great jolt over the high kerb he mounted the pavement and – CRASH! With a terrifying jar the car slammed into a wall, and came to rest at last.

A police car siren wailed in the High Street behind them. 'Come on,' said Donovan, dragging Amy from the car. There was broken glass everywhere.

Some youths at the end of the road were looking; the police were coming, so it might be a robbery. If it was a robbery they would stay to watch. Otherwise, a car crashing into a wall was not particularly interesting. Some heads appeared at windows, and a woman with a warty face and a great hairy moustache leaned out. She had seen two kids, a black boy and a girl with red hair. She had seen them, quite distinctly, disappearing into the house down the road which was known to be a den of criminals, and she would tell the police so, when they arrived.

She had seen wrong. Donovan and Amy had not gone into the house of the criminals, they had gone between two terraced houses, and swiftly to the end of a short garden. With great difficulty, and much scraping of knees, Donovan had somehow hauled Amy over the back wall. If the criminals in their house had seen, they had decided to leave well enough alone, and pretend that they had not. Amy and Donovan dropped on to rough grass, and a train thundered past, deafeningly near. They were on the railway embankment.

They ran along, keeping close to garden walls and weed-clogged fences, out of sight of windows belonging to houses in the road they had come from. People from across the railway line might see them, but they would not know those two small running figures were wanted by the police. Amy had stopped thinking, she was too frightened to think. She just stumbled on after Donovan, her breath coming in painful gasps which hurt her chest.

Donovan kept stopping. He was running from house to house now, peering through fences, and leaping to see over walls. He was looking for a way out and Amy, who had been just terrified, began to be specifically terrified of having to climb another wall.

Were they being followed? Amy glanced fearfully behind her, but she could not see very far down the line because they had rounded a bend. They must have come a long way, which was not surprising since they had been running for ever. There had never been a time, it seemed, when Amy and Donovan had not been running along this railway embankment so they wouldn't get caught by the police.

There were some railings, with thick bushes in front, and a gap just visible through the bushes. Donovan pushed into the prickly bushes and peered through the gap to see if the coast was clear. There was a garden of sorts, with a big shed in the corner. The children crawled through the gap, one at a time, and squeezed behind the shed to hide. They had no idea what they were going to do next; there was no side entrance – the only way to the road was through the house.

Exhausted from the running, and the fear, bleeding from scratched faces and hands, they crouched in their hiding place and did not speak to one another. Amy had curled into a tight little ball. She glanced sideways at Donovan, but he was looking the other way. He was a terrible boy, she thought! Donovan Grant was a terrible boy, and she must have nothing more to do with him, ever! After today she would not even talk to him; she would forget that she had ever thought he was lovely.

Donovan was pounding one fist against his hunched-up knees, and rocking slightly. His face was tense and closed, his eyes narrowed to slits. Once or twice he took breath, as though about to say something, then let the breath out as though he had changed his mind. At last, not looking at her, he said to Amy's astonishment, 'Can we still have the camp then?'

'*What*?'

'Shush, whisper, someone will hear!'

'We're going to get caught anyway,' said Amy bitterly. 'We can't escape from here.'

'Yes we can, we can. I'll think of a way.'

'No we can't, we're going to get caught, and we're going to prison. And I'm never going to see my mum and dad again.'

'We're not going to prison. Kids don't go to prison. . . . Can we still have the camp then? And the gang? If we don't get caught?'

'Is that all you can think about?' said Amy.

'Not all,' said Donovan. 'It's not *all* I think about.' He took another deep breath. 'All right, I'll tell you what else I think about . . . I'm sorry I got you in trouble, right? All right? Satisfied?'

'Are you really?' said Amy. 'Are you really sorry?'

'Yeah, I am. I am sorry. . . . Can we then . . . still have the camp? . . . Please, Amy, *please*. . . . All right? . . . Can we?'

'I suppose so.' Well he said he was sorry. He did a terrible thing, but he did say he was sorry, didn't he!

'You're all right, you are,' said Donovan with a great sigh of relief. 'You're all right, Amy Baker. I like you.'

'Hush,' said Amy, warmed and thrilled. 'Somebody's coming.'

There were running footsteps, and high-pitched voices, coming from the other side of the shed. 'It's mine! Give it to me!' '*I* want it.' 'Give it to me, I'm telling!' 'I got it first.' 'It's mine! I'm telling. Mu-u-m! Mu-u-m!' Then there was another voice, deeper, which called, 'Let her have it, you little perisher, she's younger than you!' And the first voice shouting, in sudden temper, 'It's not fair, you're always on her side, it's not fair!' There was some angry stamping, then silence. Donovan peered round the side of the shed.

A spoiled-looking girl of about six sat in the middle of a small grass lawn, clutching a very large doll. Her sharp eyes caught Donovan in the act of whipping his head back behind the shed. 'What are you doing in the garden?' said the spoiled little girl.

'Hush!' said Donovan, putting his finger to his lips. 'Don't tell anyone, I'm a detective, right?'

'No you're not, you're a boy.'

'It's a secret anyway,' said Donovan. 'Your sister can't be in it, only you.'

The spoiled little girl looked pleased that there was a secret her sister could not be in. 'Your mum can't be

35

in it neither,' added Donovan slyly. 'No grown-ups can't be in it, only me and my friend and *you*.'

'What is it a secret about?' asked the spoiled little girl.

'It's about me and my friend got to go through your house. Without nobody seeing us, right?'

'My mum and my sister will see,' said the little girl.

'If you go upstairs,' said Donovan, 'and scream and scream and *scream*, right? If you scream like that, your mum and your sister will come up to see what's happened, right? Then me and my friend can go through your house.'

'I don't like that secret,' said the little girl.

'How about this then?' said Donovan, showing her the 50p piece from his pocket. 'Do you like this?'

'Yes.' The greedy eyes gleamed.

'If you do what I say, you can have it, right? . . . If you only make out you're going to do it, I'm going to come and take it back. . . . And spank you *hard*, right?'

'All right then,' said the little girl.

She went into the house, and a few moments later, Amy and Donovan heard blood-curdling screams coming from upstairs. They ran through the kitchen, and the passage, and out of the front door. They pelted down the road, and round the corner, and round the next corner. Donovan waited for Amy to catch up. 'We can go home now,' he said abruptly. 'You go that way.'

'Aren't you coming back to my house?' said Amy. 'No.'

'*Please* come,' said Amy, suddenly terrified of being alone. 'Please, please, please.'

'Oh don't be so stupid!' said Donovan roughly. 'Silly stupid woman. . . . Silly stupid windy *girl*.'

It was just as though he had slapped her across the face. Shocked and bewildered, Amy stood gazing at Donovan, as he disappeared with rapid steps down the road. He couldn't really have said those unkind things, he couldn't. How could he when he liked her and thought she was all right? She must be imagining things again. That was the answer, she was imagining it!

Half walking, half running, Amy started to make her way home. There was a buzzing in her ears, and her head seemed not to belong to her feet. She thought it must be written all over her face that she had just been with a boy who had crashed a car, and it was amazing that no one in the street seemed to notice. For the first time in her life, she was afraid of the police. She expected policemen to pounce on her from every corner; and when she really *did* see one, at the end of the road, strolling along in his shirtsleeves, her knees went weak with fear. In a panic she turned, and doubled back, seeking another route home.

At home, Mum was laying the table for dinner, Dad was having a glass of beer, and Simon had his lego all over the floor. Everything was ordinary, and it was somehow funny to think things could still be the same all around her when she was feeling so different inside. 'Hello everybody,' Amy said, trying to sound ordinary herself.

'Where's Daniel then?' said Mum.

'If you mean Donovan, he had to go home,' said Amy.

'Have you two fell out?'

'Oh *no*,' said Amy. 'We're still going to have the camp, but another day.'

37

'What's wrong with today?' said Dad. 'You was both keen enough this morning.'

'Donovan wasn't feeling very well,' said Amy, brazening it out.

'H'm!' said Dad.

'What d'you mean, "*h'm*", like that?' said Mum.

'Just wondering,' said Dad.

'If Amy says he wasn't well, he wasn't well,' said Mum. 'Amy doesn't tell lies, you know that. I never know Amy to tell a lie. . . . Take no notice of your dad, Amy, he don't mean it.'

'Where d'you get that scratch from, Amy, on your face?' said Dad.

'Nowhere,' said Amy, feeling terrible about telling lies, when Mum had just said she never did it.

'Are you in trouble?' said Dad.

'Of course not,' said Amy bravely, and she hummed a little tune to show how unconcerned she was, and not in trouble at all, and not in the very least expecting a hammering at the door any moment, which would be the police coming to arrest her.

'How about Whatsisname?' said Dad. 'Donovan. Donovan Shifty-eyes. Is *he* in trouble?'

'What you call him that for?' said Mum. 'He's a *nice* boy.'

'He doesn't look you in the face,' said Dad. 'Ever.'

'I like Donovan, I like Donovan, I like Donovan,' said Simon, and in a rush of love and fear, Amy went to hug Simon for saying that, but Simon pushed her away, not caring much for hugs. Amy thought sadly how terrible it was going to be for Simon, having a sister who had been arrested.

'I like *Donovan*,' Simon insisted.

'Well you would, wouldn't you?' said Dad. 'He

throws his money about, doesn't he? *Somebody's* money!'

'And what's that supposed to mean?' said Mum.

'Well,' said Dad. 'You lost two pound coins, didn't you? . . . And you never found them, did you? . . . And no money never went missing in this house till that boy come into it.'

Amy gazed at Dad, her eyes round with disbelief. 'You don't think Donovan took them, do you? He never, he never! You're *horrible* if you think that! I *hate* you if you think that!'

'Well!' said Mum in astonishment.

3

A day of fear

Amy crept to school in dread, yanking Simon frantically past the police station, expecting at any moment to see a great big policeman barring her way. The police would have been doing their detecting about the crashed car, that much she knew. Probably they would have been detecting all night. It was amazing they hadn't detected as far as her yet.

As she reached the playground another thought struck her – perhaps they had detected as far as Donovan! She looked around for him, but he was nowhere to be seen. Perhaps he had already been arrested. Perhaps the police would come to school later on, for her.

Amy stood in the playground alone. She saw Cynthia, not far away, whispering in a huddle with Gloria and Lorraine, glancing over her shoulder at Amy, then whispering again and laughing, a joyless, unkind laugh. So the girls were still not speaking to her. It hardly mattered. On Friday the girls not speaking to her had been the most important thing in the world, but now all that seemed silly and unimportant, compared with the awful prospect of being arrested by the police. The bell went, and Amy dawdled to the line, wanting to be last.

Donovan was not in the line. He might just be late, of course, but Amy was terrified that he had been arrested. She felt all shaky and sick inside. There was that odd feeling again, as though her head and her feet didn't belong together, and the sounds of school around her seemed to be coming from a long way away, as though she were not really a part of this ordinary Monday morning . . .

'Fold your arms and sit up straight,' said the headmaster, who was waiting in the classroom to talk to them. Miss Elliot never said 'Fold your arms and sit up straight' because she didn't want to be that sort of bossy teacher. But the class rather liked having Mr Bassett say that – it made them feel secure, and looked after.

There was a ritual to be gone through before Mr Bassett came to the point. 'Up straight,' he repeated. 'Straight, straight backs if you want to grow! I never grew much, you see, and all because I never sat with a straight back!' This was a joke, because Mr Bassett was actually very tall. He was like a beanpole; when you looked up at him you thought your eyes were never going to reach his face. Mr Bassett's great laugh roared over the children's heads. Mr Bassett laughed a great deal at his own jokes.

'Now let me see which people have smartened themselves up for coming to school. Faces? Hair? You know what I'm going to say, don't you? Every boy must have hair as smart as mine!' And this was a joke too, because Mr Bassett had only a wispy fringe of hair above his neck. The rest of his head was as bald as an egg, and as shiny as a new penny. The class laughed happily, though they had heard all this a hundred times before. Mr Bassett was making his boring jokes, and the world was very safe.

After the jokes, however, came the lecture, and this morning it was all about Temptation. 'We must not

41

put Temptation in people's way,' said Mr Bassett. 'We must *never* put Temptation in people's way. We must look after our possessions and never, *never*, leave money in our desks . . . must we, Bharat?' *Now* they saw what Mr Bassett was getting at.

'No, sir.' Bharat's dusky skin flamed red. He looked as uncomfortable as though he had been convicted of *yielding* to Temptation, instead of only putting it in people's way.

'All right, lad, all right,' said Mr Bassett, who was really very kind and hadn't meant to upset Bharat. 'Just try to think a bit more carefully in future. You lost 50p on Friday? . . . Well now, what do you think, it's turned up! Turned up like a bad penny – sorry, sorry, I mean like a bad 50p piece! Ha, ha, ha! Come and get it. Now, what are you going to do with it? *No*, not your pocket. What will happen if you put it in your pocket? It will *walk away*, won't it! So, what are you going to do with it? . . . That's right, you are going to ask Miss Elliot to look after it for you!'

Mr Bassett frequently spoke to them as though they were about five years old, but never mind. And Miss Elliot would probably lose the money herself, but never mind that. Everyone was looking at Kevin Riley, nudging and whispering and pointing. Kevin was crying. He had been crying a lot by the look of it, his eyes were puffy, and his face all blotched. Was Kevin the thief then? He had never been known to steal before.

'Eyes this way now,' said Mr Bassett! '*This* way Michael, Andrew. That's better, I want everyone's attention because we are going to talk about Loyalty. Who knows what I mean by Loyalty? . . . That's right, Cynthia, it means when we stand up for our friends. When we help them when they're in trouble, and believe the best about them, no matter what. I'm glad you were able to tell me what Loyalty means, Cynthia, because you were not very loyal were you, on Friday? Nor you Gloria, Lorraine, Andrea, Maxine?' Their eyes were on their desks, their faces clouded with sullen shame. 'A friend was accused of something she didn't do. Wasn't she Cynthia, Lorraine? I know things looked bad for her, I understand that, but that is when we need our friends. . . . Isn't it, Cynthia?'

Cynthia was crying by now, great noisy sobs of remorse. 'All right, Cynthia,' said Mr Bassett. 'I'm glad you're sorry, but if you'd just let me go on . . . *Cynthia*! Try to control yourself, dear, I can't hear myself speak. . . . All right, now let me tell you what happened. It's a sad little story, but I know one person who is truly sorry and will never do it again. *Someone*, or some people, came into this class at dinnertime on Friday, with the foolish notion that it would be a good idea to look in people's desks. Just to see if they might be keeping something interesting inside. And of course one thing led to another. One thing always leads to another, doesn't it boys and girls? And so, you see, it wasn't just looking, it was taking! And then someone thought they were going to be caught, so they pushed the things into the nearest hiding place. And *that* is how they came to be in Amy Baker's desk!'

'Boo-hoo-hoo!' bawled Cynthia.

'And if you want to know how I found all this out,' Mr Bassett went on, 'let me tell you I have my spies. Hah – you didn't know that, did you? I have my spies. And now it's sorted out, it's finished. So we

43

want no more inquests, or post-mortems. . . . What's a post-mortem Bharat? Do you know? . . . That's right, Andrew, it's when we cut up something that's dead. Well, this is dead – *isn't it!*'

'Yes sir,' they chorused. They were willing enough – most of them had forgotten Friday's episode anyway. A weekend is a long time when you are eleven.

Mr Bassett paused at the door and looked round the class. 'Donovan Grant not here this morning?' he said with careful unconcern. 'Send him to me if he comes, Miss Elliot.' For being late, presumably.

The girls began falling over themselves to be nice to Amy. 'I'm sorry a thousand times,' said Gloria.

'I'm sorry a *million* times,' said Lorraine. 'Have a fruit chew, Amy.'

'Have some crisps,' said Andrea. 'Go on, have some more. Go on, have all of them.'

'Not in class,' said Miss Elliot. '*Please*, not in class! I mean, you know – we don't have eating in class, do we?'

'You're my *best* teacher,' said Lorraine, beaming fondly at Miss Elliot.

Cynthia had wrapped her arm heavily round Amy. She was still crying, snuffling sorrowfully into Amy's neck. It was lovely to be friends again, of course, but Amy didn't really want Cynthia snuffling damply into her neck. Cynthia's lamentations continued all the way down the stairs to Assembly, and all the way down the stairs again at playtime, and in the yard outside. It was not very comfortable for Amy, having all Cynthia's weight on her, and even less comfortable with the whole group dragging at her, all seeking to offer their embraces at the same time.

Out of the corner of her eye, and in between being pulled about by the girls, Amy saw some of the boys going out of their way to be nice to Kevin Riley, to forgive him for being the thief. They really were a very nice class. It was a pity she didn't want them, any of them, to be near her just now. She just wanted to be left alone, so she could worry about yesterday in peace!

Donovan was away from school. He wasn't late, he was absent. He had been arrested, of course. At that very moment, probably, Donovan was in the police station, being questioned. ('You had a accomplice,' the policeman was saying. 'What was her name?' 'Amy Baker,' said Donovan. 'And where does this Amy Baker live? Where does she go to school?' 'She goes to George Street, same as me,' said Donovan. 'Ha!' said the policeman with a cruel laugh. 'We've got her!')

Amy pulled away from the girls and stood with hunched shoulders and a troubled face. 'Don't be sad, Amy,' begged Cynthia. 'I won't do it again. We won't none of us do it again!'

'Poor Amy,' said Lorraine. 'Let's have a game of skipping, eh? Eh? Cheer Amy up? Come on, Amy, you can have first go!'

Although Miss Elliot couldn't manage her belongings, or sort out troubles in the class, she was really quite good at teaching, and there were some things she was specially good at; getting children to write stories, for instance. Class 4E always had story writing after play on Mondays, and today Miss Elliot was starting off in the way the children liked best. Now the squeaky-saw voice stopped being hesitant and apologetic, and took on a whole range of tones and expressions as Miss Elliot made up the opening paragraph of the story she wanted the children to write. They listened, riveted, as she gave them a chilling word picture of a school with a ghost in it.

'In the quiet of the library where was a faint, faint sighing. The boys held their breath. Then, from behind the tall bookcase came a voice. A voice which could not be earthly, because no earthly being was there . . .' The big glasses slipped off Miss Elliot's nose, and she smiled with slightly surprised triumph, as though she couldn't believe it was really her, funny little Miss Elliot, doing anything so well.

'My mum saw a ghost, one time,' said Gloria.

'What happened next in the story?' said Cynthia, knowing very well Miss Elliot wasn't going to tell them.

'That's your bit isn't it?' said Miss Elliot. She was still smiling her shy smile, and there were stains all over her teeth where she had been sucking her biro.

'You got ink on your mouth,' said Lorraine kindly. 'You're my *best* teacher though.'

'Come on everyone, *work*,' said Miss Elliot, laughing about the ink because she was always ready to laugh at herself, when she wasn't too worried to see the funny side.

'My mum saw a ghost one time,' said Gloria, getting out her books.

Amy pretended to be writing her story, but she couldn't concentrate on ghosts and haunting when the only thing she was really interested in was people being arrested. She kept turning round, hoping Donovan might have come to school after all, and slipped in when she wasn't looking – but of course he hadn't; his seat remained ominously empty.

'How do you spell "shivering"?' whispered Cynthia. She had finally cheered up, and was throwing herself into the task of story writing. Amy did not reply, so Cynthia nudged her painfully with her elbow. 'Come on, Amy, "shivering", how do you spell it?'

'Leave me alone,' said Amy, 'I'm trying to think.'

'You can think after you tell me.'

'Leave me *alone*. I've got a headache.'

'Oh poor Amy,' said Cynthia, embracing her heavily all over again. 'Poor Amy, Amy's got a headache!' She began fuss-potting in a loud voice. 'Miss Elliot, Amy's got a headache. Can I get her a drink of water? Can I take her to Mrs Raymond?' (Mrs Raymond was the Welfare Assistant, and general dogsbody around the school.)

'I should think she'd rather just have a bit of peace,' said Miss Elliot. 'I mean, you know, sort of – just let her sit quietly.'

'Yes,' said Amy, 'that is what I want.'

It was only a matter of time, of course, before the police would arrive at school to arrest her. She sat numbly, almost resigned to what was going to happen. But by dinnertime, since the police had not yet come, Amy was feeling just a little bit safer. Donovan had been arrested of course – there was no doubt about that – but perhaps he had decided to take all the blame himself. ('There was a girl with you,' said the policeman. 'Tell us who she was.' 'I will not give you her name,' said Donovan. 'Oh won't you?' said the policeman sarcastically. 'We'll see about that!' 'You can torture me if you like,' said Donovan bravely, 'but I will never tell!') How noble Donovan was! How lovely, and unselfish, and noble!

While the children were having their dinner, Mr Bassett walked through the hall. And with him was — oh disaster, disaster — a big, burly *policeman*. Amy thought she was going to faint.

'Have you got a headache again?' said Cynthia. 'Oh look — poor Amy's got her headache back! Do you feel sick, Amy? Shall I get Mrs Raymond? Shall I? Shall I tell the dinner ladies when we get in the playground? Do you want to stay in, Amy?'

'I rather go outside,' said Amy shakily.

'That's right,' said Cynthia. 'You get some fresh air. Mind out the way everybody, let Amy get some air. What you think you're doing, Maxine, breathing all over Amy? She don't want your germs, she wants fresh air.'

What Amy actually wanted was to run away; but since there was nowhere to run to, there was nothing for it but to sit on the bench under the shed in the playground, chilled with fear, in spite of the warmth of the day. Now and again Cynthia ran up to fuss over her. 'Do you want a drink of water? . . . Is your headache any better? . . . I think you're sickening for something.'

Amy's eyes were fixed on the school building, watching both doors into the playground. Every time one of the doors opened she felt a tingling terror in her hands and her feet and her tummy, because an opening door could mean they were coming for her now.

The bell for lining up jangled across the playground. The teachers were coming out to escort their classes indoors. And after the teachers, strolling together and actually laughing, came — Mr Bassett and the policeman.

How very unkind to laugh, when they were coming to arrest her! Amy's knees were as wobbly as jelly, and she tried to hide behind Cynthia. 'What's the matter with you?' said Cynthia.

'Nothing.'

'Yes there is, you're acting funny!'

'I'm not. I got a headache.'

'You're not acting like you got a headache though,' said Cynthia. 'You're acting *funny*!

'Quiet now, girls and boys,' said Mr Bassett. 'This is PC Jones, who has come all the way from the police station to . . . *arrest someone*. Is that right, girls and boys? Has PC Jones come to arrest someone? . . . Well now, they don't seem to think you *have* come to arrest anyone, PC Jones!' Mr Bassett's tremendous laugh threatened to do him some damage. His face went red, and the veins stood out on his neck. 'All right, all right, that was just my little joke. PC Jones hasn't come to arrest anyone this time – he has come to talk to us all about Safety First.'

'Come to my house,' said Cynthia to Amy, at hometime.

'All right,' said Amy, but then she remembered that the quickest way to Cynthia's house was by the railway line, right past the place where she and Donovan had crashed the car yesterday. The red car might even still be there. She would faint if she saw it. If she saw that crashed car with the front all buckled in, she would definitely faint. 'You come to my house instead,' said Amy. 'My mum will let you stay to tea.'

'All right, but we have to go to my house first to tell my mum. So I can stay out long.'

'You could phone from my house,' said Amy.

49

'I want to fetch my cardigan,' said Cynthia. 'Because it's getting cold.'

'Let's go to each other's house another day,' said Amy. 'My headache, you know.'

'It's a funny headache,' said Cynthia sharply. 'It keeps going away and coming back.'

'That's what headaches do.'

'No they don't. You're acting funny again.'

Amy made a supreme effort. 'All right, we'll go to your house and tell your mum,' she said. She would be brave, and get it over. She almost couldn't wait now, to see if the smashed car was still there.

'There's something missing.' said Cynthia. 'You know – something beginning with "S".' They collected Simon from the Infants, and he was extremely displeased to learn that he was to be dragged all the way to Cynthia's house before being taken home. 'I don't want to, Amy – I don't want to go to Cynthia's house. I DON'T WANT TO . . .'

'Well we're going, so there, so shut up,' said Amy.

'I like Donovan better than Cynthia.' said Simon, to be annoying.

'I heard that,' said Cynthia.

'Shut up Simon,' said Amy.

'I LIKE DONOVAN BEST,' said Simon.

'What's he on about?' said Cynthia.

'Nothing,' said Amy. 'Shut up, Simon.'

'Donovan came to our house,' said Simon, sensing Amy didn't want him to tell.

'Oh *did* he?' said Cynthia, in delight. '*Did* he now? Oh ho! Oh hum! *Donovan* is it, Amy? Oh ho!'

'Only 'cos he didn't have nowhere else to go,' said Amy. 'Shut up, Simon.' She jerked his hand harder than she meant to, and he set up a wail.

'Stop that noise or I'll belt you one,' said Cynthia, not meaning it.

'Let me swing,' said Simon, grabbing at Cynthia's hand with his own free one.

'No,' said Amy.

'You did with Donovan.'

'Oh *my*,' said Cynthia. 'Donovan again. What *have* you been getting up to Amy, when my back was turned?'

Amy blushed. They were nearly there. They were *there*. 'What a lot of glass in the gutter,' said Cynthia. 'Looks like somebody had a accident.'

'I wanna go *home*,' whined Simon.

The car was gone though, and that was a relief, as though yesterday had somehow been rubbed out. Then a face appeared at an upstairs window – a warty face, with a great hairy moustache on it. 'Hey you!' shouted Hairy Moustache from the window. 'You with the red hair! Yes, *you*!'

Amy looked up fearfully. 'Isn't she ugly?' said Cynthia, fascinated. 'I think she means you.'

'You was the one in that car,' said Hairy Moustache. 'With that boy, yesterday.'

'Not me,' said Amy. 'It wasn't me.'

'I wanna go *home*,' said Simon.

'Yes it was,' said Hairy Moustache. 'Don't come that! I'd know that hair anywhere.'

'There's other people with this colour hair,' said Amy, cold with terror, and shaking.

'Huh!' said Hairy Moustache, and the window was banged shut.

'It wasn't me,' said Amy, to Cynthia.

'*What* wasn't you?'

51

'I dunno, do I? . . . Anyway it wasn't me . . . Don't you believe it?'

'I wanna go *home*,' said Simon.

'Course I believe it,' said Cynthia stoutly. 'You're my friend, so I believe you, don't I? We got to believe our friends, haven't we? Mr Bassett said.'

'I want to wee wee,' said Simon, playing his last card.

'Shut up,' said Amy. 'We're going to Cynthia's house now, and then we're going home.'

'Shall I give you a piggyback?' said Cynthia, lifting Simon up.

Simon rode high on Cynthia's back. He was happy now, because he could see a long way. 'There's somebody sitting on our wall,' he said, a good minute before they got there.

'Downstairs will be cross,' said Amy.

'It's *Donovan*,' said Simon.

'It can't be,' said Amy. Donovan was at the police station being arrested, and being noble about not telling of her. So how could he be sitting on their wall?

'It *is*,' said Cynthia, greatly pleased.

'Why are you here?' said Amy, struggling with the feeling that nothing was real any more.

'*You* know,' said Donovan. He looked tense, uncertain, anxious. Oh, what had happened? *What*?

'You weren't in school,' said Cynthia.

'Don't have to go to school if I don't want to,' said Donovan.

'Yes you do,' said Cynthia.

'Not *every* day.'

'Me and Amy go every day,' said Cynthia. ''Less we're sick.'

Donovan shrugged. 'Well that's you, innit? Shall we have it now then, Amy?'

'Have what?' said Cynthia.

'I'm talking to Amy,' said Donovan. 'The gang. In your loft. Shall we have it now?' So *that* was what he was anxious about.

'Oh a *gang*,' said Cynthia with enthusiasm. 'Are we going to have a gang? Oh *great*. I can be in it, can't I? Oh great. Come on Amy, let's go and have the gang now. I can't wait.'

'All right then,' said Amy faintly.

Things were just happening to her. She couldn't control things any more, and she couldn't understand anything. Events were just taking her over, sweeping her along like a leaf in a fast-flowing stream. 'What about yesterday?' she whispered to Donovan.

'What about it?' said Donovan, not interested. 'We'll get some more kids for the gang tomorrow, right?'

4

The gang in the loft

'But what is it a gang *for*, actually?' said Lorraine. It had been fun climbing into the loft, but that seemed to be it. Nothing more was happening. It had taken days to get everyone together and now nothing was happening.

'Yeah, what *is* it for?' said Andrew, who was small, and rosy-cheeked, and silly.

'For fun of course,' said Donovan. There was a happy look on his face, not quite a smile, but pleasant enough, for the moment.

'Tell us what sort of fun,' said Cynthia.

'You know what *fun* is, don't you?' said Donovan, dismissing her. He didn't seem to have made any plans though.

'We could have some music,' said Bharat.

'Oh yeah,' said Lorraine. 'That's a good idea you had, Bharat.'

'If we had a record player,' said Bharat.

'I thought you was the boss of this gang, Donovan,' said Cynthia.

'I am,' said Donovan.

'You're not much of a boss if you can't think of what to do,' said Cynthia. 'Let me be the boss.'

'No, it's *my* gang. . . . Wait, wait, I'll think of something, right? Just wait a minute. . . . You're too impatient, right?' Donovan's eyes narrowed to slits, the fist of one hand pounding into the other. Then the not-very-nice smile lit up his face, and Amy felt shivery, and fearful. She had seen that smile before. She had seen it the time that unmentionable thing she had decided never to think about again, had happened. 'I know,' said Donovan, 'I know an idea. We'll have a gang for thinking up how to make our class more interesting.'

'It *is* interesting,' said Cynthia.

'Be better if we let off a stink bomb,' said Donovan.

'Miss Elliot wouldn't like that,' said Cynthia firmly. 'She wouldn't like that at all.'

'Oh Miss *Elliot*,' said Donovan, with a little sideways sneer.

'What you mean "Miss *Elliot*", saying it like that?'

'She's a twerpy twit twit, isn't she!' said Donovan.

Amy looked away, so as not to see the not-very-nice smile, which was spoiling Donovan's handsome looks. Andrew sniggered. 'A twerpy twit twit,' he repeated, savouring the sound of it. He sniggered again. 'Miss Elliot's a twerpy twit twit!'

'Don't you say nothing against my teacher,' said Cynthia, much put out.

'That's right,' said Lorraine. 'Don't you say nothing against Miss Elliot. She's our best teacher.'

Donovan ignored her. 'We could do it in the playground if you like,' he said. 'Have a stink bomb in the playground.'

'We could have it in the hall,' said Andrew. 'We could let it off in the hall, in Assembly.'

'Oh yeah,' said Donovan, 'so we could! We'll let if off in the hall then, right? Soon as I fix it, right? . . . I know a guy knows how to make them, right? Pong worse than Kevin Riley if you can believe that!'

'Pong worse'n Kevin Riley!' Andrew repeated,

sniggering. 'Worse'n Kevin Riley!' He rolled on the floor in exaggerated mirth, and the others began to giggle too. Amy, who was not really amused, forced herself to giggle with the rest.

'I don't think that's funny though,' said Cynthia, glowering. 'I don't think it's *kind*.'

The class seethed with suppressed excitement. Word had gone round about the stink bomb Donovan was going to get, and Donovan's popularity was going up and up. At some point, Amy noticed, Donovan had managed to change his seat, and was now sitting next to Andrew.

'It's today – pass it on!' That was Friday morning, and all over the room hands went before mouths, and hissing travelled behind hands.

'Line up for Assembly,' said Miss Elliot. 'No, *not* like that. Come on, I mean, you don't *usually* make so much noise.' Little snorting giggles were bursting out all along the line, and people were nudging one another with their elbows. There was a joke, Miss Elliot could see, and they weren't telling her what it was, and Miss Elliot was a bit hurt, because they didn't usually leave her out.

The class scuffled and tripped and sniggered its way down the stone steps to the hall. 'When's he going to do it?' whispered Gloria to Cynthia, as they sang.

'Don't ask *me*' said Cynthia, and she pursed her lips and tossed her head to show how much she disapproved. 'I think he's not a nice boy. I wish he hadn't come to our class.'

Amy was nervous. She had giggled with the rest, trying hard to believe she was having fun, when she was not really having fun at all. Why, oh *why* must Donovan do these things? Letting off a stink bomb was not as bad as that other, unthinkable, unmentionable thing he had done, but oh how she wished he wasn't going to do this either! She also wished he *would* do it, and get it over.

When was he going to do it? The waiting, and the suspense, were really painful. Andrea collapsed with hysteria, right in the middle of Mr Bassett's boring story, and Gloria had to hold her hand over Andrea's mouth, so the teachers sitting down the side wouldn't notice.

And then it happened.

There was a slight plopping sound, an explosive snort from Andrea, and a horrible, *horrible* smell. At first, most people in the Assembly thought someone had made a rude smell by accident, and they only wrinkled their noses and tried to turn their heads away. But the smell grew and grew. It filled the hall. It was disgusting and putrid, like fifty rotten eggs, all smashed at once. People started to retch, and make exaggerated sick noises.

There was a moaning and a crying and a rush for the doors. Those who were not moaning and crying were jumping up and down with glee, delighted at this gift from the blue – the chance to make a big fuss about not so very much. 'Stop!' shouted Mr Bassett. 'Stay where you are!' shouted the teachers. And some did, and some went on pushing and shoving for the doors. There was pandemonium. Children streamed into the corridor, and up the stairs. There was whooping and shouting and total chaos.

Donovan's stink bomb was a great success.

Later that morning, Mr Bassett came into Class 4E to talk to them. He tried to be jolly, and make his jokes about straight backs and neat hair, but you could see his heart was not in it. Anyway, what he had really come for, he said, was to talk about Common Sense – which he had noticed this class didn't seem to have much of, today. Oh yes, Mr Bassett's spies had told him which class was responsible for this morning's piece of silly nonsense! And let him say, let him say, that no one enjoyed a bit of fun more than he did! But things that were meant to be fun could turn out to be dangerous if people didn't think before they acted; think of the consequences, use their Common Sense.

At this point Cynthia, who had been listening very intently, began nodding her head with great vigour, and agreeing out loud with Mr Bassett. People might suppose, Mr Bassett went on, if they didn't *think*, that letting off a stink bomb in Assembly was a harmless sort of prank. ('It ain't though, is it sir?' said Cynthia.) But what if someone had been trampled, in the rush to get out? ('Yeah, that's right,' said Cynthia.) What if someone had been seriously injured? ('That's the thing, innit sir! See?') Cynthia dug her elbows into Amy's side, and gave Lorraine a push. 'That's what you got to think about, innit sir!'

'I'm not going to ask who brought the stink bomb into school,' said Mr Bassett. 'My spies have told me that already. I'm only going to say, boys and girls, that I hope everyone in this class has enough Common Sense to understand how wrong it was.'

'*Yes*, Mr Bassett,' said Cynthia.

'And enough backbone, and strength of character, not to be led astray in future.'

'*Yes* Mr Bassett,' said Cynthia vehemently.

'Hands up those who agree with Cynthia.'

All raised their hands, since Mr Bassett clearly expected them to do so. But at dinnertime Donovan was kingpin, triumphant, and crowing his success all over the playground.

'Why don't you like Donovan?' asked Amy.

'I just don't,' said Cynthia.

'But *why*?'

'He's a nuisance. He makes trouble. And he don't look you in the face.'

'You liked him first,' said Amy. 'And the gang.'

'I changed my mind.'

'I think he's coming,' said Amy.

'You've gone all red,' said Cynthia.

Donovan swaggered up. 'I got a lot more kids for the gang,' he said. 'Tomorrow afternoon, right?' His tone was very offhand.

'You didn't ought to let him speak to you like that,' said Cynthia.

'I don't mind,' said Amy miserably.

'You only say that because you love him.'

Amy was silent, struggling with herself. She had an overwhelming desire, suddenly, to confide in Cynthia. Her feelings, the muddle she was in, the funny way Donovan kept changing, and how unhappy that was making her. She opened her mouth, and closed it again. No, she couldn't say. It was all too deep, too private, to be shared with anyone.

Cynthia harangued the girls. 'You didn't ought to be in his gang. He's a trouble-maker.'

'What about you then?'

'I got to be loyal to Amy. Because I'm her best friend. And you ought to know that Lorraine, without being told.'

'Why has *Amy* got to be in it?'

'You know. Something beginning with "L".'

'Oh she *loves* him.'

'He is good-looking,' said Gloria wistfully.

'He's *bad*,' said Cynthia. 'I don't like him at all.'

So Cynthia and Amy were the only girls at the gang meeting on Saturday. There were six boys, counting Donovan, and Mum had to try very hard to go on being happy about how nice it was for Amy to have so many friends now. 'Just you be careful up there,' she kept saying. 'Mind where you put your feet.'

'Don't worry, Mrs Baker,' said Cynthia. 'I'll see they behave. Don't you worry. You sit down and do your knitting. I'll mind them!'

Downstairs was still thumping her stick and having a screaming session about the hooligans going through her hall. This cheered Mum up a bit, and she went on to the landing to scream back.

Donovan sat in the chair, and one or two of the newcomers began to complain of the hardness of the floor. 'We can get some more seats if you like,' said Donovan. 'And some carpet. We can go and look on the skips. And people's fronts, right?'

'There's plenty of carpet here,' said Amy.

'Shall we go and look on the skips then?' said Donovan, ignoring her.

'Didn't you hear what Amy said?' said Cynthia.

'Who's coming then?' said Donovan, ignoring Cynthia as well.

Six boys clambered out of the loft, by way of the

stepladder and the cupboard shelves. Various items from the shelves clattered to the ground, and Mum had to come out of the kitchen to pick them up. She was biting her lip to stop herself from being sharp with Amy's friends, but as the boys thumped and shouted their way down the stairs she shouted after them. 'Have a bit of thought for Downstairs! She's an old lady, you know!' They didn't even hear her.

Amy was sitting with hunched shoulders, her knees drawn up to her chest. 'They're rude,' said Cynthia. 'They didn't ought to treat your mum like that.'

'I know, said Amy, in a small unhappy voice, not looking at Cynthia.

The boys came back with some pieces of carpet, and the seat cushions from someone's discarded old sofa. 'Out the way, Baker,' said Donovan to Amy. 'We want to put the carpet down.'

'Don't talk to Amy like that,' said Cynthia. 'It's her house.'

'Who asked you to stick your nose in?' said Donovan.

'Yeah, you shut your gob,' said Andrew.

'It's all right,' said Amy miserably, 'I don't mind.'

'It's not fair though,' said Cynthia. 'It's not fair.' She retreated to a perch outside the curtain-walled camp, from which position she kept up an indignant monologue. 'It's not fair. You're all of you rude. You're *ignorant*. Hooligans! You got no manners . . .'

The boys sniggered together, fawning round Donovan, making fun of Cynthia. 'Ah – shut up, woman!' said Donovan.

With the cushions and carpet in place, Cynthia crept back and sat with her arm round Amy, still

61

growling and muttering. The boys had taken all the comfortable seating. 'What are we going to do now?' said Gavin, a nondescript boy, usually quiet and inoffensive.

'Yeah,' said Michael. 'What now?' He was the strong man of the class; a bit surly, but whenever Miss Elliot wanted something lifted, or reached for, Michael was proud to show off how strong he was, and do it for her.

They all looked at Donovan, waiting to be led. Donovan shifted uneasily; clearly he had run out of ideas again.

'We could play a game,' said Cynthia, coming out of her sulk.

'What game?' said someone else.

'We could play I-Spy,' said Cynthia.

Hoots of derision. 'That's a baby game! That's a sissy game!'

'It's a *good* game,' said Cynthia.

'Well we don't want to play it,' said Michael.

'All right I'll tell you,' said Donovan. 'Wait – no wait, wait, I'll tell you what we'll do, we'll look for treasure, right?'

'Where?'

'Well here, of course! This is a attic, right? There's treasure in attics, right? Well, *sometimes*. . . . What about all them cases and boxes, in the corners?'

'It's only old curtains and things,' said Amy. 'You know it is, Donovan, we looked already.'

'We'll look for treasure then, shall we?' said Donovan, to the boys.

'It's Amy's house, you know,' said Cynthia. 'Don't forget you got to ask her.'

Donovan whispered in Andrew's ear, and Andrew

sniggered. 'Say yes, Amy,' said Andrew. 'Say yes, Amy-wamy-pamy!' Donovan whispered again, and Andrew grinned and spluttered. 'Come on Amy-wamy,' he said. 'Nice Amy! Who's a nice Amy, then? Say yes!'

'Do what you like,' said Amy. She turned her head away, and curled her body into a tight little ball.

'It's all your fault,' said Cynthia angrily. 'You made my best friend upset! I hate you, Donovan Grant!'

'Shut up, big mouth!' said Gavin, who had hardly ever been known to be aggressive before. The others simply took no notice. Noisily, the gang was dispersing to the far corners of the loft; crawling, tripping, leaping across joists. Great whoops of joy sounded through the beams as first one 'treasure trove', then another, was discovered. Boxes were overturned, their contents scattered in the dust. Cases were ripped open, old clothes and books tossed around with careless abandon.

'Look at them!' said Cynthia furiously. 'Look what they're doing to your mum and dad's things!'

Amy did not want to look. She sat curled up on the carpet, her face buried against her knees. She just wanted the afternoon to be over. She wanted them all to go home. Even Donovan, even Donovan!

'I hate you, Donovan Grant,' Cynthia shouted again. 'You made them act like this! They wasn't never like this till you came! I wish you never came to our school!'

Donovan laughed, the not-very-nice smile marring his good looks. Mum, hearing the sounds of quarrelling, stood beneath the trapdoor and peered anxiously upwards. 'What's going on up there?'

'You want to see what they're doing, Mrs Baker,' said Cynthia. 'You want to tell them off!'

'Come down this minute, all of you!' called Mum.

Amy and Cynthia moved towards the trapdoor, no one else took the slightest notice. 'You deaf all of you?' shouted Cynthia. 'Amy's mum said you got to come down.'

'Cynthia Garrett is a parrot,' taunted Andrew.

'Shut up, you,' said Cynthia.

'Cynthia Garrett is a parrot,' said Andrew again.

'I'm waiting!' called Mum.

'Say that once more and you're for it,' said Cynthia to Andrew.

'Cynthia Garrett is a parrot,' said Andrew.

Cynthia launched herself at him. 'Don't!' begged Amy, but Cynthia did not hear her. Amy began to crawl out of the loft. 'And the rest of you!' called Mum. 'Now!'

Wild with fury, Cynthia staggered over the joists and Andrew backed nervously. He was an undersized boy, and Cynthia was a big strong girl. 'Save me, save me!' Andrew called in mock fear which was not all pretence – Cynthia was not playing! Everyone stopped what they were doing to watch the fight.

Cynthia hit him across the face, and Andrew put his hand up to ward off further blows. Cynthia hit him again, and Andrew balled his fist to punch her in the stomach. Cynthia grabbed his hair and pulled. 'Ow!' he yelled.

'Break it up now,' said Donovan uneasily, seeing a threat to his precious gang headquarters. Disconcerted that the others took no notice of him either, he regarded them through narrowed eyes for a moment, frowning. Then he pretended he hadn't said it anyway and just stood watching indulgently – the boss allowing his minions their fun.

They began to chant. 'Come on Andrew, come on Andrew!' Gripping Andrew's hair with one hand, Cynthia clawed his face with the other. He kicked her shins as best he could, but the summer plimsolls he wore did little damage. He kicked again with all his strength, and his other foot slipped on the joist; he fell, dragging Cynthia with him. There was a ripping, splintering, tearing sound – and Cynthia's leg disappeared from the knee downward.

Shocked silence from above, and an outburst of screams from below. Cynthia's foot had gone through the ceiling in the middle of the front room, where Simon was watching television. Simon screamed with fear and ran to his mother. Amy ran to look at Cynthia's foot, sticking through the ceiling, and screamed in fear as well. Mum screamed out of the window at Dad, on early shift this week, who was at that moment attending to some repairs on the family car, parked as usual with its insides spread over the road.

Fearing some terrible disaster, Dad crashed through the front door yelling, 'Hold on – I'm coming!' And Downstairs added her bit of course, screaming that the house was falling down, and what was going to become of *her*?

By the time Dad arrived, Cynthia had pulled her foot up, and the whole gang was climbing sheepishly out of the loft. 'Do you lot usually knock holes in the ceilings of houses you're invited into?' Dad was very, very angry.

'It wasn't me, Mr Baker.' 'I didn't do it.' 'Cynthia and Andrew had a fight, it wasn't *me*.' The disclaimers went on and on.

65

'You were fooling about, said Dad, two high spots of colour burning his cheeks. When Dad got angry, he *got angry*. 'You don't have to tell me, I know.'

'*I* wasn't fooling, Mr Baker,' said Donovan. 'The fight wasn't nothing to do with me.'

'It was *all* to do with him,' said Cynthia, weeping loudly now. 'He s-started it, he s-started it. He made them all be wicked to A-my, and A-my's mum.'

Donovan shrugged. 'She's just trying to throw the blame, right? She went mad, you should have seen her!'

'I should have liked to, if she was standing up for my family,' said Dad. He put his arm round Cynthia's shoulders and gave her a hug. 'Clear off now, the rest of you, and DON'T COME BACK.'

'It wasn't *me* though, Mr Baker.' said Donovan.

'You *particularly*,' said Dad. 'OUT – OUT!'

'It wasn't *me* though,' Donovan muttered, looking quite hurt, and hard done by.

They all went trooping down the stairs. Quietly at first, but once they reached the hallway there was a burst of defiant, jeering laughter. 'Mr Baker baked a fruit cake!' screamed Andrew, into the road. A pointless and silly joke if ever there was one, but they all seemed to find it hilarious.

'Where's Amy?' said Mum anxiously, the bubbling laughter all drained and gone.

They found her curled up on her bed, her face to the wall, and she stayed like that for nearly an hour, speaking to no one.

5

Quarrels and discoveries

By Monday, Amy had persuaded herself that Donovan was probably still lovely, after all. He was probably sorry. He'd been sorry after that thing she wasn't ever going to think about again, hadn't he? So he would probably be sorry now.

Once she got to school it would be all right, very likely. She went into a dream about it as she trudged along, dragging Simon as usual. (Donovan came up to her in the playground, his eyes brimming with tears. 'I was horrible to you yesterday,' he said, with a sob in his voice. 'I don't blame you if you won't forgive me.' 'I *will* forgive you,' said Amy, 'but you must never do it again.' 'Oh I won't, I won't,' said Donovan. 'Do you think your mum and dad will forive me too?' 'We'll go and ask them together,' said Amy. And they went, hand in hand.)

Donovan was already in the playground, kicking a football with some of the other boys. Amy stood near, hopefully, giving him a chance to notice her and say his piece about would she forgive him? He took no notice of her at all.

Amy moved nearer still; perhaps he hadn't seen that she was there. Bharat's foot sent the ball hurtling in her direction, and Donovan ran for it. 'Out the way, Baker,' he said to Amy, giving her a push. Amy felt terrible; she thought everyone must have seen Donovan pushing her in the playground.

The first lesson that morning was maths, which was the one lesson poor Miss Elliot was *not* good at. She was always getting tied up, trying to explain things, and Class 4E often finished up by explaining it all to *her*. They didn't mind. She was their very own teacher after all, so it was their job to look after her.

But today was different. Today, somehow, the whole atmosphere of the class was different. Today, for the first time, when Miss Elliot got in a muddle showing Bharat how to do long division, some people actually laughed at her! You could tell they were laughing *at* her, and not *with* her, because it was unkind laughter – jeering. Cynthia turned round in her seat, and glared at the back of the class.

'Who done that?' whispered Gloria.

'I dunno,' said Cynthia. 'Anyway, they better not do it again!'

Miss Elliot, flustered by the laughter, and put off her concentration, was tying herself up in worse knots. 'No not *there*. I mean, that's for the *answer*. . . . I know it's the answer, sort of, but it's not the *answer*. I mean it's five times. I mean six times, this number, the first one, I mean – oh Bharat, this is the way you do it!'

An echoing hiss travelled from table to table. 'I mean – sort of – I mean – sort of – oh *Bharat*. Oh *Bharat*.' Some of the boys were mocking her! They were actually mocking Miss Elliot.

Cynthia stood up in her seat. 'Who said that?' she demanded. There was a lot of sniggering, but no one admitted responsibility. 'You better stop it or else!' said Cynthia.

'It's all right, Cynthia,' said Miss Elliot, swallowing bravely. 'They're only having a bit of fun. Get on with your work please.'

'Cynthia Garrett is a parrot,' said Andrew.

'Shut up, you,' said Cynthia.

'Cynthia, *please*,' said Miss Elliot. She was much more upset than she was letting on – blinking hard, and pushing the glasses against her nose. Cynthia sat down, muttering.

'Cynthia Garrett is a parrot,' said Kevin Riley, trying to join in.

'I'm not taking that from you!' said Cynthia.

'*Cynthia*,' said Miss Elliot. In fits and starts, the morning moved towards playtime.

After play they did story writing again, and most people were still finishing their ghost stories from last week. Amy had never really started hers, because she was feeling so terrible last Monday. She was feeling terrible again this Monday, but the thought struck her that if she wrote a really good story, a really *brilliant* story, Miss Elliot would ask her to read it out to the class. Amy thought the ghost could be Mr Bassett, who had died of laughing at one of his own jokes, and come back to haunt the school, and creep up behind all the people whose backs weren't straight enough, and blow down their necks. . . . And Donovan would be impressed all over again, and think how she wasn't boring like the others. And look at her hair, which he seemed to have stopped noticing.

Those who had finished their stories could write another one of their own choice. Or they could do silent reading if they preferred, Miss Elliot didn't mind. A large number of the boys chose silent reading, only they didn't do it very silently.

'*Quietly*, Gavin,' Miss Elliot had to keep saying. '*Please* Andrew, you're disturbing the people who are writing.' Donovan wasn't doing anything noisy, but the not-very-nice smile was on his face, and he was making signs at the others to stir them up. Cynthia saw him doing it. 'Stop that, Donovan Grant! Stop making faces, behind Miss's back!'

'Cynthia Garrett is a parrot,' said Gavin.

'You're the parrot!' said Cynthia furiously, 'if you can't think of nothing new to say, only copycat things!'

'Garrett the parrot,' said Michael. 'Miss Elliot, did you know Garrett the parrot put her foot through the ceiling in Amy Baker's house?'

Raucous laughter from various sources accompanied this disclosure. 'I don't know what you're talking about,' said Miss Elliot. 'And I don't think I want to know. I mean – it's not nice to tell tales, is it? I mean – it's sort of – *you* know.'

'I mean, it's sort of, *you* know,' mocked a whispering voice.

'That was you, Donovan Grant, and you can't say it wasn't!' said Lorraine.

'Me? Not me! I never done nothing!'

'Don't you believe him Lorraine,' said Cynthia. 'He's crafty, that's all. He's crafty, Miss Elliot, and he's rude, and he's making all the boys rude. Us girls don't like him. Us girls are on your side.'

'Who cares about you?' said Andrew.

'Yeah, who cares about you lot?' said Gavin.

'*Please* get on with your work,' said Miss Elliot. Her hair was so messy where she had been rubbing at it, she looked rather as though she had been pulled through a hedge backwards.

After dinner, Class 4E had art.

The classromm walls were plastered from top to bottom with fabulous artwork inspired, surprisingly enough, by Miss Elliot. In some places, to be truthful, *executed* by Miss Elliot. Although she was such a mess herself, Miss Elliot's classroom walls were actually quite wonderful.

The class was making collage pictures in groups; cut-outs, stuck down on the background Miss Elliot had tried to persuade the children they had designed all by themselves. Cynthia's group was doing a jungle scene, Bharat's group was doing a football match, Andrew's group was doing a seaside. Donovan was in Andrew's group.

The disturbance started with bursts of furtive laughter, coming from the boys who were working on the seaside picture. 'I think they're doing something rude,' said Gloria.

'They're always rude these days,' said Lorraine,' 'I don't know what's got into them, they didn't use to be like that.'

'I don't mean that sort of rude, I mean the other sort of rude,' said Gloria. 'You know, *nasty*.'

Andrea giggled, snorting into her crooked arm. 'Shut up laughing, Andrea,' said Lorraine. 'It's not funny, you know.'

'That's right,' said Maxine, 'It's not funny.'

'I know,' said Andrea.

'How would you like it if you was Miss Elliot?' said Gloria.

'I *know*.'

'Well then—'

There was another outburst of sniggering from Andrew's group. The boys had their heads together, and Donovan seemed to be drawing something.

71

There was whispering, and more not-very-nice laughter, and then some sort of discussion. 'No!' 'You can't do that!' 'Put it away now!' 'You'll get in trouble!' 'Go on then, I dare you!'

'Come here a minute, Miss,' called out Donovan.

'I'm busy just now,' said Miss Elliot, who was helping Hansa's group. With a few deft strokes, Miss Elliot transformed the landscape of Hansa's picture. 'There,' said Miss Elliot, to Hansa. 'You've made a really good job of that now!'

'Come *here* though,' said Donovan, 'we got something to show you.'

'All right, what is it?' said Miss Elliot, moving across to their table. She peered through the big glasses, then drew in her breath. 'Donovan!' she reproached him, blushing scarlet.

'Don't you like it, Miss?' said Donovan innocently. 'Isn't it good enough to go on our picture?' The other boys were stifling half-embarrassed laughter behind their hands, admiring Donovan's cheek.

'Tear it up and put it in the bin,' said Miss Elliot. 'I mean – you know – that's the only thing to do with it, tear it up!'

'Oh Miss!' Donovan taunted her. 'You don't mean it, Miss! Not after we worked!'

'Donovan, *please*,' said Miss Elliot.

'We thought it could go here, Miss' said Donovan. 'In the water.' Andrew's rosy face was puce now, he did not know how to contain himself. He was having a *great* time.

'Stop that sniggering!' said Miss Elliot sharply, and everyone looked round, because they had never heard Miss Elliot speak like that before. 'Put that thing in the bin, Donovan. I shan't tell you again.'

The unpleasant giggling died away, and one or two of the boys had the grace to look ashamed. 'But what's wrong with it?' Donovan persisted. 'Tell me, I want to know.'

'The bin!' said Miss Elliot, with tight lips.

'Put it in the bin, Donovan, like Miss said,' said Cynthia.

'You keep out of it, Garrett the parrot,' said Donovan.

'Yeah – you keep out of it,' said Andrew.

'That's enough!' said Miss Elliot.

'Big-mouth!' said Gavin to Cynthia, ignoring Miss Elliot even though she *was* trying to be strict.

'All right, *I'll* put it in the bin,' said Cynthia. She lunged at the boys' table, trying to snatch the offending picture. Donovan guarded it with his arms, laughing at her – a laugh with no heart in it. Cynthia pushed at Donovan's arms but Donovan was a strong boy and she couldn't move him. He laughed at her again. 'Leave off, Parrot!'

Frustrated and stung, Cynthia lost her head and did a dreadful thing. Bending down, she bit Donovan hard, on his bare arms, to make him let go. Donovan gave one yell, then his face twisted up with anger and he began to hit Cynthia in real earnest. His face went dark and he was hitting Cynthia, and hitting her, and hitting her. And Cynthia, after the first shock, gave back nearly as good as she got.

It was terrible. There had never been a fight in Class 4E before, never. Most of the children watched in stupefied silence, but Andrea began to scream and cry, and the Asian girls hugged each other in fear. 'Shall I get Mr Bassett?' said Lorraine, and she went, without waiting for Miss Elliot's reply. Helplessly

Miss Elliot blinked, and pushed her glasses against her face, and waited for someone else to sort out the trouble.

Miss Elliot was shaking, after Mr Bassett yanked Donovan away by the back of his collar, and the tears were trickling down her cheeks. She wiped them away from under her glasses, and they trickled down some more. 'Look what you done!' said Gloria to the boys. She put her arm round Miss Elliot, and led her tenderly to her seat. 'Sit down, Miss Elliot, have a rest.' She shot a look of withering contempt at Andrew and his group.

Amy crouched beside Cynthia, who was weeping distraughtly in a heap on the floor. 'Never mind,' she kept saying. 'Never mind.' She couldn't think of anything else to say. She was so confused she didn't really know if she was on Donovan's side or Cynthia's.

Lorraine grabbed the dirty picture, which still lay on Andrew's table. Andrew tried to snatch it, and hide it under his desk, but Lorraine was quicker. She gave the picture one disdainful glance, then tore it into small pieces and dropped them in the bin. She blew on her fingers, as though to remove a bad smell.

One by one the children went back to their work, but there was no joy in it any more.

Cynthia had been quite badly bruised by Donovan's pummelling, but her self-esteem had suffered more damage than her skin. She had *bitten* someone. The shame of it! Cynthia wept with enthusiasm and abandon all afternoon. The other girls tried to console her. They didn't blame her in the least, they said. They would have done exactly the same themselves, they said, probably, had they been brave enough. They had just got her dry-eyed when Mr Bassett sent for Cynthia too, to have a word with her about the biting – and, of course, that set her off all over again.

At hometime, usually, groups of 4E girls mingled freely with groups of 4E boys. Today there were two distinct camps – unfriendly, taunting one another. 'How's Garrett the parrot?' shouted Andrew. Cynthia was sick to death of that joke, but she managed not to rise to it. She would keep out of trouble, she would just ignore their stupid jibes.

'Shut up, Andy Pandy,' shouted Lorraine.

'Didn't know parrots bite, did you?' said Gavin to the other boys. Their jeers filled the air. 'Bitten anybody else lately, Parrot?' 'Perhaps she's a dog, not a parrot!' 'You mean a cat!' 'Yeah, a wild cat!' 'A rat!' Donovan was smiling his not-very-nice smile. Lorraine pointed at him scornfully. 'I rather be a parrot than a pig like him!'

'Don't you say nothing against my best mate,' said Andrew, leaning on Donovan.

'Who'd want him for a mate?' said Gloria, with a shudder. 'I think I rather have a bee.' (She meant a wasp.)

'Amy Baker doesn't think so,' said Andrew.

'We all think so,' said Lorraine.

'Amy doesn't,' said Andrew, 'she *loves* him.'

'I don't,' said Amy. 'I don't.' But the hot blush covered her freckles. She could even feel it spreading down her neck.

'Amy loves Donovan, Amy loves Donovan!' crowed Gavin, jumping up and down.

'Amy loves Donovan!' said Kevin Riley, trying to join in.

The boys didn't want *him*. They felt like being nasty to the girls, and they felt like being nasty to poor smelly Kevin as well. 'You shut up,' said Michael, turning on him. 'What do *you* know about it?'

'You said, though,' said Kevin.

'It's nothing to do with *you*,' said Andrew. 'You're a tea-leaf, aren't you? A thief!'

'No I'm not,' said Kevin.

'You are then, you was caught! Don't make out!'

Kevin's eyes filled with tears. 'It wasn't only me.'

'Leave him alone,' said Donovan, suddenly uneasy.

'What's wrong?' said Andrew.

'I said leave him alone, that's all,' said Donovan.

'That's funny,' said Cynthia to Amy. 'That's funny, Donovan sticking up for Kevin! That's very, very funny.'

Next morning Maxine strutted into the playground looking very important, and pleased with herself. The dull, heavy face was quite animated for once. She found Lorraine, and whispered something in her ear. 'No!' said Lorraine, looking pleased as well.

They looked around for Gloria and Andrea, and the four girls went into a huddle, whispering with their heads together. Cynthia, watching with Amy, began hopping up and down. There was a secret, and she wasn't in it. 'Let's go and see,' she said, and they ran across. 'Come on, tell! Tell me and Amy!'

'No,' said Gloria.

'Come on, don't be mean,' said Cynthia.

'It's not mean,' said Andrea. 'It's mean to tell. Amy loves him.'

'You give it away Andrea, saying that,' said Gloria.

'Give what away?' said Cynthia.

'Nothing,' said Gloria. 'It's nothing. . . . Shut up Andrea, shut up giggling like that.'

'Give *what* away?' said Cynthia. 'I shall keep asking till you tell. So come on, tell!'

'All right,' said Lorraine. 'Maxine knows something about Donovan Grant. Something bad. Something *very, very* bad.'

Amy's heart slid into her shoes. She dreaded to hear, and she couldn't wait to hear.

'Well?' said Cynthia. 'Come on.'

'My mum knows one of the dinner ladies at Norfolk Street School,' said Maxine, all lit up with pride and triumph.

'So?'

'My mum's friend knows why Donovan Grant leave.'

'I know why he left,' said Amy. 'He left because he didn't like it there, he said.'

'Oh yeah, he *said*,' said Lorraine, with heavy sarcasm. 'I bet that's what he *said*.'

'All right, what really happened then?' said Amy. The suspense was so dreadful she could hardly breathe.

Lorraine paused. One or two of the others opened their mouths and drew breath as if to speak, but Lorraine stopped them. 'No, let me, let me . . .' She paused again, then brought it out. 'He was EXPELLED.'

'What!'

'It's true,' said Maxine. Her eyes gleamed with pleasure. All the girls had round gleaming eyes. They were all enjoying themselves very much.

77

'Well, come on,' said Cynthia. 'Come on, tell us quick. What did he do wrong?'

'Everything!' said Maxine. 'He did play tricks, and he steal money, and he make the other boys steal money, and he make everybody bad in the class, and he throw the chairs about one time, when he did get his temper up.'

'And that's why he got expelled!' said Cynthia. 'I *knew* he was a troublemaker! I said, didn't I? Didn't I say Donovan's a troublemaker?'

'My mum's friend said, "you name it he's done it,"' said Maxine proudly.

'Tell about the car,' said Gloria.

'The car?' said Amy, weak with terror.

'A teacher's car. Donovan did drive it down the road,' said Maxine.

'What!' said Cynthia. 'He really drive a real car? Oh he's a nuisance! He's a troublemaker! Didn't I say? Didn't I say, Amy? Anyway, you can't love him now, thank goodness!'

'It nearly crash, said Maxine.

'He's the worst boy I ever met,' said Cynthia. 'He's a *horrible* boy, he's a *nuisance*. Anyway, I did say!'

Maxine whispered in Lorraine's ear. 'Oh yeah,' said Lorraine. 'There's something else.'

There couldn' be *more*, Amy thought. Already there was a buzzing in her ears, and she felt giddy. Another shock would be more than she could bear.

'Well come on, come on,' said Cynthia. 'You are so slow to tell, Lorraine. You are slow as a tortoise, do you know that?'

'I don't want to say this bit,' said Lorraine.

'All right,' said Gloria, '*I'll* say. 'It's not about Donovan, it's about his dad. Maxine's mum's friend said, she said . . . that Donovan's dad . . . is . . . in . . . prison!'

'Tell me my story, Amy,' said Simon.

'I don't feel like it,' said Amy.

'Oh *Amy*!

'Shut up and go to sleep, and stop nagging me for stories all the time, when I don't feel like telling them.'

6

War!

She wanted to tell him she knw – about his dad, and about being expelled, the whole shameful list. She wanted Donovan to know that she knew, but was going to be loyal; she was *never* going to tell. The others would probably blab it about, but not her, not Amy. If Donovan knew how loyal she was going to be, perhaps he would like her again, and say nice things to her sometimes, like before.

She looked at him from across the playground, and wondered if she dared. It was early in the morning and he was all by himself, kicking a ball against the wall. Amy was alone as well, so she couldn't make any excuse to herself about the others noticing what she was doing. She looked, and looked away, and looked again.

She began to meander across the playground, casually, as though she were not really going anywhere in particular. Donovan went on kicking his ball.

Had he seen her coming? Amy stopped and swallowed. Her heart had begun to beat a bit faster and she felt sick. She swallowed again, and started to make a big circle – a circle which would take her right to where Donovan was, when she had finished stepping round it.

Donovan went on kicking his ball.

'Hello,' said Amy. Her voice sounded timid and

faint in her own ears, and she cleared her throat to make it stronger. 'Hello,' she said again.

'Yes?' said Donovan, still kicking his ball.

'I just said hello,' Amy's courage was ebbing fast; she felt foolish and conspicuous, and she thought everyone must be looking at her, making up to a boy who wasn't interested.

'Is that all you come to say then? Just hello?'

'No. There was something else.'

'Hurry up then. . . . Well, come on, I'm listening!' His voice was impatient and abrupt, and he still hadn't looked at her.

'I . . .' The words wouldn't come. She was so afraid of saying it wrong, and being rebuffed, that she couldn't say it at all.

'If you got anything to say, say it,' said Donovan. 'And if not go away, Baker, because I'm busy.'

'All right, it's not important.' Feeling quite cold, and dead inside, Amy trailed back across the playground. That was it; she wouldn't try any more. Donovan liked her once, or he'd seemed to, and she didn't know where she'd gone wrong, but whatever the cause, the split was too big to be mended now. Or anyway, it was too big for her to mend. Suddenly the little speech she had planned, about being loyal, and keeping Donovan's secret – that little speech seemed silly, and she was quite glad she hadn't made it.

'Will you get the globe down for me please Michael?' said Miss Elliot. 'I'm afraid I can't quite reach it.'

'In a minute,' said Michael.

'I should like to have it *now*, actually,' said Miss Elliot.

'In a minute,' said Michael, quite rudely. 'I'm busy.'

81

'Michael!' said Cynthia. 'Miss wants it now!'

'Shut up, Parrot,' said Andrew.

'Miss Elliot should have sat up straighter,' said Donovan. 'Then she'd be tall enough to get it herself.'

The boys fell about laughing at Donovan's joke. He had been away for a couple of days, bunking off again no doubt, and the boys were delighted to see him back. 'They're getting to be *awful*,' whispered Lorraine.

'And we know whose fault *that* is,' whispered Cynthia.

'Shall we tell them?' whispered Gloria. 'You know, what Maxine said. About Donovan was expelled.'

'No,' said Cynthia. 'They're too awful. They don't *deserve* to know.'

There was something wrong with this reasoning, Amy thought, but she was glad they weren't going to tell the boys about Donovan. He'd be shamed then, before everyone, and in spite of everything, she couldn't bear the thought of seeing him shamed. She wanted him to be sorry, for all the bad things he'd done, but she didn't want him shamed. She wanted him to be lovely, like she used to think he was when she first met him.

The boys were whispering behind their hands, and passing notes. 'They're up to something,' said Cynthia. 'Miss Elliot, the boys are up to something! I know their tricks!'

'What's the matter with you, Parrot?' said Andrew.

'Her nose is bothering her,' said Michael.

The boys fell about laughing again, and Cynthia scowled. 'I'll find out what it is,' she muttered. 'I'll find out what it is, you see if I don't find out what it is! You just see!'

The weather had been wet, on and off, for several days, and this afternoon there was a drenching downpour, which meant the children could not go out to play. Cynthia stood outside the boys' toilet, at the end of the top corridor, trying to hear what they were saying; but then Amy and Gloria came along and found what Cynthia was doing. 'That's not nice,' said Amy.

'You spoiled it,' said Cynthia crossly.

'It's not nice, listening to people's private conversations,' said Amy.

'Well, I got to find out what they're up to haven't I?' said Cynthia. 'It's sure to be something bad you know! That Donovan can't think of any good things to do, only bad things. You didn't ought to love him, Amy.'

'He might change though,' said Amy. 'One day.'

'Huh!' said Cynthia. 'Anyway, I don't know why you have to love *anyone*. You won't catch *me*.'

'Gloria does,' said Amy. 'She loves Michael, don't you Gloria?'

'Only a bit,' said Gloria.

The rest of the afternoon was not very happy. The children were restless and niggly, from not being able to let off steam in the playground. There was bickering, and unkind laughter in Class 4E's classroom and not much else. They were supposed to be working on individual projects, which meant there was a great deal of glue, and paint, and sheets of coloured paper around the room; and as the afternoon dragged to a close, more of these materials on the floor than on the desks.

'Clear up now,' said Miss Elliot, ten minutes before hometime. The girls, and some of the boys, started to do as they were asked. Donovan lounged on his desk, breaking a packet of green crayons into little pieces; his cronies lounged with him, still laughing and joking in rough voices, and trampling the muck into the floor.

'Why don't you clear up, when Miss Elliot said?' said Cynthia.

'Shut up, Parrot,' said Andrew.

Donovan threw a piece of green crayon at Cynthia, which hit her on the cheek and really stung. 'That's for telling me what to do! Nobody tells me what to do!'

'And nobody throws things at me!' said Cynthia furiously.

'Try to ignore him, Cynthia,' said Miss Elliot. 'I mean – you know – just *try*.'

'Try to ignore him, Cynthia,' mimicked Donovan quite audibly, in a high voice.

Cynthia lunged at him, but this time Gloria and Lorraine grabbed her, and held her arms. She struggled wildly, but could not free herself from their grasp.

'Come on Parrot, come on Parrot,' mocked Andrew, grinning and jumping up and down.

With one frenzied jerk, Cynthia drove her elbow into Gloria's chest, and when Gloria cried out with pain and let go, Cynthia clawed and punched with her free hand at Lorraine. Lorraine let go as well, and stood nursing a wounded cheek, hurt and surprise in her warm brown eyes. Cynthia trembled. She was free, but her anger was spent. She threw herself into a chair and scraped the chair around to face the wall. She kicked at the wall with her feet, and the noisy sobs began.

The bell went, and the class began putting chairs on the tables, and straggling to the door. The room was still a shambles. 'Clear up *first*,' said Miss Elliot, but either they didn't hear her, or they had stopped taking notice of what she said. With no consideration for their teacher, boys and girls alike pushed towards the cloakroom.

'Come back!' In the face of this outrage, Cynthia forgot her personal woe. 'You lot come back and tidy up the room!' She followed the crowd to the classroom door, and bawled at them down the corridor. 'Litter-louts! Lazy good-for-nothings!'

'We'll do it,' said Amy. 'Don't worry, Miss Elliot, me and Cynthia will clear up for you.

'Don't cry, Miss Elliot,' said Cynthia. 'Look – here's Andrea come back as well. And Lorraine, and Gloria . . . and Maxine. Don't cry, we're all going to help you.'

'Miss Elliot is our *best* teacher, isn't she girls?' said Lorraine.

Miss Elliot was weeping quietly. She was blowing her nose and pretending to have a cold, but really she was breaking her heart because her nice class was falling apart, and she was helpless to stop it happening. And he *promised*, *he promised*. Well, she would just have to stop it. She would have to learn to be strict like all the other teachers which up to now she hadn't needed to be. Miss Elliot bent down with the girls and worked with them, stuffing waste paper into the bin.

'Look what I found,' said Gloria.

'What is it?' said Lorraine.

'It's got writing on it.'

'It's signed *from Andrew*.'

'It says "METIN" – what's METIN?'

'He means MEETING, he can't spell. What a dunce! And "SEEKRT" – what's SEEKRT?'

'I know, I know,' said Cynthia. 'They're having a secret meeting. See, I told you. I did tell you, didn't I? I know their tricks, they're having a secret meeting!'

'How babyish!' said Gloria.

'It's all about doing bad things though,' said Cynthia. '*I* know their tricks! They're still having that gang, aren't they? They got a new secret place, haven't they? They're having a meeting to talk about doing more bad things! I know their tricks!'

'Pity we don't know where their secret place is – eh, Miss Elliot?' said Lorraine.

'That's right,' said Maxine.

It was raining again next morning, so everyone wore macs and coats to school. The cloakroom smelled damp and steamy from all the wet coats. There would be more indoor play today, most likely.

Miss Elliot smiled at them all very bravely as they came in, but you could see how sad and worried she still was really. 'You lot got to behave yourselves today!' Cynthia scolded them.

'That's enough from you, Parrot,' said Andrew.

There was a banging of desk lids and a succession of noisy complaints and accusations about lost pencils, etc. There were scuffles and aggressive voices. There were little plops of explosive laughter as the boys displayed to each other, under cover of their desk lids, the contents of the small tins and boxes they had brought to school.

'There's something *bad* in those tins,' said Cynthia darkly. 'I know their tricks!'

86

'What tins?' said Amy.

'Oh you never notice *anything*,' said Cynthia.

Then the boys were all asking to go to the toilet. One after another, exaggerated innocence on every face, they put the request to Miss Elliot, who didn't like to say no. 'You're like a lot of Infants!' said Gloria scornfully. 'They're a lot of babies aren't they, Miss Elliot? All asking to go to the toilet, like a lot of babies!'

'They're up to something,' said Cynthia. 'I know their tricks!'

'That's the last person I'm going to let out this morning,' said Miss Elliot.

At playtime the message came round that although it was raining, there was to be outdoor play after all. The children were to put on their coats, and go under the shed in the playground. This was always a miserable sort of play, and they straggled to the cloakroom without enthusiasm, wishing the time away.

Maxine put on her coat, and put her hand in her pocket to find a tissue. She screamed.

Gloria screamed too, and threw her mac on the floor.

Andrea was having hysterics. Her head was thrown back, her eyes popping wildly as her shrieks pierced the roof.

Lorraine was shuddering, and banging her coat against the pegs. 'Get away, ugh! Get away!'

Fearfully, Amy put her hand into the pocket of her own coat. Her fingers touched something. Something cold, and slimy, and wriggling. She could feel the colour draining from her face, and she thought she was going to be sick.

Cynthia was very angry indeed. 'It's worms, it's worms, they put worms in our coats!' Beside herself with rage and disgust, she kicked and stamped at the wriggling things on the floor. Over the coat pegs appeared a row of grinning boys' faces. 'What's the matter, Parrot?' Andrew's head shouted, above the din. 'Something wrong?'

Then Mr Bassett came, striding on his beanpole legs towards the scene of the disturbance. The row of boys' faces disappeared like magic from above the coat pegs. Mr Bassett towered over the girls. 'Cynthia Garrett! Good heavens child, what *are* you doing to God's creatures?'

'They're disgusting, they're disgusting,' said Cynthia, kicking some more.

'Stop it this instant!' said Mr Bassett, and Cynthia did stop, because it was unusual to hear Mr Bassett speaking so sharply. 'They're not disgusting at all, they have their place in the world as you have. Not in the cloakroom though. . . . All right, Cynthia, all right dear, I can see you're upset. . . . Now, Cynthia, don't cry. Do you want me to have to *swim* back to my office? You want me to *drown* perhaps. . . . Well, I must say, you're producing enough water to drown us all. Now where's someone sensible? Ah – Bharat, pretending not to be there! Just find a bag or something, lad, and collect up these things, and put them in the caretaker's garden. They'll be quite happy there.'

'Aren't you going to tell the boys off, for putting them in our coats, sir?' said Lorraine.

'After you shattered their eardrums with your screams?' said Mr Bassett. 'They'll be stone deaf, they wouldn't hear me! All right lads, a joke's a joke –

just don't do it again.' And he chuckled, to show everyone what a good sport he was really.

The girls were furious.

'It's not fair!'

'Mr Bassett should have told the boys off, it's not fair!'

'He done that 'cos he only likes the boys!'

'Yeah – Mr Bassett don't like the girls, only the boys!'

'Mr Bassett is a unfair pig.'

'Mr Bassett is a mean old baldy.'

'He's a *cow*.'

'Mr Bassett is too tall. He's not like a human bean, I think he come from Mars really.'

'Yeah – he got a extra pair of arms under his coat, like Amy's story. I see them sticking out.'

'It's not fair though.'

'The boys ought to have a punishment'

'I know, let's *us* punish the boys.'

'Oh yeah.'

'What shall we do?'

'Let's put worms in their coats,' said Maxine.

'Nah, not that, not that, something different.'

'Let's put spiders in their coats.'

'Who's going to collect the spiders though?'

Cynthia gave a great sniff, and swallowed the last of her tears. 'I got a better idea,' she said. 'Let's follow them, and find where their gang is, and spoil it.'

'Oh *yes*.'

'I don't want to do that,' said Amy.

'Well, you got to whether you like it or not,' said Cynthia firmly. 'We'll follow those boys after school. Right, girls? Right everybody? And if they don't go to their meeting tonight we'll do it next day, or next day, or next week. . . .'

It was quite fun really, quite exciting, stalking the group of boys down the road, seven girls counting Andrea's little sister. At first it wasn't necessary to hide, because this was most people's way home anyway. But at the end of George Street the boys turned off towards the big main traffic road, which was dangerous to cross with so many cars and lorries hurtling by, four lanes abreast. No one from George Street School lived the other side of the main traffic road.

'I wonder where they're going,' said Lorraine.

'Don't let them see you,' said Cynthia. 'Hide round the corner. . . . *Now*! No, get back, get in this doorway!'

'It's all right,' said Lorraine, 'they're not looking. They're too busy thinking about their wrong things they're planning to do.'

'I think they're going across the main road,' said Gloria uneasily.

'My mum said I mustn't,' said Maxine.

The boys streamed over, without waiting for the green pedestrian signal. Vehicles hooted them angrily. 'My mum said I mustn't,' said Maxine. 'I'm going home.'

'My mum said I mustn't too,' said Lorraine.

'Go on home then,' said Cynthia. 'Lot of use *you* are!'

They crossed the main road by the lights. 'My mum will worry if I'm late and I didn't tell her,' said Lorraine, still with them after all.

'Well we won't be late,' said Cynthia. 'We won't be

late. Not really late. Let's just see where they go. It can't be much further. . . . Look out, hide, hide!'

'They're going in the cemetery!' said Andrea.

'*Oooh*!' said Andrea's little sister

'I'm not going in the cemetery,' said Andrea. 'There's ghosts in the cemetery, I ain't going in there.'

'Br-r-r-r-r,' said Andrea's little sister.

'There's *not* ghosts,' said Cynthia. 'Dead people isn't the same as ghosts. Dead people can't hurt you, you're silly if you think that.'

'My mum saw a ghost one time,' said Gloria.

'I'm going home,' said Andrea.

'I'm going home too,' said Lorraine. 'I don't like ghosts.'

'You're just silly,' said Cynthia. 'You know that? You're just silly! Me and Amy's not scared of ghosts, are we, Amy?'

'No,' said Amy, only half listening. There was no space in her mind for thinking about ghosts. What was eating her up was that she was being against Donovan. She was being on Cynthia's side against Donovan, and that made her feel all mixed up, and horrible, because she didn't want to be against Cynthia either. She just hoped Donovan would somehow not have to see her, being on Cynthia's side against him.

'Come on then,' said Cynthia. 'You and me and Gloria follow the boys in the cemetery.'

'My mum saw a ghost one time though,' said Gloria.

'She *would*,' said Cynthia, exasperated. 'You and me then, Amy . . . Amy?'

'We can't spoil their gang with only two,' said Amy, hopefully.

'I know but – just see where they got their meeting. Just that. Then we'll go home. Then we'll go home I promise. . . . Amy?'

'All right,' said Amy.

They passed through the big main gates. The boys, eight or nine of them, whooped and played as they moved along the path between the tombstones. 'Hide!' said Cynthia. 'Case they look back. Till we see which turn they take.' The girls crouched in the space between two big graves. 'I don't know why they come all this way,' Cynthia grumbled. 'Give us so much trouble following them! Why don't they just have their meeting under the shed at school?'

'Oh no,' said Amy, 'that's too ordinary.' She understood well enough why it had to be the cemetery. She understood how coming to the cemetery made it an adventure. Personally, she only liked adventures when they were in books, or inside her head, where it was safe and you couldn't get in trouble. But some people liked taking risks, and Amy understood that. She knew people weren't always the same as each other.

Cynthia peeped round the tall headstone. 'They're turning, come on!' The girls bent low, as they ran along the path. 'My back aches, running like this,' said Amy. 'Don't make such a fuss,' said Cynthia. 'Come on, faster. . . . Oh hide again, hide. Keep your head down, Amy, they going to see! They going to see your hair. You didn't ought to have hair like that, like a fire-bush, it's a nuisance.'

Her hair, her hair! Donovan would see her hair and know she had come to spy on him! Amy took off her mac, and covered her head with that. The rain had finally stopped, and there were patches of blue sky between the banks of pink and grey cloud. The wet grass smelled sweet, and the sweetness hurt because it was such a sad thing she was doing. Amy lay full length on the wet grass, and breathed in the sad sweetness. 'Don't do that!' scolded Cynthia. 'You'll get your dress all soaked. You'll catch your death. You'll catch PEWNOMIA!'

'Where are they now?' asked Amy.

'They've gone in a little house,' said Cynthia.

'Shall we go home then?' said Amy. 'Now we've seen where they go?'

'No, not yet, not yet . . . I know, I know, I know what we'll do. We'll creep up and listen.'

'*Cynthia!*'

'What's wrong?'

'You not supposed to listen to people's private conversations.'

'Oh pooh! . . . Come on, we got to find out. We got to find out all the wrong things they're planning to do. Amy?'

'I don't want to.'

'I know you don't *want* to. I know that. The thing is . . . are you my friend.?'

'All right then,' said Amy unhappily.

The boys were all inside the little house; there was a heavy iron door, partly open, through which their muffled voices floated. Over the doorway were two stone angels, grimy with age, and round the other three sides of the mausoleum a hedge of tall bushes – a perfect screen. Twigs snapped as Cynthia and Amy squeezed themselves between the hedge and the stone wall, but the noise was drowned out by the excited clamour inside. Cynthia stood as near the open door as she dared, and Amy stood behind her, anxious and miserable, wishing not to be there.

The hoots and shrieks and horseplay inside went on and on. 'They're just mucking about,' said Amy.

'Wait,' said Cynthia.

'Shut up, you guys – shut up, shut up now, *listen*,' said Donovan, above the din.

'Wriggle wriggle, slimy wriggle!' Andrew's delighted squeals bounced around inside the tiny house. 'Wriggle, squiggle, didn't they scream!'

'Shut up now though, right?'

'It was good, it was good.'

'Listen though, listen, listen to me . . .' Donovan could not get them quiet.

'He's not much of a boss, is he?' said Cynthia, pleased that Donovan was not having it all his own way.

'LISTEN! I got something good to say. . . . No listen, listen. . . . You want to hear it? Right then listen. We finished with the worms, right? That wasn't nothing, that wasn't no big deal. I got a much more better thing we can do, right?'

'All right,' said Michael, 'what?'

'You're not all listening.' Someone coughed, and someone else giggled. 'All right, now I'll tell you. Now I'll tell you what we're going to do—'

'To the girls?'

'Yeah, to the girls . . .'

'Goody goody gumdrops!' 'Wriggle wriggle!' 'Make them scream again?' 'Ah-h-h-h-h-h!'

'All right, you don't want to listen, I won't bother to tell you . . .'

'Ah come on!' 'Come on, Donovan!' 'Come on, we won't muck about no more.'

'All right. . . . How about we write shaming things about them, right? All over the walls at school, right? And outside. . . . Right?'

There was a subdued silence.

'Cynthia Garrett is a parrot,' suggested Andrew.

'No not that, that's silly,' said Donovan. 'Something much worse than that.'

'It's not silly,' said Andrew, put out. 'It's good. It makes her go mad. Anyway, I don't know nothing bad about Cynthia really. I don't think there *is* anything.'

'Doesn't have to be true,' said Donovan. 'We can make it up.'

'That's mean,' said Bharat. 'You can't write it if it's not true.'

No one else spoke. 'All right, forget it,' said Donovan.

'You *can* write it if it's not true,' said Gavin. 'Serve her right, nosy old parrot!' 'Yeah, serve her right!' 'Come on, what else can we write?'

'We can write things about Amy Baker,' said Andrew, sniggering. 'You don't mind, do you Donovan? You know what you said about Amy Baker!' There was whispering, and raucous laughter.

'We can write "Gloria loves Michael",' said Gavin.

'You ain't writing my name,' said Michael. 'I'll punch your head in if you write my name.'

'Only joking.'

'No but – you're not writing my name. Nobody's writing my name.'

'We could write about Miss Elliot,' said Donovan. 'How about that?'

'She's a *nice* teacher,' said Bharat in a troubled voice.

95

'She's soft. She's twitty,' said Donovan.

'Nobody's writing my name,' said Michael.

'All right, we get it,' said Donovan. 'Nobody's writing your name.'

'You can write Miss Elliot's name if you like,' said Michael. 'She gets on my nerves. "Michael do this. Please Michael do that." Who does she think she is telling me to do things? I'm not her slave!'

'We could write "Miss Elliot loves Mr Bassett",' said Gavin. 'That upset the girls as well. That make them shout!'

Hoots of merriment.

'We didn't ought to do it though,' said Bharat. 'I don't think we ought to do that.'

'Are you soft too then?' said Donovan, scornfully.

'Bharat's soft,' said Andrew. 'Bharat's soft as pudding!'

'Rice pudding!' 'Treacle pudding!' 'Rhubarb pudding!' 'Ha, ha, ha!' 'He's a sissy!' 'You're a sissy, Bharat!'

'Only joking,' said Bharat unhappily.

'Shall we get some chalk then?' said Andrew. 'Off of Miss's desk?'

'Nah, chalk rubs out too easy.' Donovan sounded pleased. They were with him now, he had them all with him. 'We want something going to be there a long time. Going to shame them a long time. Going to shame that parrot's lot a long time. . . . We'll do it in paint, right?'

'Paint comes off easy,' said Gavin. 'You just wash if off, it's easy.'

'I don't mean paint out of school you know,' said Donovan. 'I mean proper shiny paint. Like you paint doors with – that sort of paint.'

'The thing is though, we haven't got none of that sort of paint.'

'*I* know where to get some, leave it to me,' said Donovan. 'Right?'

The girls had heard most of it, and what they hadn't heard they guessed. Cynthia seethed with rage as they scurried home. 'Wicked things! Wicked awful things! What do they have to listen to that Donovan for? It's all his fault, they wouldn't think of it by themselves! They never done bad things before he come! Did they, Amy? . . . Amy? . . . Isn't it all that nuisance Donovan's fault!'

'Yes,' said Amy, but she wasn't thinking about the bad things the boys were going to do, she was wondering what shaming thing it was that Donovan had said about her, to Andrew. Humiliated, and hurt beyond words, she panted to keep up with Cynthia.

'I wish Bharat went on standing up for Miss Elliot, don't you Amy?' said Cynthia, not looking at Amy's stricken face. 'Don't you wish that? I use to like Bharat, didn't you? I use to think Bharat was a really nice boy. . . . We got to stop those hooligans, haven't we? Those nuisances . . . oh!' Cynthia stood still suddenly, and clapped her hands to her head in horror. 'Oh *Amy*, you forgot Simon! We *both* forgot Simon!'

7

Red paint

'See?' said Cynthia. 'You should have come. I told you. Didn't I tell you? You should have come. Shouldn't they, Amy? They should have come!'

'My mum saw a ghost one time though,' said Gloria.

'We got to stop him doing it,' said Lorraine.

'I know we got to stop him, I know that,' said Cynthia. 'The thing is – how?'

'Tell Mr Bassett,' said Gloria.

'Mr Bassett isn't no good,' said Cynthia. 'Remember something beginning with "W"? Remember? Remember he blamed us instead of the boys? Remember?'

'Yeah,' said Lorraine, 'Mr Bassett only likes the boys.'

'That's right,' said Maxine.

'Tell Miss Elliot,' said Andrea.

'NO,' said Cynthia. That's the very thing we're not going to do, Andrea. Poor Miss Elliot! We're not going to tell her that Donovan is going to write "Miss Elliot loves Mr Bassett" all over the road. Poor Miss Elliot! Do you want to make her cry, Andrea?'

'That's right, Andrea,' said Maxine. 'Fancy you wanting to make our best teacher cry!'

'Miss Elliot loves Mr Bassett,' said Andrea, giggling.

'It's not funny Andrea,' said Cynthia sharply. 'So

shut up laughing all of you, and think. Come on *think*. Use your brains that God gave you. And you, Amy! You got to think as well. . . . Come on, Amy, *wake up*. I'm talking to you!'

Amy struggled to focus her attention on what Cynthia was saying. Something about Mr Bassett, and Miss Elliot – and Donovan. Donovan was going to do something terrible, and she ought to feel it was important what Donovan was going to do, but she couldn't. The important thing was what Donovan said to Andrew. Something that wasn't very nice, about her . . . And the other thing that was important was that thing she had decided she was never going to think about again, only it wouldn't *let* her not think about it!

'We could hide the paint,' said Andrea, giggling again.

'That's a good idea you had, Andrea,' said Cynthia. 'That's a *good* idea. . . . Don't you think that's a good idea, Amy, to hide the paint?'

'What paint?' said Amy.

'Oh I lose my patience with you!' said Cynthia.

'That's right,' said Maxine.

Donovan was in the playground, and he had a plastic bag with something heavy inside. 'I bet that's the paint,' said Gloria. 'I bet he pinched it from somewhere.'

'Yeah, I bet,' said Maxine.

'We have to watch him,' said Cynthia, 'and see where he goes to put it.'

Donovan went nowhere. He brought the plastic bag into class, and hung it over the back of his chair. Every now and again his hand crept back to feel if the bag was still there, and he looked pleased in a sly sort of way.

'When shall we take it, Cynthia?' said Lorraine.

'Playtime,' said Cynthia. 'We'll hide in the toilets, and when everybody's gone downstairs we'll creep back to the classroom and take the paint.'

'All of us?'

'Not all of us, you silly great idiot, Maxine! Not all of us. Me and Amy. . . . Amy? . . . All right then, me and Lorraine. Me and Lorraine will get the paint at playtime, and pour it down the loo.'

Cynthia lifted the heavy plastic bag from Donovan's chair. 'It *is* paint! See? See, I was right, Lorraine! I said, didn't I? Didn't I say he was going to get paint?' She looked again. 'It's *red* paint. What a cheek to paint our names in red paint! Don't you think that Donovan's got a cheek, Lorraine?'

'There's somebody coming,' said Lorraine. 'Quick, hide the paint!'

Cynthia sat down heavily at the nearest desk, the plastic bag with the paint in it clutched between her knees, under her skirt.

'What you doing sitting in my desk?' It was Kevin Riley, come back for something or other. His nose was running, as usual; the sad pale face had dark shadows under the eyes, and round the mouth.

'You're not supposed to be here,' said Cynthia.

'I got permission,' said Kevin, 'if I'm quick.'

'Be quick then,' said Cynthia. 'and blow your nose.'

'You're sitting in my desk?'

'So?'

'Get out of my desk!' He hadn't much spirit, and he

was used to being pushed aside, but this was invasion of his personal space, and too much to be tolerated. 'You get out of my desk, Cynthia Garrett!'

'She's not hurting your desk,' said Lorraine.

'She's hiding something. She got something in her lap.'

'So?' said Cynthia. 'It's none of your business.'

'I want to see.' He tugged at her skirts.

'Leave me!' Cynthia was outraged.

'I think you thiefed something.'

'You can talk!'

He hung back then, stung, and his eyes filled with tears.

'No use crying,' said Cynthia sternly. 'You done that Kevin, you know it. You made my best friend in trouble that time. It was really mean what you done to Amy, and you never said, and you let everybody think it was her. You should be ashamed of yourself!'

She was ranting at him to distract attention from the tin of paint in her lap, not to be cruel, but to the boy who had no friend, ever, her words cut like knives. 'I never done it though,' he blurted – and immediately began shifting his feet, looking at the girls with hangdog eyes, as though scared he had given something away.

'What you mean?' said Lorraine.

'Nothing,' said Kevin.

'If you never done it,' said Cynthia, 'how come you let everybody think you did?'

'I dunno,'

'Yes you do. How come?'

'I dunno, I said.'

'You're stupid, Kevin, do you know that?' said Cynthia. 'You're stupid and you're telling lies. I

think you done it all the time, you're just making out
. . . Wait a minute though, *wait a minute*. . . . I
remember! . . . I remember you said you never done
it one time, and the boys was going on at you, and
Donovan Grant told them to leave you alone. I get it,
I get it. . . . It was Donovan, wasn't it? It was
Donovan took those things and put them in Amy's
desk!'

'No.' The tearstained face looked terrified.

'I think you're just scared to say,' said Cynthia. 'I
think you're scared Donovan's going to beat you up.'

'Did he *say* he would beat you up?' said Lorraine,
with interest.

'No,' said Kevin.

'Never mind if he *said*,' said Cynthia. 'Kevin knows
he's wicked, don't you Kevin, and *you* ought to know
it Lorraine, without being told!'

'I'm going down to play,' said Kevin.

'NO!' said Cynthia. She jumped up to grab him,
and the paint tin fell out of the plastic bag, with a
clatter, and began rolling across the floor. Lorraine
barred Kevin's way as well, and he gave up the
struggle. The paint tin came to the end of its roll.
'That's Donovan's,' said Kevin.

'So?' said Cynthia.

'He's going to go mad. Ain't you scared?'

'No,' said Cynthia.

'You're scared of everything, Kevin,' said Lorraine.

'Don't be unkind, Lorraine,' said Cynthia. 'Listen,
Kevin, I got 5p. You can have 5p if you tell us what
secret things you know about Donovan Grant. . . .
Eh?' she wheedled, '5p?' The sad eyes gleamed,
momentarily. Poor Kevin never had any money to
spend.

Silence.

'All right,' Cynthia persisted. 'I tell you what. I tell you what, Kevin. You tell us what secret things you know about Donovan Grant and you can be our *friend*.'

The sad eyes gleamed again, hope mingling with unbelief. 'Can I?'

'He can, can't he, Lorraine? He can be our friend, can't he? . . . There, Lorraine says you can!'

'What must I tell?'

'You know – that day – all those things in Amy's desk.'

'Donovan made me come, didn't he?'

'Yeah, I'll believe that all right,' said Cynthia. 'That's what Donovan does. He makes people do wrong things, he's a nuisance.'

'He said "Let's go and see what we can find in people's desks."'

'But *you* never took them, Kevin, did you? It was *him*.'

'No! No, I never! I swear.'

'Don't you worry, Kevin,' said Cynthia. 'We know you wouldn't do a mean thing like that. We do, don't we, Lorraine? Don't we know Kevin wouldn't do a thing like that, and just sit there that time, and let everybody think it was Amy?'

'He *did* sit there and let everybody think it was Amy,' said Lorraine.

'He didn't mean to though. You ought to understand that, Lorraine, without being told. It wasn't Kevin's fault, it was Donovan's. Donovan made him stay quiet, didn't he, Kevin? We know his tricks. We know what he was going to do with this paint if we hadn't of taken it. Don't we Lorraine? He was going

103

to write rude things about us in the road. And Miss Elliot.'

'What?'

'You heard. And blow your nose. And close your mouth, you look like a goldfish. All the boys are in it, they think Donovan's the best thing since sliced bread. And we're not telling you how we know about it neither. You got to be our friend a bit longer before we tell you *all* our secrets. We'll let you help though. We'll let you help us get the tin open, so we can pour the paint down the loo.'

The lid was very tight. Kevin tried with Cynthia's 5p piece, but he was so overcome with the wonder of being someone's friend at last, that his fingers were all wobbly, and Cynthia had to snatch the tin and the 5p piece away from him, because she was afraid playtime would be over before they managed to get rid of the paint. Her own fingers were not strong enough to use the 5p piece, and neither were Lorraine's, but luckily Cynthia thought of the spoon that was kept by the sink, for dishing out powder paint. They all had a go at opening the tin with the spoon, and Kevin was the one who finally got it off, which made him feel very happy and useful – but also resulted in a great deal of red paint being on his hands.

'Wash it under the tap,' said Cynthia. 'Go on, Kevin, wash it off before somebody sees.' But the paint was sticky, and wouldn't come off. 'Hide your hands then,' said Cynthia. 'Put them in your pockets.'

'Hurry, hurry, hurry,' begged Lorraine. 'Playtime's going to be over.'

The paint wouldn't all go down. They kept pulling

the flush, but the paint still clung in a sticky mess, all around the toilet bowl. They tried to rub it off with paper, but they only got paint on their hands. Without thinking, Lorraine rubbed her hands on her dress, and now there was paint on her dress as well. 'Look what you done!' Cynthia scolded her.

'The bell's going to go,' said Lorraine, in a panic.

'All right, calm down, calm down,' said Cynthia. 'We shall just have to hide our hands too. What shall we do with the tin?'

'I don't know, I don't know!'

'We'll put it out the window, on the ledge,' said Cynthia. 'Oh no that's no good though. They'll see it from the outside.'

'They going to see the paint in the toilet anyway.' said Lorraine.

Donovan was beside himself with rage. His anger seethed and boiled behind the darkened face, filling the room with silent threat. His eyes, looking at no one, were narrowed slits. He slumped in his desk (the shoulders in the rough-dried shirt hunched around his ears), refusing to work, or even get out his books. Miss Elliot, on the principle of leaving well enough alone, pretended she had not noticed that anything was wrong.

Amy cringed. Even when she wasn't looking at him, she could feel Donovan's anger, only just contained beneath the surface. She didn't know about the paint in the lavatory, but she knew the plastic bag had disappeared from Donovan's chair, and she could see how guilty and excited Cynthia and Lorraine were – whispering to one another and keeping their hands hidden under the table. The

105

tension in the air was like a piece of elastic, stretched to breaking point, and ready to snap at any moment. 'It wasn't me,' Amy wanted to say to Donovan. 'It wasn't me took your paint, it wasn't!'

Something must happen soon. If something didn't happen soon, the smouldering volcano that was Donovan would burst, and erupt, and spill disaster all over the room. Perhaps the volcano would burst and erupt anyway. The waiting was terrible; it was a relief, on the whole, when Mr Bassett came in and told them all to fold their arms and sit up straight because he had something important to tell them.

There was a mystery that needed solving, Mr Bassett said, and his spies had fallen down on the job for once, so there was a need for some good detectives to help solve this mystery. Perhaps there were some good detectives in Class 4E. They would call it The Mystery of the Red Paint. Could anyone tell Mr Bassett anything about Red Paint? No one? Then perhaps everyone would be good enough to put their hands on the tables, and Mr Bassett would come round and see for himself.

He stared at the back. The boys did not mind putting their hands on the tables. Since their hands were innocent of paint they were, in fact, quite eager to show them. The questions that followed might be awkward, but at least their hands were not going to incriminate them. And meanwhile, it was going to be quite interesting to find out who had taken Donovan's paint.

Poor Kevin! He was white and shaking as Mr Bassett took his wrist and turned it to inspect the palm. 'Well I never!' said Mr Bassett. 'The Red Demon in person! Explain yourself young man!'

Kevin's mouth opened and closed, but no actual sound came out.

'Speak up, I can't hear you. I want to know how this paint got on your hand. Both hands, I see.'

'Don't know.' The words were just audible.

'Don't *know*? Red paint all over your hands and you don't know how it came there? Well, well, well, we must have a little pixie in the school, who pours paint all over people's hands when they aren't looking. . . . Is that it? Is that it . . . No? . . . How, then?'

'Don't know.'

'Did *you* bring paint to school, Kevin? To brighten up the classroom perhaps? I must say this dingy old building could do with a lick or two of paint. Was that it then?'

'Don't know.'

'Well now, if I had brought paint to school, if I had taken the trouble to bring a tin of expensive gloss paint to school, I should be *quite annoyed* to find someone had poured it down the girls' lavatory. Are you annoyed about that, Kevin?'

'Don't know.'

'You don't even know if you're annoyed? I wonder if anyone else is annoyed.' Mr Bassett's gaze wandered round the room. 'What about you Donovan Grant, are *you* annoyed?'

'No, sir.' He wouldn't look at Mr Bassett though, and his voice was hoarse and thick.

'Really? I thought you were looking a bit out of sorts. My mistake, my mistake! Let's have a look at the rest of the hands, shall we, Miss Elliot? What about the ones I haven't seen yet? We still don't know who poured the paint down the girls' lavatory, do we?

And left the tin on the window ledge, for the whole of George Street to see! Ah, *Cynthia*! And *Lorraine*! Now that's a funny place to put nail polish! I never saw a girl put nail polish on the ends of her fingers before, did you, Miss Elliot? Nor up her arms, nor all down the side of her skirt! I wonder what your mother is going to say about that Lorraine!'

No answer.

'In any case, I can't imagine what possessed you to pour paint down the toilet, Cynthia. Such a wasteful thing to do, apart from the mess! Whatever made you do it, dear?'

'Donovan was going to write rude things.' Donovan's face was a picture. How did she know that?

'What!' said Mr Bassett, as though such a thing were quite beyond the bounds of possibility.

'It's true,' said Cynthia. 'Donovan was going to write rude things about us, with the paint.'

'You astonish me,' said Mr Bassett. 'Tell me more.'

Cynthia closed her lips tight. She was not going to tell Mr Bassett about going to the cemetery. Mr Bassett didn't like the girls, only the boys. Mr Bassett would say they didn't ought to have gone to the cemetery. He would say they didn't ought to have listened. Mr Bassett was a mean old Martian, and she wouldn't tell him any more, so there!

Mr Bassett pretended she had told him anyway. 'So it was *your* paint, Donovan.'

Silence.

'Donovan?'

'I suppose so.'

'You *suppose* so?'

108

'Yeah, all right, it was.'

'You brought it to school then?'

'Like you said, to brighten up the class.' He was swallowing fiercely, controlling himself, but only just.

'There, I thought that must be the explanation! Ha, ha, ha! And Cynthia poured it down the toilet for you! Ha, ha, ha! What a tiresome little girl you are, Cynthia, pouring the paint down the toilet after Donovan took so much trouble to bring it to school! . . . It's a *joke*, Cynthia, don't look like that! My goodness you are spoiling your pretty face with that sulk! Don't you think so, Miss Elliot? And talking of pretty faces – yes, we've finished with the paint, the paint's buried. I mean drowned. Ha, ha, ha! Only no more, boys and girls! Do you hear me? *No more paint.* What was I saying? Oh yes, pretty faces – I hope you all remember the photographer is coming this afternoon. So pretty faces please, all the girls, and hair as smart as mine boys, hair as smart as mine!'

Mr Bassett ran a hand over the shiny dome of his head. 'Do you notice, Miss Elliot, how quite a few boys in this class have forgotten to have hair as smart as mine?' He coughed as he said this, in a slightly embarrassed way, since Miss Elliot's own hair was looking, as usual, like a particularly ragged birds' nest.

The volcano was still rumbling. Not quite so dangerously, gathering force for a new thrust, perhaps. Something was going to happen soon.

They were still whispering together, Cynthia and Lorraine, their hands cupped over their mouths. Every now and again they shot furtive looks in her direction, so Amy knew they were whispering about her. She felt lonely, and left out, and when Gloria and Andrea and Maxine were invited to join the whispering, Amy felt more lonely and left out than before.

She skipped by herself in the playground, pretending not to notice that the others had a secret from her. She thought about Donovan and the paint, and about how much nicer it would be if Donovan owned up, and said he was sorry, instead of saying that silly thing Mr Bassett didn't really believe. ('Yes Mr Bassett,' said Donovan, with tears in his eyes, 'I did bring the paint to school and I was going to write rude things with it, but I didn't mean to do wrong. I didn't think really, and I will never do it again.' 'That's all right lad,' said Mr Bassett. 'We won't have any inquests or post-mortems.')

Shyly, in case they were still talking about her, Amy wandered towards her friends. 'Oh *hello* Amy,' said Cynthia, 'we were just saying about Kevin. Weren't we girls! Weren't we just saying about Kevin! We were, weren't we!'

This declaration was accompanied by vigorous nods, winks and nudges, 'What about Kevin?' said Amy, as though she believed that was really what they were talking about.

'Well, he's going to get beat up now, isn't he! Stands to reason, he's going to get beat up. Donovan's going to beat him up, for helping us with the paint.'

'You don't actually *know* Donovan beats people up though,' said Lorraine.

'Where are your brains, Lorraine?' said Cynthia pityingly. 'Donovan's bad, isn't he? And bad people beat people up, don't they? Stands to reason.'

110

'You don't *know* it though,' said Lorraine.

'All right, I'll find out,' said Cynthia. 'If you're so fussy I'll find it out. Satisfied?'

She eavesdropped shamelessly; in the cloakroom, outside the boys' toilet, her sharp ears straining to catch every word. 'They're all going to beat him up,' she said. 'Told you!'

'All of them?'

'All of them. After school.'

'Poor Kevin!'

'It's Donovan's fault,' said Cynthia. 'He made them be like that. He's a troublemaker. He's a nuisance.'

'Poor Kevin!'

'It's no use saying poor Kevin like that, Lorraine,' said Cynthia. 'We got to *do* something about it.'

'Tell Mr Bassett,' said Gloria.

'I'm surprised at you Gloria,' said Cynthia, 'to say such a silly thing. You know Mr Bassett only listens to the boys, and he don't like the girls. You know that. So *we* got to protect Kevin. Now he's our friend we got to protect him. We got to put him in the middle of us and take him home, so the boys can't get him.'

'I got to go straight home tonight, my mum said,' said Gloria.

'My mum said that too,' said Andrea.

'That's right,' said Maxine, 'and mine.'

'What's your excuse?' said Cynthia, to Amy.

'I got to take Simon,' said Amy miserably.

'Anyway, me and Lorraine aren't scared, are we?' said Cynthia.

'No,' said Lorraine, wishing she had the courage to say 'Yes.'

111

It was hopeless, of course. What could two girls do against a great crowd of boys? They were waiting round the corner, and they snatched the luckless Kevin and held him. They were baying for his blood, and it was not a pretty sight to see. Cynthia made a futile attempt to snatch him back, but the boys just made fun of her, and two of them held her arms so that she was helpless between them, crying with rage and frustration, and fury directed against Lorraine, who had run off while she could, and was standing at a distance, her back pressed against someone's garden wall for comfort.

'Here he is, Donovan!' screamed Andrew. 'We got him, we got him! Donovan's going to show him! Good old Donovan!' Those who could get near enough were all holding Kevin, inviting their leader to exercise his right; his right to punish this little worm, who had spoiled their fun.

Kevin's face was ashen with fear. In desperation he lashed out. 'I'll tell, I'll tell! If you hit me, I'll tell what you done!'

'What did I do?' said Donovan. 'What did I do for you to tell?' There was a vague stirring in his memory – about something a long time ago, weeks ago, so he couldn't properly remember what it was. And anyway he didn't want to hit this poor weak thing in front of him, this poor weak thing that nobody liked. It was expected of him, because of what this poor weak thing had done, but he didn't actually want to do it. 'Anyway, who told?' said Donovan. 'You didn't know nothing about it, so somebody must have told!'

'Don't know,' said Kevin. 'Don't know!' He didn't know. If he knew he would tell. To save his skin he would tell. Was he going to be let off anyway? Hope and fear consumed him – it was a pitiful thing to watch. Donovan looked away, and his gaze fell on Bharat.

'*You* done it!'

'What you mean?' Donovan's face had twisted suddenly with a new bitterness, and Bharat was alarmed.

'You told the girls. You went and told the girls about the paint!'

'No I never!'

'Yes you did! You didn't want us to do our plan, so you went and told, you dirty squealer, you!'

'No, no!'

'He never!' 'Not Bharat!' 'You shouldn't blame Bharat, it weren't him!' The boys were sure that Donovan had made a mistake, but Donovan was not listening to them.

'I know something you don't know, Donovan Grant!' shouted Cynthia, but Donovan did not hear her either.

Donovan advanced on Bharat, and his eyes were narrowed to slits, and his shoulders were up, the bent arms pumping, the fists clenched so the knuckles showed white. 'No, no!' Bharat backed, frightened. Donovan hit him.

'Leave him, Donovan!' Two boys tried to pull Donovan away from Bharat but tentatively, not quite sure where their loyalties were supposed to lie. Donovan twisted from their grasp, kicking and elbowing them out of the way to get at this new enemy. Bharat! Whose dad wasn't in prison, and whose mum would never throw *him* out of the house. Who didn't have to do anything special to make himself liked, because everyone liked him anyway. It

113

wasn't fair, it wasn't fair! Donovan lashed out at the unfairness of it, smashing the pleasant face with his fists.

'Go on Donovan, go on Donovan!' That was Andrew, coming in on Donovan's side. 'He did tell, he did tell!' Andrew was screaming with excitement. 'You give it to him, Donovan!' 'Yeah, it was Bharat, it was!' Gavin thought it was Bharat too. Well, it had to be, didn't it? There wasn't anybody else.

Bharat was on the ground, and Donovan was kicking him. Bharat wasn't much of a fighter, and he didn't know how to defend himself. 'Help me!' he begged – and by this time most of them would have liked to, only they couldn't quite make up their minds.

Bharat was hurt. His nose was streaming blood, and he was all doubled up, where Donovan had kicked him in the stomach. 'That's enough!' said Michael suddenly. Donovan went on kicking Bharat. 'I said that's enough!' Michael shouted, grabbing at Donovan with powerful arms, and yanking him away.

'Leave me or I'll do you too!' Donovan was beside himself. He turned on Michael now, his eyes brimming and hot with rage.

'Do me then!' Michael squared up. The crowd backed away to give them space. One or two began ministering to the injured Bharat. 'Michael, Michael!' the chant began, softly at first, just a few voices, then louder and louder, swelling to a shout. 'Come on Michael! Come on Michael!' The boys holding Cynthia let her go and she ran to join Lorraine, still against the wall. The girls clung to each other, and screamed until their voices cracked, for Michael to win the fight against Donovan.

114

The tide had turned. It had trembled and dithered, unsure of direction, and now it was racing away. 'Michael!' 'Michael!' 'Michael!' The fight was short and decisive. Donovan was strong, but he hadn't a chance against Michael. With bruised eyes and damaged pride, he flung away from his adversary. 'Don't have to fight you if I don't want to!'

The tide had receded still further, but Andrew and Gavin were still with Donovan, stranded on a bleak shore now. 'All right,' said Andrew. 'Donovan don't have to fight you if he don't want to!'

'Donovan's a better fighter than you anyway, Michael,' said Gavin illogically.

'Michael's a thickhead anyway.' said Andrew. 'He can't do nothing clever, only fight.

'Hooray, hooray, hooray!' cheered Cynthia and Lorraine. 'Michael won! Hooray!'

The crowd melted away.

The tide had gone out – right out now. With hurt and puzzled eyes, Donovan watched it recede.

8

Secrets come out

Amy's thoughts were like a bagful of fleas – hopping and jumping all over the place. One minute she was longing to hear about yesterday, what happened when the girls took Kevin home; and the next minute she didn't want to know at all. She wanted to draw a curtain, and cover it all up, and not hear any more about it, ever.

It was Saturday, and her turn to go to Cynthia's this afternoon, and she couldn't get out of hearing about Kevin then, even if she wanted to. She was dreading Saturday afternoon, and she couldn't wait for it to come.

'I got to get new shoes for Simon,' said Mum. 'And I got to go to Sainsbury's. You can come, Amy. Make yourself useful and mind Simon in Sainsbury's. If you can keep yourself in the same world as the rest of us two minutes on end! Honestly, Amy, you're a laugh! I never know such a absent-minded child in my life. Wouldn't notice Father Christmas coming down the chimley less somebody shout "Oh look – there's Father Christmas, coming down the chimley!"'

She went on and on about it, all the way to the High Street. She had been very upset, that day Amy forgot to bring Simon home, but now she had got over being upset, she decided it was a great joke. She told the story to everybody, with great shrieks of laughter, which was very embarrassing for Amy; just now she was talking in such a loud voice, she might as well be telling the street – which was even more embarrassing. Amy lagged behind, holding Simon very firmly by the hand so no one could accuse her of forgetting him again. 'Keep up, keep up!' Mum shrieked back at her. 'Can't let you out of sight, you might forget where we're going.' The cascading torrent of Mum's laughter splashed the whole road.

Amy went into a dream. Perhaps Donovan changed yesterday, all of a sudden, all of a sudden, after she went home. ('It's all right, Kevin, we aren't going to hurt you,' said Donovan. 'We forgive you what you done. We going to let you off, aren't we boys? You can join our gang if you like.' Kevin smiled, and everyone was happy ever after.)

Outside Sainsbury's there was a woman with a warty face and a great hairy moustache. 'It *was* you,' said Hairy Moustache, as though she and Amy were continuing the conversation they had weeks ago, in the road by the railway. 'I'd know that hair anywhere!' She spoke aggressively, in a very accusing voice.

'What's she on about?' said Mum, to Amy.

'Nothing,' said Amy.

'Let's go in Sainsbury's,' said Simon. He was not interested in this conversation, and he had been promised a packet of Smarties from Sainsbury's if he was good.

'This your daughter?' said Hairy Moustache, to Mum.

'In case it's any of your business, which I don't think it is, yes,' said Mum.

'She crash somebody's car, you know. Did you know that?' said Hairy Moustache.

117

'Let's go in Sainsbury's,' said Simon. 'Mum, Mum, let's go!'

'Don't be ridiculous,' said Mum, to Hairy Moustache.

'Mum, *Mum*,' said Simon.

'Shut up or I'll clip you one,' said Mum. 'All right you, if you got something to say, say it!'

'She crash somebody's car, three-four weeks ago,' said Hairy Moustache.

'Don't you make accusations like that!' said Mum furiously. 'Who do you think you are?'

'I know it was her, I see her red hair.'

'What about it? Lot of people got red hair. *I* got red hair. Perhaps you like to accuse *me* of crashing somebody's car. Course I can't drive, but that don't matter, oh no! I can't drive, but I crash people's cars because I got red hair.'

'Don't you get nasty with me,' said Hairy Moustache. 'I was a witness. There! I was a witness, I see it all. And that boy she was with. It was a Sunday.'

'You want to watch your trap,' said Mum. 'You going to be up in court else.'

'And that tricky girl's going to be in court an' all!'

'You asking for a fat lip?' said Mum.

'Who's going to give it to me then? You?'

Amy thought she would die. Was Mum really going to hit Hairy Moustache? 'Mum,' whined Simon. 'Let's go.'

'Yeah, good idea,' said Mum. 'We had enough of this conversation. Some *people*.'

She went on muttering "some people, some people" all through the shopping. But when they were home she rounded on Amy. 'Come on then, Miss Madam, what's it all about?'

'What's what all about?' said Amy, beginning to shake.

'You know. Don't make out. What you been up to?'

'Nothing.'

'Do you think I'm stupid or something? Three-four weeks ago? That's when you was with that Donald! What was all that how's your father about somebody's car then?'

'Nothing. It wasn't me. That lady made a mistake.'

'One good thing about you, Amy, you weren't never a liar. So you haven't had any practice at it, so you aren't no good at it. So I know you aren't telling me the truth because I can see you're scared. You're scared I'm going to find something out. . . . Darn it, I remember . . . that day you come home late for your dinner. *That* was Sunday. Your dad thought you were in trouble. I remember, he didn't believe you that time!'

'*You* believed me,' said Amy desperately.

'Well I don't now,' said Mum. 'So don't you mess me about, Amy. You spit it all out and get it over. What happened?'

'Nothing,' said Amy. 'That lady made a mistake.'

'No she didn't'

'Yes she did.'

'She didn't.'

'She did.'

Mum's face tightened, and she went into the kitchen, banging the door. There was a heavy atmosphere all through dinner, with Mum speaking only a few words to Amy, and Amy not speaking at all. After dinner, Amy put on her anorak. 'What you putting that on for?' said Mum.

'It's too cold to go out without a coat.'

'And where do you think you're going?'

'Cynthia's. It's my turn.'

'I don't care whose turn it is. You're not going anywhere till you tell me the truth. You're staying in this house till I get it out of you. I don't care if it takes all day. I don't care if it takes a week. I don't care if it takes a month of Sundays, and your dad going to agree with me I *know*, when he comes home.'

'But Cynthia's expecting me.'

'That's all right, I'll phone up her mum and say you got a bad stomach.'

'That's a lie!'

'Look who's talking!'

She meant it. Sick and cold, Amy dropped into the armchair and drew her knees right up to her chest, her feelings as tightly curled as her body. An appalling future stretched before her. Days, weeks, months, with faces coming at her, clamouring at her, shrieking at her – 'Tell! Tell! Tell!' And it was unthinkable to tell. How could she tell such a dreadful thing to anyone? She must go on denying it. All she had to do was keep on saying it wasn't her, Hairy Moustache made a mistake.

But they were going to go on at her. They were going to keep her prisoner, and not let her go to Cynthia's, or to school, or anywhere. They were going to shout at her, and shout at her, and Dad was going to get really angry, like he did sometimes with his face all red and his voice not kind any more, and she wouldn't be strong enough, or brave enough, to stand it. She would tell in the end, and what would become of her then? 'Up in court,' Hairy Moustache said. And what would become of Donovan?

She must never tell.

'Whizz-zz-zz-zz!' Simon, on hands and knees, was propelling his toy car round and round the armchair.

'Get off!' Amy burst out at him. 'Get off and leave me alone!'

'Don't take it out on him,' said Mum.

Amy went into the bedroom and climbed on to her bunk. But the bedroom was Simon's as well, and there was no certainty of privacy. 'Why can't I have a room to myself?' she shouted.

'You know why,' said Mum. 'Because there isn't another room, that's why! Or perhaps you'd like your dad and me to move out of our room for you. Would that suit you, Madam? We could kip down in the passage I daresay. Or have a couple of hammocks in the bathroom.'

'I wish Downstairs would die,' said Amy.

'Wash out your mouth!' said Mum, shocked. 'That's a wicked thing to say!'

Amy hardly cared that she had been wicked. It was only to be expected, the way today was going. Downhill. Like the big slide in the park – down, down, speeding up and you couldn't stop. And a great pit of disaster at the bottom.

She thought about Donovan. What would happen to Donovan, when she told? When they dragged it out of her, as they surely would. She could say Donovan made her do it, and they might let her off a *bit*, if she said that. But what would happen to Donovan? He said kids didn't go to prison, but what if he made a mistake about that? What if they put Donovan in prison and it was all her fault because she told? And she still didn't know what Donovan said to

Andrew about her, but she didn't want him to go to prison, and she *wouldn't* tell, she *wouldn't*.

One day Donovan would find out that she had protected him, and hadn't told – and that would be lovely. ('You're a brilliant girl, Amy,' said Donovan, with tears in his eyes. 'You're the most bravest girl I ever met. You stood up for me, and I didn't deserve it, and I haven't been very nice to you but I will make it up to you.' 'Oh Donovan,' said Amy.)

Dad came in later, home from driving his Underground train. He sat on the edge of Simon's bunk and said, 'What's this I'm hearing about, love?'

And Amy told him everything.

They weren't a bit angry with her, once she had told. Mum was angry with herself, even. 'I'm a thoughtless cow,' she said remorsefully, 'going on at you like that, Amy, when you was so worried! I could *kill* that Darren though.'

'It wasn't your fault, love,' said Dad. 'I daresay plenty little girls would do the same in your place, he's a good-looking lad. But you see, Amy, what you got to understand, he's a bad 'un! He's a bad lot! No good. It's a pity, but there it is – there are some people like that, and you got to learn to steer clear of them.'

'Are you going to tell the police?' said Amy, still fearful.

'Nah,' said Dad. 'It's a long time ago now. Least said soonest mended, eh? But you got to promise something, Amy. You got to promise not to have nothing more to do with that boy. All right?'

Amy was silent.

'Come on now,' said Mum. 'You promise, like your dad said.'

Amy sighed. What was she losing after all, if she did promise? Donovan didn't want anything to do with *her* any more anyway, he made that very clear. Perhaps he never did like her really. Perhaps he just used her, to get started with his gang. To get the use of the loft. 'All right,' she said, 'I promise.'

'I know,' said Dad. '*If* it's a nice day, and if we can get your mum out of bed in time, and if the carburettor hasn't packed up – how about we go to Brighton for the day, tomorrow?'

'Oh yes,' said Amy, cheering up.

'We'll take Cynthia with us, if you like.'

'She has to go to church,' said Amy. 'And Sunday school.'

'Just us then. The Baker family. How about that?'

'Oh yes,' said Amy.

She was enormously relieved. Now it was gone, she suddenly realised how the stone weight of guilt, kept to herself all these weeks, had been cutting her off from her family, from everyone. But it was over, it was over! She had gone all the way down the slide, helter skelter, because she couldn't stop. And after all there was only love, and understanding, at the bottom.

She would do what Dad said. She would forget about Donovan. She would, she *would*.

'You look all right, you got rosy cheeks,' said Cynthia.

'We went to the seaside,' said Amy. 'The car didn't break down once.'

'You supposed to have a billy attack.'

'What's that? . . . Oh, you mean a *bilious* attack. Yeah, it was terrible. All pains.'

123

Cynthia looked at her sharply. 'Funny you got better so quick.'

'It was a quick sort of thing.'

'Well come on, come on, ask about my news,' said Cynthia, hopping up and down with impatience to tell.

'All right,' said Amy. 'What is your news?' She was only asking out of politeness, of course. She wasn't really interested.

'Donovan didn't beat up Kevin after all, and I don't know why he didn't beat up Kevin but he beat up Bharat instead and all the boys stuck up for Bharat, well *nearly* all of them, and it was good, and then Michael beat up Donovan and it was good, and Michael won the fight, Amy, it was good, and all the boys went off Donovan. Except for Andrew and Gavin. And it was *good*.'

Amy's eyes wandered round the playground. 'Donovan's all by himself.'

'That's because Andrew and Gavin haven't come yet, and if they're away Donovan won't have no friends.'

Unbidden, and unwanted, a pang went through Amy. 'He looks miserable,' she said.

'Serve him right!'

'No but – he looks really miserable.'

'You're not *sorry* for him?'

'Well – a bit.'

'All right, all right, I'll tell you something. You wait till I just tell you something. You won't be sorry for Donovan when I tell you this. You're going to *hate* Donovan when I tell you this.'

Amy swallowed. What nasty thing was she going to hear now? She listened in stricken silence, while

124

Cynthia related the story of Kevin and the stolen goods. 'And that's your lovely Donovan,' said Cynthia triumphantly. 'That you love so much!'

Amy did not answer. What was there to say? Suddenly it was all too painfully clear that what Cynthia had told her made no difference really. What Donovan said to Andrew made no difference really. What Dad said, yesterday, made no difference. She looked at Donovan, and she was hurt for him, and hurt for herself.

'So now do you hate him, like I said?'

'No,' said Amy.

'You're mad, Amy,' said Cynthia. 'You're really mad, you know that? You're *increbidle*. I think you've lost your marbles!'

9

More trouble

The next week was half term, and since the weather was fine, Cynthia and Amy spent most of it at the playground, in the park. Some days Donovan was there as well. The first time they saw him he looked dejected and subdued, but he was pushing the roundabout for some small children who screamed with delight as Donovan made the roundabout spin faster and faster. Presently Gavin arrived, fawning and eager, and Donovan looked a bit happier after that. The boys swarmed up the high climbing frame, calling to one another.

'Let's tease them,' said Cynthia. During the past few weeks she had aquired a taste for drama, and since drama was lacking just now, it was necessary to create some.

'Leave them alone,' said Amy.

'Oh you *would* say that,' said Cynthia.

She ran to the foot of the high frame and shouted up. 'Had any good fights lately?' Then she ran back quickly.

The boys ignored her, so she tried again. 'Beaten anybody up lately?' she taunted them. She ran a few steps, inviting chase, but the boys were not interested. Cynthia trailed back to Amy, still glancing hopefully over her shoulder now and again. The boys went on doing their balancing tricks on the climbing frame. 'Let's go somewhere else,' said Cynthia to

Amy. 'The park is *boring*'

The next day the girls had Simon with them, so they were stuck in the park anyway. 'There's Donovan,' said Simon, running joyfully to greet him.

'You come back!' said Cynthia. She fussed at Simon, pleased with the excuse to draw attention to herself. 'He's not a nice boy, Simon, you didn't ought to talk to him.' Donovan pushed Simon on the swing, and Cynthia ran across to snatch him back. 'Leave him alone, he's Amy's little brother, not yours!' She looked sideways at Donovan, hoping to provoke some retaliation, but he only shrugged his shoulders, and slouched away.

'I *like* Donovan,' said Simon, disappointed.

'He's wicked!' said Cynthia. 'He's boring too,' she added. 'Now he doesn't do bad things any more.'

The photographs had come at last. Miss Elliot had them in a pile on her desk, and was holding them up, one at a time, for the whole class to see. Amy was very pleased with hers. She thought she looked quite lovely in it, saintly and wistful; the red-gold curls hung softly round her face, and the freckles hardly showed. She wondered if Donovan was admiring her photograph, and she peeped to see, but he was busy at that moment, with something inside his desk.

Cynthia was pulling a face in her photograph. Her mouth was all twisted to one side, and the class laughed, rather unkindly, when they saw it. Cynthia was very much put out. 'Shut up you! Shut up, Andrew, I saw you laughing! They didn't ought to laugh, did they, Miss Elliot? It might be them one day, mightn't it? Anyway, *I* don't care!'

Donovan's photograph was stunningly handsome.

127

He was not smiling in it, which was good, because his usual smile was not very attractive. His expression was inward-looking, and brooding, and more than a little bit sad. Amy thought Donovan looked lovely in the photograph. She wished she could have one of Donovan's photographs for herself.

The children had to take their photographs home and bring back the big envelopes with either the returned pictures, or the money to pay for them, inside. Miss Elliot collected the big envelopes as they came back, and put them in her drawer. You had a few days to decide whether you wanted to buy your photograph or not, and most people brought their envelopes back on Monday, after the weekend, when their families had had a good chance to look at them. Some of the pictures were so good that people had ordered extra ones, to be Christmas presents for aunts and uncles and grandparents. The money for the extra ones was inside the big envelopes as well. Miss Elliot's drawer was so full of bulging envelopes, on Monday morning, that the drawer wouldn't shut properly.

Miss Elliot intended to take the photograph envelopes to the school secretary at playtime, to be locked up in a safe place. But just before play, Mr Bassett came in to ask if Miss Elliot had finished filling in the report forms yet, because he was waiting for them, rather, and of course she *hadn't* done them, because she was always behind with everything, and she was so agitated at the thought that Mr Bassett was going to be cross with her, that she forgot all about the photographs.

After play, Miss Elliot's drawer was still bulging. At dinnertime, Miss Elliot was in a great hurry to get to the bank. She had only 10p left from the weekend, not even enough for her bus fare home. The bank was in the High Street and she would just have time, if she ran all the way, to draw some money and be back in time to do second sitting dinner duty. She was so anxious about getting to the bank that she forgot all about the photograph money *again*.

Cynthia noticed that Miss Elliot had forgotten the photograph money. 'Miss Elliot—' she said.

'Not now, Cynthia, *please*. . . . Any time but now, I *beg* of you! Where's my cardigan? . . . Where is it? Where's my bag? . . . I know they're here *somewhere*.' Miss Elliot flustered about, scattering mounds of books and papers and assorted junk, looking for the missing articles.

'Here they are, Miss Elliot,' said Cynthia. 'Miss Elliot—'

'Not now, Cynthia,' said Miss Elliot, preparing to fly down the corridor. 'When I get back—' she flung over her shoulder. Not looking where she was going, Miss Elliot tripped over a couple of spilled crayons, and nearly fell. As it was, she twisted her ankle, and had to hobble the rest of the way down the stairs.

'She going to break her neck one of these days,' said Lorraine.

'Good job she got us to look after her,' said Gloria.

'She's our *best* teacher though.'

'Oh yes.'

'Do you think we ought to get the photographs?' said Lorraine. 'And take them to the secretary?'

'Lorraine!' said Cynthia, shocked. 'You *know* we're not supposed to touch Miss Elliot's drawer without permission. You ought to know that without being told! I'm surprised at you, to say such a thing.'

'Suppose somebody thief them though?' said Lorraine.

'There's only one person in this school who does really bad things,' said Cynthia. 'And I'm going to watch him all through dinnertime.'

She watched, as she had said she would. All through dinner, and afterwards in the playground, Cynthia did not take her eyes off Donovan Grant. As usual, the fourth-year boys were playing football. Donovan was back with the main group now, sometimes. Not their leader any more, not liked, but tolerated, just about. Even though the rumours were beginning to circulate. Donovan twisted and weaved, pursuing the ball; Cynthia, from her own corner of the playground, watched, not once losing sight of the curly head, as it plunged in and out of the crowd. There could be no doubt about it, Donovan did not leave the football game, even for a moment.

For all that, when Class 4E got back to their room, the photograph envelopes were missing.

'Your drawer's shut, Miss Elliot,' said Cynthia. 'Look – it wouldn't shut before, and now it is!'

'Oh, Cynthia, don't fuss!' said Miss Elliot. She was worried about the report forms, which Mr Bassett was going to be cross about; and about her bank balance, which was in the red and she hand't realized it; and about her twisted ankle, which was swelling up and hurting a great deal. She was still forgetting all about the photograph envelopes.

'But Miss Elliot,' said Cynthia. 'The *photographs*.'

She remembered then! Sick with foreboding, Miss Elliot pulled open the drawer. There was the usual mess of broken pencils, notes from home, and various confiscated items – but the only photograph envelopes were the stiff ones, the ones being returned. 'Perhaps I put them somewhere else,' said Miss Elliot, forlornly clutching at straws.

'You didn't,' said Cynthia. 'You put them in your drawer. I tried to tell you but you wouldn't listen. I did try to tell you, Miss Elliot, I did try—'

'Shut up, Cynthia,' said Lorraine. 'You going to make Miss Elliot upset.'

'Let's look for the envelopes,' said Andrew. 'Come on, everybody look!' He himself made a great performance of ransacking desks, cupboards and the waste bin. Gavin climbed on a chair and inspected the high shelf where the globe was kept. 'Don't be silly,' said Cynthia. 'They couldn't have got up there!'

'What do you know about it, Parrot?' said Andrew.

'They were in Miss's drawer,' said Cynthia. 'I saw them.'

'Somebody thiefed them, Miss Elliot,' said Lorraine. 'Somebody come in dinnertime, and thiefed them out of your drawer.'

There was whispering all around the room. 'Who said my name?' said Donovan defensively. He stood up, his face darkening. 'Somebody said my name! Somebody want to say I done it? Come on and say it then, say it! Right? Come on, I'm waiting!'

'It couldn't be Donovan actually,' said Cynthia. 'I was watching him, all dinnertime.'

'Ha, ha, ha!' Donovan's laugh was not pleasant, but perhaps you couldn't blame him.

'Shall I get Mr Bassett?' said Lorraine.

'No,' said Miss Elliot quickly. 'Not yet.' She

131

dreaded telling the headmaster she had made a mess of something else. The worst mess yet! How much money was involved, Miss Elliot wondered. She decided to try to find out. 'Listen, no listen, listen everyone . . . oh listen, *please*!' The noise, which had been getting pretty loud, stopped. 'Just think,' said Miss Elliot desperately. 'I mean *think*, all of you, who had money in their envelopes? Who can remember what they brought?'

They added it up, and it came to over thirty pounds. Miss Elliot's heart sank into her shoes. She already had an overdraft at the bank – how could she find another thirty pounds to replace the missing photograph money? Not to mention the envelopes the money was supposed to be in, with the names and the order forms. She would have to tell Mr Bassett. But she *couldn't* tell Mr Bassett, she couldn't tell the headmaster she had been so silly as to leave over thirty pounds in an unlocked drawer, when there was a known delinquent in the class!

Donovan Grant had been passed from school to school, and he always ended up in trouble. It was almost a foregone conclusion that Donovan would end up in trouble. Yet how could Donovan be the thief this time? Cynthia Garrett, bless her, had been watching him all through dinnertime. Who, then? Someone from another class? Miss Elliot decided to copy one of Mr Bassett's ideas. 'I want you all to be detectives,' she said. 'I want you all to be spies. I mean – see what we can find out, just *us*. I mean, sort of, let's keep it a secret just for now, just for our class. Just till after play, perhaps. Someone might hear something in the play-ground . . . or something. Well, *something* might turn up. I mean – oh everybody help me, please.'

'Poor Miss Elliot,' said Gloria, at playtime.

'I think Miss Elliot's going to get in trouble for losing that money,' said Andrea.

'That's right,' said Maxine.

'She might have to pay it back herself,' said Lorraine.

'That's right,' said Maxine.

'Poor Miss Elliot, we got to find it for her,' said Cynthia.

'Anyway, it wasn't Donovan,' said Amy.

'And we all know that pleases *you*,' said Cynthia sourly. She was really annoyed that the thief couldn't be Donovan. 'Listen everyone – no listen, listen, listen to me – if it was you took that money what would you do with it, where would you hide it?'

'Put it in my coat pocket,' said Lorraine.

'In my shoe,' said Andrea.

'But it's too big to go in those places,' said Cynthia. '*Think*, everybody. Use your brains that God give you to think with. All those envelopes? You couldn't put all them in your shoe.'

'In my pocket then,' said Lorraine.

'They'd still stick out.'

'In my school bag,' said Andrea.

I don't think I'd put it in my school bag,' said Gloria. 'Mr Bassett will search our school bags when he comes.'

'But he's not coming if we can help it,' said Cynthia. 'Miss Elliot's going to get in trouble from Mr Bassett if he comes. Because Mr Bassett's a mean pig and he doesn't like the girls, only the boys.'

'Miss Elliot isn't a girl,' said Lorraine. 'She's a lady.'

'She's nearly a girl though,' said Cynthia.

'I should take it out,' said Andrea suddenly.

'Take what out?'

'The money,' said Andrea, giggling at nothing as usual. 'I should take it out of the envelopes, so it don't take up so much room.'

'You're not so silly as you look, are you Andrea?' said Cynthia.

'Oh yeah,' said Gloria, 'and then I should tear up the envelopes and hide them somewhere.'

'Where?'

'In the dustbins. I should just keep one envelope for the money to be in.'

'That's right,' said Maxine.

They searched the dustbins in the playground, but there were only empty crisp packets, and sweet papers. They searched in the girls' toilets, and peered through the railings to see if anyone had thrown the envelopes into the road. There was nowhere else to look, until they should be allowed into the building again, after play.

Going up the stairs, Lorraine found the envelopes, all screwed up and stuffed behind a cupboard on one of the landings.

'All right,' said Miss Elliot, giving in, 'go and get Mr Bassett, Lorraine. He'll have to know about it now.' Her face was white and miserable, and she had sucked her biro so hard, and with such poor aim, that the ink was all over one cheek. 'You got ink on your face,' said Maxine. And Miss Elliot burst into tears.

'Never mind, Miss Elliot,' said Gloria, embracing her, 'you still got us.' She used her own tissue to wipe the ink off Miss Elliot's cheek.

'We won't let Mr Bassett be cross with you,' said

Andrea. 'We'll *protect* you. We won't let him shout at you.'

'Mr Bassett doesn't shout at people anyway,' said Amy.

'Well just let him *try*,' said Cynthia. 'Just let him *try*!'

Mr Bassett did not shout at Miss Elliot. He was annoyed with her for being so careless, certainly, but he was much too kind to let that show. 'Well now, well now,' said Mr Bassett, with a heartiness he did not feel, 'a pretty kettle of fish *this* is, but I'm sure we can sort it out. . . . *When* did you say this money turned up missing?'

Dinnertime? Mr Bassett groaned inwardly. And they had been out. Whatever was the silly woman thinking about, letting the children out of the room without calling him first? If she had called him they might, just might, have found the money on someone's person. Anyway now that the alarm had been raised, and the children had been out, the money would certainly be hidden somewhere outside. Perhaps even outside the school grounds. It was not at all unknown for a child to slip out and back at playtime, without the teacher on duty noticing. Donovan Grant, for instance, was quite slippery enough to do that. You can't accuse people without evidence, though. Oh dear – Miss Elliot *did* have a lot to learn.

'Turn out your pockets and your school bags,' said Mr Bassett, wearily. 'And open your desks. You all know why this is necessary.'

'They haven't found it, they're still looking,' said Gloria.

Mr Bassett, Mrs Raymond, and the caretaker had spent the hour between play and hometime ransacking the school building for the missing money. They had searched in all the hidey holes they could think of, including the tumbledown room at the top of the school, and inside the lavatory cisterns.

'I wish it could have been Donovan took it,' said Cynthia.

'Are you sure you watched him *all* the time?' said Lorraine.

'Every single minute,' said Cynthia. 'Every little titchy teeny second. . . . Hang about, hang about, I got an idea! I got an idea! I got an idea, you lot! I was watching Donovan, but I wasn't watching Andrew or Gavin.'

'Oh yeah,' said Lorraine.

'I know something, I know something,' said Gloria.

'Come on then.'

'Give me a chance, I'm trying to think. . . . Listen – remember when we was coming up the stairs after dinner? Remember Donovan and Gavin was having a fight at the back? And Miss Elliot said "No fighting on the stairs." Remember?'

'It was only a play fight,' said Maxine.

'*Exactly*,' said Cynthia triumphantly. 'It was a play fight. An excuse to be last, so the others wouldn't see.'

'Wouldn't see what?'

'Wouldn't see Gavin give the money to Donovan, of course.'

'Why did he give it to Donovan though? If Gavin took it, why didn't he keep it himself?'

'Because that was their plan,' said Cynthia. 'I know that Donovan, I know his tricks. Gavin took it, and Donovan hid it. Donovan knew people going to suspect him, so he made Gavin take it.'

'What about Andrew?' said Lorraine.

'Oh *he* was in it,' said Gloria. 'I bet Andrew was in it. I bet Andrew helped Gavin sneak in. Andrew's good at sneaking in, you know.'

'I think you're talking rubbish,' said Amy.

'Oh you *would* think that!' said Cynthia.

'All right,' said Amy. 'What did Donovan do with the money then?'

'Hid it of course, like I said.'

'Yes, but *where*?'

'*I* don't know, do I?' said Cynthia. 'I don't know *everything*. You can't expect me to know everything, Amy. You got to be reasonable.'

'I think I see something,' said Maxine. 'I think I did see something sticking out of Donovan's shirt, when he come into the classroom.'

'You never saw it,' said Amy. 'You're making it up.'

'Shut up, Amy,' said Cynthia.

On reflection, all the girls thought they remembered a mysterious bulge in Donovan's shirt earlier that afternoon.

'It wasn't there when he stood up.' said Andrea.

'What you mean, when he stood up?' said Cynthia. 'What you talking about?'

'When he stood up,' said Andrea. 'When people said his name, and he stood up. Remember?'

'He must have put it somewhere else by then,' said Gloria.

'He never had it,' said Amy. 'You all made a mistake.'

'Shut up spoiling it, Amy,' said Lorraine.

'I know, I know,' said Cynthia. 'Donovan went to the toilet.'

'No he never.'

'He did,' said Cynthia. 'Before we come in the classroom. He asked Miss, don't you remember? And Miss said "A pity you didn't think of that in the playground." And Donovan said "We was busy playing football." And Miss said "All right this time."'

'I didn't notice that,' said Amy.

'Oh you never notice anything,' said Cynthia.

Some of the others hadn't noticed either, but they all tried hard to remember doing so.

'When he come back,' said Maxine, 'when he come back, there wasn't nothing sticking out of his shirt no more.'

'You didn't see that, you just imagined it,' said Amy.

'You're spoiling it again, Amy,' said Cynthia.

'All right, Cynthia,' said Amy, 'if you're so clever, you still haven't thought where he could have hid the money. You say it was in his shirt, and he asked to go to the toilet and he put it somewhere else. . . . All right, where did he put it? You just tell me that!'

'I don't know,' said Cynthia.

'You don't know neither, Amy,' said Lorraine.

'That's right,' said Maxine. 'You don't know neither, Amy.'

Amy wanted to point out that she couldn't be expected to know, since she didn't believe it anyway, but she didn't want to antagonize the girls any more so she only said, 'If they took it out of the envelopes it will be all loose coins. How can Donovan have all those loose coins in his shirt?'

'They saved a big envelope, remember?' said Gloria.

'That's right,' said Maxine. 'The money was in a envelope, and I see the sharp corner sticking out of Donovan's shirt.'

Amy wanted to say she didn't believe Maxine saw any such thing, she thought she remembered it because she wanted to remember it. But if she said that they would all turn on her, and she didn't want them to turn on her, and she didn't want Donovan to be guilty, like they said. She didn't, she didn't, she didn't!'

That evening Cynthia had a bright idea, and she telephoned Amy to tell her about it. 'Remember about the paint?'

'What paint?' said Amy.

'You know, the red paint Donovan brung to school.'

Oh, *that* again! 'What about it?'

'Remember where me and Lorraine put it?'

'Down the loo.'

'I mean the tin. Remember where we put the tin?'

'Not really.'

'Outside the window, on the window sill. Donovan could have hid the money outside a window.'

'It would notice from outside, like the paint tin.'

'Well I know that. Who don't know that? Mostly it would notice, I agree with you. But the envelope is not as big as a tin. He could put it behind somewhere, perhaps. Somewhere you couldn't see, from outside. *Amy*, don't you think that's a good idea I had?'

'Tell Mr Bassett,' said Amy. 'If you think that, you better tell Mr Bassett.' She didn't want any more to do with it, and she didn't want Cynthia to have any more to do with it. She didn't want to have to talk about it any more, and she wanted Cynthia to shut up saying bad things about Donovan, even if they were true.

'Tell *him*,' said Cynthia. 'Tell that spider-legs Martian? I'm surprised at you, Amy Baker, saying such a unlikely thing!'

'What then? What are you going to do?' Amy was sick of the whole subject. When was it going to end?

'I'm going to school early tomorrow morning,' said Cynthia. 'I'm going to look all round the windows and see where Donovan could have hidden that money. Perhaps it's still there. Wouldn't it be good, Amy, if the money is still there? . . . Amy? You still on the telephone? . . . Oh, I thought you gone away. I said, wouldn't it be good if it was still there?'

'Yes,' said Amy.

'So are you coming with me?'

Silence.

'Amy? . . . I said, are you coming with me?'

Silence.

'Amy?'

'I think I rather not.'

Cynthia, on the other end of the line, was silent also. Then she said, quite coldly, 'All right, you had your chance. I'll ask Lorraine. . . . I rather you though. I *much* rather you.'

'No don't,' said Amy, torn and anguished. 'Don't ask Lorraine!'

'Well make up your mind!'

'All right,' said Amy miserably, 'I'll come.'

10

Disgrace

Cynthia was in the playground, and Cynthia was very excited. 'There!' she said. 'That's where he put it! I bet that's where he put it!'

She was pointing to a small sash window, halfway up the tall school building. Alongside the window was a drainpipe, running all the way down to the playground, and half a metre or so above the window, a little piece of horizontal drainpipe, joining the long vertical one at the side. '*That's* where he put it,' said Cynthia. 'Behind that pipe. I can see it, I can just see the corner of it, sticking out.'

'*I* can't see anything,' said Amy.

'You would if you had proper eyes.'

'All right,' said Amy, 'What is it the window of?'

Cynthia screwed her face into a hideous frown, to aid concentration. 'That's our class, and that's the library, and that's 4C – and that little window is down the stairs we don't come up. On the landing. By the boy's toilet. There!'

'Doesn't prove nothing though.'

'You're increbidle Amy, like I said! Don't you *want* the money to be found?'

Amy had not thought of it like that. She supposed the truth was, she didn't really care much whether the money was found or not. She only cared whether Donovan took it.

'I wish we had a excuse to go inside,' Cynthia

fumed. 'Don't you wish that, Amy? All right, *I* wish it.' Cross and frustrated, she grabbed at the drainpipe, and made a clumsy, futile attempt to climb up it. Aware of another pair of eyes watching her, she turned round, ready to snap. 'What you looking at?'

It was Kevin Riley, and the sight of him made Cynthia even crosser, because she had a guilty conscience about Kevin Riley. She had promised to be his friend, and since the day of the paint she had *not* been his friend. She had actually forgotten to be his friend. So now, uncomfortable with herself about the broken promise, she took it out on him. 'Go away, Kevin Riley, this isn't nothing to do with you!'

The sad eyes brimmed. 'All right,' said Cynthia ruthlessly, 'turn off the waterworks. Can you climb?'

'A bit.'

'Can you climb this drainpipe?'

'Cynthia!' said Amy, 'you can't make Kevin climb up there, it's dangerous!'

'Shut up Amy. . . . Can you, Kevin?'

'I dunno.'

'Try . . . I'll be your friend again, if you try.'

Kevin knew now that Cynthia didn't mean it about being his friend. He didn't blame her. In his heart he knew he wasn't much of a friend to have. Without much hope his hands grabbed the pipe and he started, painfully and awkwardly, to climb. 'Go on,' Cynthia encouraged him. 'You're doing good, Kevin. Go on, you're nearly there!'

He stopped, and looked down. 'How much further?'

'Only not the next window, not the next window, but the next! Nor far,' she lied. 'You're nearly there.'

Kevin looked up. 'I can't,' he said.

'Come down!' said Amy. 'We're all going to get in trouble.'

'Shut up, Amy. I'm surprised at you, being such a coward! Kevin's not a coward, are you, Kevin?' She knew she was behaving badly, trying to push him. She knew she only had to be a little bit patient and there would be an opportunity, probably, to explore the landing window from inside. But some perverse demon was driving her, and the worse she felt about what she was doing, the more she went on doing it. 'Go *on*, Kevin.'

'I'm scared,' said Kevin piteously, clinging to the drainpipe.

'I'm scared too,' said Amy.

'All right,' said Cynthia crossly. 'Everybody's scared. I'm surprised at you, Kevin, to be scared at such a thing, but I suppose you better come down.'

'I can't,' said Kevin.

'Don't tell me you're scared to come *down*. Coming down is nothing to be scared at. Me and Amy will catch you.'

Kevin began the descent – but through sheer fear he lost his grip and fell heavily, grazing his elbow and his knee. 'Now we done it,' said Amy.

'Stop moaning,' said Cynthia. 'And you, Kevin! You ain't really hurt, only a little bit. . . . And it's one good thing,' she added, brightening, 'because now me and Amy can take you in to Mrs Raymond, to get the knee washed.'

The girls escorted the pathetic casualty indoors. They should have gone straight back to the play-ground of course, but they didn't; they went to the top floor, then down the stairs by the boys toilet, to the half landing where the little window was. The window was already open at the top. 'Look how small it is,' said Amy, relieved. 'He couldn't get out there. Your idea must be wrong.'

'My idea is not wrong,' said Cynthia. 'He must have stood on the window sill and put his arm through the space. And *that*, Amy Baker, is what *we're* going to do. Now.'

'It's too high,' said Amy.

'Put your hands together, and I can climb on them,' said Cynthia. 'You ought to know without being told, Amy, that's the way to do it.'

Cynthia was very heavy. 'You're hurting me,' said Amy.

'Don't make such a fuss,' said Cynthia. 'I nearly done it, I nearly—'

'WHAT DO YOU GIRLS THINK YOU'RE DOING?' said a loud voice. Mr Cousins was the worst-tempered teacher in the school, and it was bad luck to be caught by him. 'Trying to commit suicide it looks like! On second thoughts, don't bother to tell me, I can't be bothered to listen. Get back to the playground where you should be. Hop it, scram. Get lost. Disappear . . .'

Donovan asked to be excused. 'Look, Amy,' said Cynthia, 'Donovan's going to be excused.'

'What are you whispering about?' said Lorraine.

'It's a secret,' said Cynthia.

'It's about the money, isn't it?' said Lorraine. 'That's not supposed to be a secret. It wasn't a secret yesterday.'

'Well it is today,' said Cynthia. 'It's just between me and Amy now. Isn't it, Amy?'

'Yes,' said Amy sadly.

'Miss Elliot,' said Cynthia, 'I left my bag in the playground, I only just noticed.' She kicked her bag under the table as she spoke, so Miss Elliot wouldn't see she had it all the time. 'Can I go and get it?'

'All right Cynthia but, you know, sort of, be *quick*.' She had worried all night about the missing money, and her eyes had great dark circles.

'Can Amy come with me? Case it got lost?'

'All right,' said Miss Elliot, who still didn't like to upset people by saying 'No'.

Cynthia led the way, along the corridor towards the boys' toilet. 'I thought we were going to the playground,' said Amy.

'God didn't ought to waste his time giving you brains,' said Cynthia. 'For you not to use them. . . . We're going to catch Donovan aren't we? Getting the money, out of the window.'

Amy's heart began to hammer. It might be true that the money was hidden where Cynthia said it was. She prayed hard that Cynthia had made a mistake.

At the little landing, Donovan was already on the window sill, his arm through the top opening – reaching, reaching, his hand against the wall outside.

'Caught you!' said Cynthia. She was so excited she could hardly get the words out. Donovan's head whipped round to face his accuser. 'What you doing here, Parrot?' For the moment, he was clearly thrown.

'What are *you* doing here, more like it!' Her triumph was making her dizzy.

'There's a bird's nest,' said Donovan slyly. 'I was looking for a bird's nest. I see it outside, from the playground, right?'

145

'Perhaps there really is a bird's nest, Cynthia,' said Amy. '. . . I didn't see it though.'

'You never see anything, Baker,' said Donovan.

He had hurt her again. Hope and eagerness drained from her face, and she pressed herself into a doorway, wishing the ground would open and swallow her up.

'I hate you, Donovan Grant,' said Cynthia. 'And I know what you're looking for really. You're looking for the photograph money.'

'You're mad,' said Donovan.

'You put it there yesterday, and now you're looking for it.'

'I'm looking for the bird's nest, I told you!'

'All right, prove it,' said Cynthia. 'Show me the bird's nest.' She grabbed at the back of Donovan's shirt, and hauled herself on to the window sill beside him.

'You can't reach it,' said Donovan. 'It's too high for you.'

'That's rubbish, Donovan. I'm as tall as you nearly.'

She stretched and groped. The tips of her fingers touched the drainpipe above the window. Donovan jumped to the floor and tried to pull her down. 'It ain't a bird's nest, I made a mistake. . . . Let's get back to class, eh? . . . Right? You two coming back to class?'

'No.' Cynthia clung to the window frame, to stop Donovan from pulling her down. 'Help me, Amy! Help me!'

Amy shrank further into her doorway. She couldn't get hold of Donovan when he didn't want her to, she couldn't!

'Help me, Amy! If you're my friend you got to help me!'

She did it. She grabbed Donovan round the waist and pulled. It gave her a funny feeling, to be holding Donovan like that. Donovan lost his balance and staggered backwards. Cynthia stood on tiptoes, and her groping fingers found the envelope folded over and over, and tucked behind the drainpipe. Just where she had said it would be.

For a moment, it looked as though Donovan was going to snatch the envelope from her. He was swallowing fiercely, his hands clenching and un-clenching at his sides. 'What's that then?' he said in a thick voice, forcing the words out.

'As if you didn't know!' said Cynthia. She shook the envelope, so Donovan could hear the coins jingling about inside.

'Sounds like money,' said Donovan, trying to sound surprised.

'That's right,' said Cynthia.

'I thought it was a bird's nest.'

'No you never.'

'Prove it, right? Prove I never thought it was a bird's nest.'

'I'm not going to bother to prove it, I'm going to take the money to Miss Elliot,' said Cynthia.

'No, don't do that, don't do that!' Donovan looked at her sideways, through narrowed eyes. 'What about we share it . . . eh? We share it, right?'

'Donovan! It's the photograph money!'

'Oh all right, take it! Go on, take it! . . . What you waiting for? Take the money to Miss Elliot, like you said.'

'Come on, Amy' said Cynthia. 'And don't you go

147

running out of school, Donovan Grant. I know your tricks.'

'Run out of school? I'm not running out of school. I got nothing to run out of school for. Right? What I want to run out of school for?' said Donovan, who had been considering doing just that.

Cynthia linked arms with Amy, and Donovan shuffled behind them, stiff and tense, desperately casting his mind about for a way out of *this* one.

Mr Bassett also had worried in the night, about the missing photograph money. He had wondered if he ought to call in the police, but it was probably too late to do that now. And anyway, you don't call the police to investigate members of your own family! The children of George Street School were Mr Bassett's family. The good ones, and the bad ones, they were all his family, and he would do the best he could for all of them. For Donovan Grant, even, standing in front of him now, and clearly guilty.

'How did you know the money was there, Donovan?' said Mr Bassett.

'I didn't,' said Donovan. 'I thought it was a bird's nest.'

'Think again, lad,' said Mr Bassett.

'All right then,' said Donovan, 'how did *she* know? Garrett the parrot – how did *she* know it was there?'

'Well, Cynthia?'

'I guessed.'

'You *guessed*!'

'I thought it out,' said Cynthia. 'I—.' She had forgotten the stages of her own reasoning. She had thought it out very cleverly, she knew that, but just for the moment she couldn't remember how she had done it.

'See?' said Donovan. 'She don't know herself.'

'Can you explain it, Amy?'

'I don't know.'

'Try,' said Mr Bassett.

'Cynthia thought there was some other boys in it,' said Amy. It was the best she could do for Donovan, so he wouldn't have to take all the blame himself.

'Is that right?' said Mr Bassett, to Donovan.

'I don't know nothing about the money,' said Donovan. 'I thought it was a bird's nest.'

'Perhaps someone asked you to hide it,' said Mr Bassett cunningly. 'Perhaps someone asked you to look after the envelope for them, and you didn't have time to see what was inside.'

Driven into a corner, desperate for a way out, Donovan agreed. 'Oh yeah, I remember now, that's what happened.'

'Who asked you to hide it?'

'I think it was Gavin.'

'You think?'

'It was Gavin . . . and Andrew. It wasn't nothing to do with me. I didn't know what was inside the envelope, right? They said to hide it for them, so I did.'

'And this morning,' said Mr Bassett, 'this morning they said get it for them, I suppose, so you did.'

'That's right. It wasn't nothing to do with me really.'

'Stand up Gavin, and Andrew,' said Mr Bassett.

In the other half of their double desk, Andrew sat with his back pointedly turned towards Donovan.

His shoulders were heaving, his face angry and hurt. Suddenly Andrew moved; he flung his desk open, and began gathering armfuls of books. Then he staggered to his feet with the books, and transferred himself and his possessions to the emtpy place next to Kevin Riley. A wan smile flitted over Kevin's face. This was his lucky day, after all.

Gavin was crying. He had never been in trouble like this before. Now his mum and dad were going to be called up to school and he was going to get a beating, most likely, but that wasn't the worst, that wasn't the worst! The worst was he'd been used, and told on, and betrayed. One thing was sure, he was never going to speak to that Donovan Grant again, never, never, *never*. Not if he lived to be a thousand years old!

'Donovan's not going to have no friends, now,' said Cynthia joyfully. 'He's not going to have no friends at all, because he made Gavin and Andrew be bad and then he told on them, and he tried to get out of it himself. And it serves him right. Hands up those who think it serves him right. . . . See, Amy, five against one! Mr Bassett's a good headmaster, isn't he, to find out all the truth in the end? Hands up those who think Mr Bassett's a good headmaster! . . . *I* think he's a good headmaster too. And I'm a good detective, aren't I? Hands up those who think I'm a good detective! . . . Poor Gavin and Andrew, it wasn't their faults, it was all that nuisance Donovan's fault! I'm going to say something nice to Gavin and Andrew at playtime, because it wasn't their fault. Hands up those who are going to say something nice to Gavin and Andrew at playtime! . . . All right, Miss Elliot, I'm going to get on with my work now. I'm

going to do it *now*, Miss Elliot, I'm just starting, look!
. . . Dear Miss Elliot, you're my *best* teacher!'

'Donovan's mum hasn't come yet,' said Cynthia.
'Andrew's mum been, and Gavin's mum been, but
Donovan's mum hasn't come.'

'You mean his gran,' said Amy. She had been
sneaking looks at Donovan all morning, her heart
wrung with pity for the misery and apprehension on
his face. She had expected he would truant today, but
probably he had been warned not to.

'All right, his gran,' said Cynthia. 'It's all the same.'

Just before dinner the classroom door was suddenly
flung open. No knock, no greeting to Miss Elliot, just
the classroom door flung open, and a rough, rasping
voice shouting directly at Donovan. 'There you are! I
see you, you little devil, you!'

'It's Donovan's gran,' whispered Cynthia, her cup
of happiness now full.

Donovan's gran was a slovenly looking person,
with a lined face and dyed blonde hair showing grey
at the roots. She wore cotton trousers too tight for
her, and a T-shirt with tea stains down the front. The
cardigan draped round her shoulders had two
buttons hanging off, and she was smoking a cigarette.
In her hand was a fattish nylon holdall.

Donovan's gran threw the holdall on to the
classroom floor. 'There's your stuff! You can go
round your mum's tonight and stop there. I ain't
having you in my house no more!' The tail of ash on
the end of her cigarette quivered and fell.

Apart from the noise Donovan's gran was making,
there was a deathly hush in the classroom. Everyone

watched this piece of free entertainment with keen interest. Eyes swivelled from Donovan's gran to Donovan, and back again. 'You done it this time!' Donovan's gran shouted at him. 'You're no better than your dad, and you're going to end up same place as him!'

Donovan found his voice then. He had been sitting in stunned and angry silence, but now he leapt to his feet and began shouting back. 'Don't you say nothing against my dad, right?'

'I'll say what I like against you dad! He's inside again. Because he don't know the difference between his property and other people's. All right, teacher, I know I'm shaming him in front of his mates. Might as well try shaming him for a change, nothing else seems to work. All right, I'm going, I'm going, you don't have to push me!'

Miss Elliot was not the sort of person to push anyone, of course, but she *was* trying to coax Donovan's gran out of the classroom. Miss Elliot was looking terribly upset.

'He never done it!' Donovan's eyes were filling with angry tears. 'My dad never done it, right? He was framed, he told me! He always gets framed.'

'If you believe that you'll believe anything!' said the slovenly person in the doorway. 'Anyway you stole that money from your teacher, else you made some poor sucker do it for you. Same thing, only worse. You've had your last chance far as I'm concerned, so help me!'

Donovan was trembling all over. His hands clenched and unclenched, and his face had gone dark. 'He never done it! My dad never done it!' His voice was choked with rage and tears.

'I bet he did,' said Michael.

Donovan picked up his chair, and threw it at Michael. Michael ducked, and one leg of the chair caught Bharat on the back of the head. 'Stop it!' said Miss Elliot to Donovan, but she had no idea how to make him stop. He picked up the spare chair next to him and threw that – wildly, anywhere.

He had gone quite, quite berserk. He rampaged round the room, throwing chairs, tipping over desks, shouting bad words. And Miss Elliot watched it all helplessly, the nice eyes behind the big glasses round with fear and horror, while Donovan wrecked the class.

But for Amy, cowering with the rest, it was as though a great light had begun to shine. The light had first flickered into being when that horrid gran appeared, and throughout the chair-throwing it grew brighter and clearer. But it's not really his fault, she thought. *It's not really his fault.*

'*I* stopped him, didn't I, Miss Elliot?' said Michael proudly.

'Yes, Michael,' said Miss Elliot. 'Thank you. I mean, I don't know what I'd have done without you.'

'If he does it again,' said Michael, 'you can just ask me.'

'All right,' said Miss Elliot, still badly shaken, 'I will.'

'You're a good rescuer, Michael,' said Cynthia. 'Like I'm a good detective.'

She went on and on in the playground. 'Good job for Michael, eh? Who thinks it's a good job for Michael? . . . Who thinks that? Who thinks Donovan might have killed somebody? Isn't Donovan terrible?

I think he's the most terrible boy in the world. Don't you think so, Amy? . . . Well, you must think so *now*.'

'I think it's not his fault,' said Amy.

'What you mean it's not his fault?' said Cynthia. 'Course it's his fault! Whose fault is it then, if it's not his? He flung the chairs, didn't he? Who flung the chairs then, tell me that!'

'Michael said about his dad though,' said Lorraine.

'I don't mean that,' said Amy. 'I don't mean because what Michael said. I mean about he's got a horrible gran.'

'*So?*' said Cynthia. 'He's got a horrible gran, what about it? *He* doesn't have to be horrible, just because he's got a horrible gran!'

Amy could not explain any more, she just knew she was right. She struggled to give her thoughts form, and order.

'Mr Bassett should give Donovan a really bad punishment,' said Cynthia. 'What punishment do you think Donovan ought to have?'

'He did ought to be expelled,' said Maxine.

'Yeah,' said Andrea.

'And good riddance,' said Gloria.

'I think he's unhappy,' said Amy.

'Well, *course* he's unhappy,' said Cynthia. 'You do say obvious things sometimes, Amy! Course he's unhappy, he *made* himself unhappy. Look – all the boys liked him first, right? And then he beat up Bharat, so the boys went off him, right? And then he got Andrew and Gavin in trouble, and he tried to blame it all on them, so they went off him, right? So now he's unhappy because nobody likes him and it's all his fault. . . . Who agrees? . . . You see, Amy, everybody agrees with me, so it's five against one.'

'I mean he was unhappy before,' said Amy. 'Before he done any of those things he was unhappy. He was unhappy because he got a horrible mum, and a horrible gran, and it made him get a bit nasty.'

'That's rubbish, Amy,' said Cynthia. 'You're mad. Who thinks Amy's mad?'

Unexpectedly, though, Cynthia found she was less than comfortable in her own mind, and at playtime in the afternoon she hung back, to enlist Miss Elliot's support. 'Donovan Grant is a *terrible* boy, isn't he, Miss Elliot? Don't you think Donovan Grant is the worst boy in the world? *I* think he is, anyway.'

'He does sort of do terrible things, I agree,' said Miss Elliot. She ran her fingers through her messy hair, a vague attempt at tidying it, and Cynthia saw that she had been biting her nails. 'You been biting your nails again, Miss Elliot,' she said sternly.

'I know,' said Miss Elliot. 'I will try harder not to do it.'

'It must be because of Donovan,' said Cynthia, to comfort her. 'I think he's enough to make anybody bite their nails. . . . Amy's sorry for him. She thinks he's only bad because he's unhappy, but I think he should have a really serious punishment for what he done this morning. . . . Don't you, Miss Elliot?'

'I agree with Amy,' said Miss Elliot.

'What?' Cynthia frowned at Miss Elliot, for saying what she didn't want to hear. 'You don't think he should be punished?'

'I think he *is* being punished,' said Miss Elliot. 'I mean, you know, he's sort of all on his own now, isn't he!'

155

'Serve him right,' said Cynthia. '. . . Miss Elliot, did you know Donovan was expelled from his other school?'

'Yes, I know.'

'Did Mr Bassett know?'

'Yes, he knew too.'

'Why did Mr Bassett let Donovan come to our school then? When he done all those bad things in his other school? . . . Donovan spoiled our class didn't he, Miss Elliot? . . . I think he spoiled our school.'

'Well you see, it's like this, it's sort of . . . Well, what we were hoping, Mr Bassett and I, we were *hoping*, that this nice class might help Donovan. And he promised to try, if we gave him a chance. . . . I expect it was my fault it didn't work,' Miss Elliot added humbly.

'It's not your fault, Miss Elliot,' said Cynthia. 'Don't let me hear you say such a thing! It's Donovan's fault because he's horrible. Anyway, *I* think so.'

Miss Elliot tried once more. 'Cynthia, do you think your mum would ever . . .? I mean, what I'm trying to say is . . .'

'Yes,' said Cynthia. 'What are you trying to say?'

'Well I can't really say it actually,' Miss Elliot floundered on. 'I mean, I can't say it but . . . Oh Cynthia, *think*. Think how lucky you are! Suppose you, sort of, hadn't been lucky like that?'

'*Dear* Miss Elliot,' said Cynthia. 'I don't know what you're on about.'

The next day Cynthia was very quiet, scowling and moody on the edge of the group. 'What's the matter with you?' said Lorraine.

'I'm thinking,' said Cynthia.

'What d'you mean, thinking?'

'Thinking, of course! You know what thinking is, don't you? You don't do much of it yourself, but you ought to know what it *is*.'

'She got the hump,' said Andrea.

'No I haven't,' said Cynthia, 'I'm just thinking. . . . All right, if you must know what about . . . I told my mum last night, about Donovan Grant.'

'So?'

'And my mum said, it's disgusting what his gran done. Coming up to school and shouting private family things for everybody to hear! And my mum said she wouldn't *think* of showing any of her kids up in public. And she said she wouldn't think of throwing any of us out of the house *whatever* we done. And she thinks Donovan's gran is cruel. . . . And she is sorry for Donovan and she says you can't really blame him.'

'*What*!'

'You heard. . . . Well it's not his fault he does bad things, is it? How would you like it if your gran come up to school and shame you in front of everybody? How would you like that then? And if she throw you out of the house like you were a old bag of rubbish or something? . . . And his mum throw him out before that, didn't she, Amy? Didn't you tell me, his mum throw him out of the house a lot of times! See? His mum is just as bad as his gran, and how would you like that? . . . And if your dad was in prison? You would be down in the dumps then, I *bet*. Donovan does all these things because he's down in the dumps and you ought to know that Lorraine, without being

157

told. . . . And I think we ought to start being a bit nice to Donovan now. . . . Anyway, that's what I think.'

11

Into danger

'The others don't want to be in it,' said Cynthia to Amy. 'They still think Donovan's just wicked. But we know, don't we? It's lucky we got more brains than that lot. I wouldn't like to be that stupid lot, would you Amy? . . . Well, come on, when shall we start?'

'Start what?' said Amy.

'You know, being nice to Donovan. Because it's not his fault.'

Amy glanced across at Donovan, skulking sullenly in his corner of the playground. He was kicking his heels against the wall behind him, and he looked fierce, and menacing. 'Do we actually have to be nice to him?' she said. 'Couldn't we just be sorry for him?'

'What's the use of being sorry for people if you don't *do* nothing about it?' said Cynthia. She prepared a careful smile and walked across the yard. 'It's a nice day, isn't it?' she said politely, to Donovan.

Donovan turned his head away.

'Well I mean, it's not a *very* nice day. It's a bit cold actually, but it might be sunny later, don't you think?'

Donovan went on drumming his heels against the wall, still looking the other way.

'If the clouds would blow away,' said Cynthia.

'Get off, Parrot!' Donovan snarled at her.

'All right, *be* like that!' said Cynthia.

'What a misery-guts!' She complained to Amy. 'He don't deserve people to be nice to him. I think I wasted my time.' But a bit later, she said 'It's only because he's unhappy, isn't it? I think he must be really, *really* unhappy to be nasty to people when they're only making conservation. Don't you think that?'

'I *told* you that's what I think,' said Amy. 'It's awful. I can't *stop* thinking about it.'

'Well *do* something then! I tried, why not you? You should stop looking so miserable, and try to cheer him up. I don't wonder Donovan went off you when you got such a miserable face! I nearly went off you myself one time, only you're my friend, and you always been my friend, and you always will be my friend. . . . So you should just pull yourself together, and that's all I got to say about it.'

On the way home, Amy went into a dream about doing something to cheer Donovan up. ('I know they're all against you,' said Amy, 'but you can rely on me. I want to help you.' 'Do you really?' said Donovan humbly. 'Yes I do,' said Amy. 'And I am sorry your gran is so horrible to you, and I think they made a mistake to put your dad in prison, I think he was innocent all the time.' 'You're the only friend I got,' said Donovan.)

Amy dropped Simon's hand while she was dreaming all this, and he ran ahead, skipping and leaping along the kerb. A large van mounted the pavement, and Amy ran to snatch Simon back. 'You got to stay with me!' she scolded.

On Sunday the weather was brilliant, for once, and Dad said they should go to the seaside again. Dad only had every other Sunday off, and the Sundays he was free were usually the ones it chose to rain. Amy found bathing things and towels, and Mum made sandwiches, and everyone was excited about the outing – and then, surprise, surprise, the car wouldn't go properly! Mum and Amy unpacked the seaside things, and Dad took the car to pieces. Dad enjoyed taking the car to pieces almost as much as driving to the seaside, but everyone else was very disappointed.

Feeling flat, and let down, Amy went to the park by herself. Mum called after her to take Simon, but Amy pretended she didn't hear.

Donovan was in the park. He was mooching about on the big swings, scowling and brooding and only looking at the ground. Amy went to the little swings, and the sun was hot, beating down on her head. She watched Donovan from a distance, and thought about all the stories she had read, where the goodies made the baddies good, just by being kind to them and pointing out their mistakes. ('You see, Donovan,' said Amy patiently, 'you have to be nice to people if you want them to be nice to you. You aren't supposed to beat people up when they haven't done nothing wrong, and you aren't supposed to tell lies about them. I suppose you didn't understand that before.' 'Nobody ever explained it to me, only you,' said Donovan gratefully.)

Amy thought Donovan looked at her. Only for a moment, but she felt a little thrill of excitement. Could she go up to him? Did she dare? She had put on her prettiest sun-dress for going to the seaside, and although she didn't often think about what she wore, she was glad about the sun-dress now.

She would do it, she would really do it. Amy slipped off the swing and took three paces towards Donovan before she lost her nerve. She went back to the swing and sprawled across it on her stomach, running with little steps to make it go, then drawing her knees up to enjoy the rhythmic motion which was helping her to think. She was going to pull herself together. She was going to *do* something. In a minute. In one more minute.

Amy stopped the swing, and levered herself upright. She peeped round at Donovan and saw that he was swinging himself really high. His face was tense, and he was gripping the chains of the swing so his knuckles showed white. Higher and higher went the swing, and the chains looped upwards. At the highest point, Donovan's head was towards the ground, he was almost upside down. Amy felt sick and dizzy watching him, and she found herself imagining that the swing went so high it made a complete circle over the top, and came down the other side.

Amy shut her eyes so she couldn't see the swing making a circle over the top, and when she opened them the swing was slackening pace, and Donovan was still safely in the seat. She would do it now. As soon as the swing stopped. However nasty you look Donovan, she thought, I'm going to speak to you, so there!

She took a deep breath, and marched across to the big swings. She sat on the one next to Donovan and tried to smile, though her face felt stiff as treacle. Donovan turned his head the other way.

'Hello,' said Amy. She was doing it! She was also breaking a promise, and she felt uncomfortable about

162

that, but not very. You couldn't always keep promises. Not always. Anyway, she would think about the broken promise another time.

Donovan did not answer her.

'We were going to the seaside, but the car wouldn't go,' said Amy.

'What you telling me that for?' said Donovan.

'Just making conversation.'

'Well don't. I don't want you to make conversation. I don't want anybody to make conversation.'

'Just because the boys are nasty to you, you don't have to be nasty to me.' said Amy. It was quite easy now she had started, she was amazed at how easy it was.

'I don't care who's nasty to me.' said Donovan. 'It ain't nothing to me. And I can be nasty to who I like, so leave it out, Baker!'

'It's because you're unhappy though,' said Amy. 'Don't you understand that?'

Donovan was furious. 'Who says I'm unhappy? Who says that?'

Amy recoiled. Why was he so angry with her? What had she done wrong?

'I'm *very* happy actually,' said Donovan. 'So get away and leave me alone, right?'

Amy climbed off the swing with dignity, and withdrew a few paces. Donovan looked at her sideways, his face working. Once or twice he seemed about to speak, then changed his mind. Finally he dropped his head and chanted indistinctly at the ground. 'Amy Baker's bo-o-ring! Amy Baker's bo-o-ring!'

'What was that?'

'I said Amy Baker's boring. You deaf?'

It was like being punched in the stomach, but she persevered. 'You didn't use to think that.'

'Well I do now.'

'I suppose you just used me really,' said Amy bravely. 'Like you done Gavin and Andrew.'

'No I never.'

'No?'

'No. . . . Satisfied? Now leave me alone.'

'You don't *really* want to be left alone. You want to have friends, don't you?'

'I got plenty friends, right? I got the guy that made the stink bomb, remember? He's *fourteen*.'

'Why aren't you with him then, if he's your friend?'

'Ah, shut up! Anyway I don't want *you*.' Again the punch in the stomach.

Donovan slipped off the swing and gave it a great push, leaping out of the way so as not to be struck when it came crashing back. Then, head down, he strode off across the park.

Amy followed.

In one way she was amazed at herself, following Donovan across the park, and in another way it seemed only the natural thing to do. He turned once, and saw her coming. 'Don't follow me!' he threatened.

Amy kept on going.

Donovan stopped, and waited for Amy to catch up a bit. When she was near enough to hear properly, he said, 'All right, I'll tell you something stop you following me! . . . You want to hear it? . . . You sure? . . . All right, I'll tell you . . .' He had put it out of his mind a long time ago. But it came back now, because it was useful. 'You *sure* you want to hear it? All right then, *I* put them things in your desk that time.'

'I know,' said Amy.

That shook him. '*You know?*'

'Yes, I know.'

'How did you find that out?'

'I'm not telling you. You're not the only one that knows things.'

'Don't you mind then?'

'Not much.'

'Ah – you're just stupid!'

He strode away, and Amy trotted after him. He was really uneasy now, not understanding. Once more he kept looking back, and at last he stopped to shout again. 'All right, I'll tell you something else . . . You asked for it, I'll tell you, right? Right? . . . All right, this is it. . . . I took *two pounds* out of your house one time. Right?'

Amy swallowed hard.

'*Now* will you stop following me?'

'No.'

They were leaving the park by the far exit. It was late morning by now, and the pavement sizzled in the heat. Donovan began to run, and Amy tried to run after him, but she was soon out of breath, and there was a stitch in her side. She couldn't keep this up, she would lose sight of him in a minute.

Donovan turned a corner. He was still skirting the park, along the road which led back towards the railway line. Where would he go after that though? Sick with disappointment, Amy's steps slowed. It was no good. She couldn't do good to Donovan after all, she would have to give up trying.

Round the corner Donovan was dawdling. Waiting for her! Amy thought, with another little thrill of excitement. I guessed it right. He doesn't want to be lonely really, but he's all muddled up. He doesn't want me to follow him, and he doesn't want me not to follow him.

As soon as he saw her, Donovan ploughed on again – fast, but carefully not too fast. Amy thought, I guessed it right, I guessed it right! It's like when I get muddled up sometimes, when I want to do two things, and they're both different. It's like that, only Donovan's muddled up ever so much more than me, I think he's muddled up all the time.

Crossing the road bridge over the railway line, Donovan bent and picked something up from the gutter; someone's old Coca Cola tin, or something. Then he hoisted himself on to the wall and sprawled there, waiting for Amy to catch up.

'What are you doing on that wall?' said Amy.

'Guess!' said Donovan. A train came past, and Donovan hurled his Coca Cola tin.

'You'll get in trouble,' said Amy.

'Who's worried?'

'*I'm* worried.'

'Oh, *you!*'

Donovan dropped off the wall and turned back towards the park. Once across the bridge though, he seemed to change his mind, and turned left along the railings, by the railway embankment. On this side of the railway line there was a gate, often padlocked, but open today. There were men in bright orange overalls, working a long way down the line. 'They'll see us,' said Amy, but Donovan took no notice, apart from a sly backwards glance, to make sure she was still following. He wants me to come really, she thought, fear and exultation churning around together inside her.

166

The rough bank smelled of summer. Donovan picked some small stones out of the grass, and put them in his pocket. There was a great metal thing over the rails, something like a bridge. Donovan gripped one of the upright struts, and began to climb. There were horizonal struts as well as vertical ones, but far apart. Donovan swung his feet to grip the horizontal strut above his head, and hauled himself up by his hands. 'Don't!' shouted Amy. 'Donovan, don't! You'll be killed!'

He didn't know what she knew. He didn't have a dad who drove a train on the Underground. Her dad had told her about the live cables joined up to that metal thing. If you touched one of the cables, if you just touched it with your little finger, you would frizzle up and die, because of the electricity inside. 'It's electric!' she screamed at Donovan. 'It's electric! Those greeny things, they're electric!'

Donovan looked down at Amy, smiling his not-very-nice smile. 'Try and stop me, Baker!' he taunted.

She couldn't believe it. She couldn't believe he'd risk getting killed on purpose! 'Don't you understand, Donovan? You can die!'

'Don't matter.'

'*What?*'

'I said, don't matter . . . I don't care if I die!'

'*I* care,' said Amy.

'Well don't! I didn't ask you to! . . . Where's this electric then? Which way? Is this the way to the electric, Baker?'

'Come down, Donovan,' she implored him. '*Please* come down.'

'I'll come down when I'm ready . . . I'll come down when *I* want to come down.'

Amy scrambled over the grass, and stood at the foot of the bridge-like structures. So terrified of the cables was she, that she was afraid of the struts themselves, though she knew the danger was not there. Frantic with fear, she nevertheless grasped the strut now, and tried to haul herself up, like Donovan. If she could grab him, if she could just grab him, she could hold him away from the cable, perhaps.

The metal strut was hot from the sun. Amy gripped it, and pulled on her arms, but the strut hurt her hands, and her arms were too weak anyway. She gave up, blowing on her stinging hands. 'Come down!' she begged again, but he only laughed, jeering, way above her.

A train was coming. Amy hunched up on the bank, her knees tight against her chest. The train roared past. Amy had a horrid waking dream about how she tripped and fell onto the rails and she couldn't get up again, and the train went over her. She peeped to see if Donovan was still on the bridge thing, or if the train thundering past made him fall. The train going over her was only imagination, it hadn't really happened; Donovan on the bridge thing was sickeningly real.

He was right at the top, sprawled and grinning and brandishing a stone in his hand. 'I got it!' he boasted. 'This is for the next one, right?' He wriggled on his perch, and moved nearer to the cables.

'Stop!' Amy shouted. 'Stay where you are, Donovan, and don't go any further, *please*.'

'Which way mustn't I go? This way? Is this the way I mustn't go?'

'Those greeny things I said about. You're getting near! You're going to be frizzled up!'

'Which way did you say?' he called again to taunt

her. 'I didn't hear you! Is this the way I mustn't go?' He wriggled further still, purposefully hanging over, closer and closer to the terrible cables.

Amy began to scream. She stood on the bank, and screamed and screamed and screamed. Down the line, the orange-clad figures began to run. 'Hurry! Hurry!' Amy screamed at them.

Donovan's back was to the orange figures. 'You're tricking me, Baker,' jeered Donovan. 'Nobody ain't coming, I know!' He wriggled again, enjoying Amy's distress. Suddenly Amy couldn't bear it. Suddenly it was all too much. Gulping for breath, and with great dry sobs, Amy ran up the bank, and through the open gate, and on to the road.

At home, Dad was still enjoying himself with the broken-down car, and Mum was putting the picnic sandwiches on the table for dinner. 'That's all there is to eat,' she said, 'so you needn't bother to turn your noses up. Not my fault your dad got a rubbish car. I kept telling him to sling it, but he won't listen to reason, will he? That heap's part of the family, your dad'd go into mourning if it died, so there it is, we're stuck with it. . . . What's the matter with you, Amy?'

'Nothing.'

'Yes there is, you're as white as a sheet. . . . Where you been all this time?'

'Like I said. Up the park.'

'On the swings?'

'Yes.'

'Something's happened, hasn't it? You're not to go up there by yourself any more.'

'Nothing happened in the park, honestly,' said

Amy, forcing her voice through the roaring sound inside her head.

'Oh *I* know what's wrong with you, you got a touch of the sun! You shouldn't have stayed up the park so long, Amy. You know you can't take it. Now you going to be sick, aren't you? Silly girl! Go on in the bathroom quick!'

She only just made it.

At least she had an excuse for not wanting any dinner, otherwise she could see nothing but disaster, every way she looked. Lying on her bunk, with the window curtains drawn because, mercifully, Mum had remembered that was the right treatment for sunstroke, Amy rewrote the last bit of the morning in her mind.

(Amy held the iron thing, and it was like a knife cutting her hand, but she didn't mind that. Amy was incredibly brave, and incredibly strong. She didn't care how much her hands were hurting, she went like lightning up the iron thing and caught hold of Donovan. It was all right to catch hold of him, even if he didn't want her to, because she was saving his life. 'Leave me alone,' said Donovan, struggling. 'I will not let you go till you come down,' said Amy. 'Leave me!' said Donovan, kicking her in the face. 'No!' said Amy, being incredibly brave.' 'I don't want to die really,' said Donovan. 'I know you don't,' said Amy. 'You were just making out.' 'Help me down,' said Donovan. 'You're all right now I'm here,' said Amy, saving Donovan with her incredible strength and bravery).

It was comforting, a bit, pretending things had happened the way she would have liked them to, instead of the way they actually did. But it didn't get rid of the horrible picture in her mind, of Donovan sprawled across the bridge thing, inching purposely towards the greeny cables. Nearer and nearer he inched, in Amy's mind, and the railway men were coming, but they were too slow. 'Come down!' shouted the railway men, but Donovan laughed, and wriggled nearer the cables, to tease them. . . . And then he screamed! One terrible, piercing, haunting scream – before he was frizzled up for ever!

She was all alone in her fear. She would like to tell Mum, she would like to tell Dad, but she couldn't of course, because they would be so angry with her about breaking her promise. Mum would say she was wicked to break her promise, and tell a lot more lies, and she was getting too good at it. Dad would say Donovan was a bad lot, and she was supposed to steer clear of him, wasn't she? And she was a silly stupid little girl not to do what he told her. And it only served Donovan right if he got frizzled up on the railway. And anyway Amy mustn't get mixed up in it, and now she must promise again, and they would go to the seaside on his next Sunday off, if the weather was fine.

And if Donovan was dead, she was never going to want to go to the seaside again. Ever.

Of course, of course, it would be on the news! If Donovan was dead it would be on the six o'clock news from the BBC. They always had the six o'clock news in their house, when Dad was at home. Amy looked at the bedroom clock. Only half past three! How could it be only half past three, when she so desperately wanted it to be six o'clock? She closed her eyes and willed the time to go faster . . . and faster . . . and faster . . .!

Amy opened her eyes and looked at the clock again. Oh no! Oh no, it *couldn't* be, she *couldn't* have! She could, and she had. She had fallen asleep, and the time was just ten minutes past six. She had missed it!

Perhaps the news was still on though. Perhaps they kept the bit about Donovan till last. It was usually something about bombs or earthquakes first. Amy scrambled off the bed and ran into the front room. There was a lovely smell of roast chicken. Mum was laying the table, and Dad was reading the *News of the World*. 'I want the telly on.' She turned the switch. 'That's not the news, why isn't it the news?'

'Because it's Sunday,' said Mum. 'The news is later Sunday. . . . Why you so interested in the news all of a sudden?'

'I haven't missed it then?'

'No. I said. Another ten minutes. Anyway it's only a lot of Northern Ireland, and bombs.'

'I'm interested in Northern Ireland,' said Amy.

'Oh? You never was before.'

'Well I am now.'

'Good,' said Dad.

'I suppose you have been having about it in school,' said Mum.

'That's right.'

'They don't half fill the kids' heads up these days. . . . I must say you're looking a bit better, Amy. You had a good sleep then? We're having dinner tonight, seeing we didn't have it dinnertime. Nice big chicken I didn't feel like cooking this morning. Anyway we had to eat up the sandwiches. Waste not want not. Could you manage a bit, Amy? *Amy*, I'm talking to you! The chicken, could you manage a bit? Try, anyway . . .?

'Hush!' said Amy.

There was nothing about Donovan on the television news. Perhaps the railway men saved him after all. Perhaps he only got in trouble for climbing on the iron thing, and throwing stones at the trains.

Perhaps that was all it was.

Perhaps!

12

A Secret Plan

There had been one beautiful day, and once more the skies were full of rain clouds. Donovan had not come to school. 'Bunking off again!' said Cynthia. 'How can we do our being nice to him, if he doesn't even bother to come to school?'

'I don't think he's bunking off,' said Amy. With the sight of that empty seat, her worst fears had come streaming back. Mounting and growing as the minutes passed, and hope died that he might be just late.

Amy was supposed to be weighing things, in a corner of the room with Cynthia, and she kept making silly mistakes, because she couldn't concentrate. 'What's the matter with you?' said Cynthia impatiently. 'And what's up with your face? You look as though you just seen a ghost.'

'I think Donovan's dead,' said Amy.

'What!'

'I think he's dead. I think he got electrocuted on the railway.'

'Don't be silly,' said Cynthia. 'You must have had a bad dream. You are getting all muddled up with your dream.'

'No, it was real,' said Amy.

'Tell me,' said Cynthia.

Amy told her. 'It wasn't on the news though. It would be on the news wouldn't it, if Donovan got electrocuted on the railway? Would that be important enough, Cynthia, to be on the news?'

'Excuse me interrupting,' said Miss Elliot, 'but when are you two going to, sort of, do some work?'

'Sorry, Miss Elliot,' said Cynthia. 'We're just going to do it now, Miss Elliot.'

'It would, wouldn't it, Cynthia?' said Amy. 'Be on the news?'

'The news people might not know about it yet,' said Cynthia.

'*Oh*!'

'It might be on the news tonight.'

'Oh I can't wait, I can't wait,' said Amy.

'Well you shouldn't have run away,' said Cynthia. '*I* wouldn't have. . . . Never mind,' she added kindly. 'You can't help it if you aren't as brave as me.'

'I was brave a *bit*,' said Amy.

'Poor Donovan,' said Cynthia. 'He must be mad! He must have gone mad from all his unhappy things! Poor Donovan!'

'Don't tell Lorraine,' said Amy.

'Tell Lorraine? What do you take me for, Amy, a blabbermouth or something? Really, I'm surprised at you! I'm not telling any of that stupid lot! I wouldn't tell that stupid lot for a hundred million pounds. They haven't got the brains to see Donovan's not wicked really, only unhappy. And mad. They probably be *glad* he got frizzled up. . . . Perhaps it's in the paper!'

'Oh yes, yes,' said Amy. 'Oh, let's look in a paper! Where can we find a paper?'

'Use your eyes, Amy, there's one right in front of you – well, nearly! On Miss Elliot's table, look!'

'You ask her,' said Amy.

175

'Miss Elliot, can me and Amy have a lend of your newspaper?'

'Cynthia, *really*,' said Miss Elliot. 'You've already wasted the last ten minutes chattering.'

'We want to see about Northern Ireland,' said Amy. 'About the bombs.'

'Oh – all right then' said Miss Elliot, not quite sure about it. She supposed children must be encouraged to take an interest in current affairs, even if it *was* the wrong time and place altogether. 'Just for a minute, and then you'll have to work extra hard – I mean, to make up.'

'We will, Miss Elliot, Don't worry, Miss Elliot,' said Cynthia. She fussed over the pages. 'Northern Ireland, we don't want that. Bombs – we don't want that! You're getting nearly as clever as me though, Amy, to think of saying it. There's nothing in the paper about Donovan. . . . Perhaps he's sick, Amy. Let's go round his mum's after school.'

'May I have my paper back now please?' said Miss Elliot. 'Before you, sort of, mess it *all* up. . . . And how about some work?'

'Get on with your work, Cynthia,' said Lorraine. She had observed the exchange of secrets and was feeling a bit jealous. Especially as she was missing Gloria, who had gone off to Jamaica for six weeks, lucky thing! 'Cynthia gossips too much, doesn't she Miss Elliot?'

'Some people got important things to gossip *about*,' said Cynthia.

'We don't know where his mum lives,' said Amy.

'It's in the register,' said Cynthia. 'Everybody's address is in the register, and you would know that,

Amy, if you didn't go about everywhere with your eyes shut.'

Miss Elliot was bending over Michael's table. 'Parrot's looking in your register,' said Andrew.

'Just a minute, Andrew,' said Miss Elliot.

'But Parrot's looking in your register!' said Andrew.

'That will do all of you,' said Miss Elliot, who was getting quite good at being firm now, when she put her mind to it. 'Particularly you, Cynthia.'

'Sorry, Miss Elliot. I won't do it any more, I promise. . . . Let me write it down before I forget,' she said, to Amy.

'That's not his mum's address, that's his gran's,' said Amy.

'That's all right,' said Cynthia. 'We'll go to his gran's.'

'But he doesn't live there any more.'

'What have you done with your brains, Amy?' said Cynthia. 'His gran will know if he's been frizzled up, won't she!'

'What about Simon?' said Cynthia.

'Simon?'

'You know, that little thing in the Infants. That little nuisance thing. We better take him to your house first.'

'Oh we can't, we can't!' said Amy. 'My mum's going to the dentist. She's going to be out, I nearly forgot. We'll have to take him with us.'

'He'll moan,' said Cynthia.

'He'll have to moan then,' said Amy. 'Come on hurry, hurry. Hurry, Cynthia, I think it's going to rain again.'

'I wanna go *home*,' said Simon.

'Shut up, and I'll buy you a lolly,' said Cynthia.

'You haven't got any money,' said Amy.

'You're tricking me!' wailed Simon.

'Now look what you done, Amy!' said Cynthia. 'All right Simon, I'll give you a piggyback. And you better not be as heavy as last time.'

Amy stood still in the middle of the road. 'Oh!' she said.

'Come on then,' said Cynthia. 'We don't want to stop for "Oh".'

'I just remembered – Donovan's gran doesn't get home till late. He told me. A long time ago.'

Cynthia considered. 'If he's frizzled up, she'll be there.'

'How do you make that out?'

'Well, its stands to reason, she won't go to work if he's frizzled up. She'll be home, crying.'

'Crying? Her?'

'She'll cry if he's dead,' said Cynthia. 'People always cry when people are dead. And they get sorry for what they done, when it's too late.'

'So if she's not there,' said Amy, in sudden hope, 'if she's not there we'll know Donovan's all right, shall we? Shall we, Cynthia?'

'Are we going to see Donovan?' said Simon.

'No,' said Cynthia.

'But you *said*, I *heard* you.'

'You're not supposed to listen to other people's conservations,' said Cynthia, who did it all the time.

'Shall we Cynthia?' said Amy. 'Shall we know?'

'Let's see when we get there?' said Cynthia.

They splashed through puddles to the front door.

178

The name on the bell said MRS BOWERS. 'That's not Donovan's name,' said Cynthia.

'His gran's name's different to his,' said Amy.

'Oh yeah,' said Cynthia, 'like Andrea's mum's name is different to Andrea's. TOP FLAT MRS BOWERS,' she read. She looked up. 'The curtains are all drawn over. Oh *Amy*, the curtains are drawn. Oh Amy.'

'What is important about the curtains?'

'When people draw the curtains over, it means somebody's dead.'

'Are you sure?'

'I think so,' said Cynthia.

'Is Donovan dead?' asked Simon.

'No,' said Cynthia.

'Let's ring the bell,' said Amy.

They rang, and rang, and nothing happened. 'She must be not in,' said Cynthia.

'So if she's not in crying, he must be all right,' said Amy hopefully.

'I dunno,' said Cynthia. 'She might be round his mum's crying. I think she *would* be round his mum's crying. Oh Amy. Oh poor Donovan. Oh, Amy.'

'Let's ring the bell again,' said Amy. 'Perhaps she didn't hear. Perhaps she's deaf. Perhaps she's out the back.'

They rang, and rang, and rang.

'Look!' said Amy. Somebody upstairs was moving the curtains. Part of a face appeared briefly, then disappeared. 'I think it was her, Cynthia. I think it was!'

They waited, but nothing more happened.

'I wanna go home,' said Simon.

'Shut up,' said Cynthia. She put her finger on the bell, and held it there. The remorseless jangling

179

inside the house went on and on. 'It's no good,' said Cynthia. 'She's not going to answer. I think we might as well go home.'

'Can I have a piggy bank?' said Simon.

'Shut up, Simon,' said Amy. 'Shut up bothering us. Can't you see we're worried?'

'I wanna piggy bank,' said Simon.

'Why didn't she come?' said Amy.

'I told you,' said Cynthia. 'She's crying behind the curtains. Because Donovan got frizzled up on the railway.'

'What's frizzled up?' said Simon.

'You're not supposed to be listening,' said Cynthia.

'I'm going to try again,' said Amy. 'I'm not giving up, I'm not! I know she's in there, I'm going to *make* her come down, I'm going to *make* her.' She put her finger on the bell, like Cynthia.

'I think we wasted our time,' said Cynthia.

'I wanna go home,' said Simon.

'I don't care what you want, I'm staying here,' said Amy. She turned her face to the wall, and pressed her forehead against the bell, instead of her finger. She closed her eyes, and willed Donovan's gran to come down the stairs.

'She's coming to the window!' said Cynthia. 'Look, Amy, she's coming!'

Above their heads, the curtains were being jerked aside, and the sash window wrenched upwards. 'Go away!' said Donovan's gran, in a very cross voice.

'We come about Donovan!' yelled Cynthia.

'He's not here,' said Donovan's gran, banging the window shut again.

Amy put her finger on the bell once more. 'That's

right,' said Cynthia furiously. 'You do that, Amy. Miserable old cow won't talk to us, when we come all this way! She ought to be glad we take so much trouble. I think she's very, very rude. She got no manners. Miserable old cow!'

'Come on, miserable old cow,' said Simon.

There were footsteps on the stairs inside, and the front door fell open sharply. Donovan's gran stood there, looking very angry, and very ill. 'What's the matter with you kids?' she demanded. 'Haven't you got any manners?' She was wearing a frayed and grubby dressing gown, and her dyed blonde hair looked as though it had not been combed all day. Her eyes had dark circles all round them. 'Have you been crying?' said Cynthia.

'Crying, no! Running to the loo all night more like it. *And* all day. Must be something I ate.'

'Oh, you're *ill*,' said Amy, relief surging over her like a warm tide.

'What you sounding so pleased about?' said Donovan's gran sourly. 'It's no joke, I can tell you. Up and down all night I was! *And* sicking into the bowl!' She coughed, leaning against the doorpost. She was still smoking a cigarette, and her fingers were stained brown. The nails had black dirt under them as well. Amy looked at the dirty fingernails, and the grubby dressing gown, and the face with yesterday's make-up on it, and she thought it was no wonder Donovan's gran got ill, eating so many germs. Her fastidious soul recoiled from all that dirt. She thought about Donovan, with his rough-dried shirts that were always clean, and it suddenly occurred to her that he probably washed them himself.

181

'I'm sorry we disturb you,' said Cynthia, when the racking coughs subsided. 'We come about Donovan.'

'He's not here, I told you.'

'Do you know where he is?'

'At his mum's, I suppose. It's nothing to do with me. I told him last night. You go back to your mum's, I said. Your mum can't palm you off on me every time something goes wrong, I said. I'm not having no more of it, I said. You go back to your mum's, I told him. Last night.'

'You saw him last night?' said Amy. 'Are you sure? Are you *sure*?'

'You trying to call me a liar then?'

'No, no, not that. It's just he wasn't in school today, and we was worried.'

'Worried? You don't want to worry about *him*. He can look after himself all right! In trouble of course, as usual. Police brung him home to warn his mum. Nearly up in court this time, they only *just* let him off. His mum send him round to me to take him off her hands, 'cos she's sick of him in trouble and I said, you go back to your mum's. I said, it's her responsibility not mine, and anyway I got troubles of my own with this bad stomach. And he went. With his things he brung. And he never come back 'cos I waited to see. So that's where he is. At his mum's.'

'*Thank* you,' said Amy, her heart dancing. 'Oh *thank* you, *thank* you.'

'Don't know what you're thanking me about,' said Donovan's gran. 'Anyway, can I go back to bed now? . . . You sure? . . . You sure you don't want to ring my bell a bit more? Give me a headache on top of—?'

'Bye,' called Cynthia, with a wave and a big smile. 'We didn't want to hear about her sicking in the bowl

182

again, did we?' she said to Amy, as they scampered down the road.

'Why was the miserable old cow sicking in the bowl?' said Simon.

'Don't ask silly questions,' said Cynthia.

'Is Donovan dead?'

'*No!*' said Amy joyfully.

'Why did we go to the miserable old cow's house?' said Simon.

'Listen, Simon,' said Amy. 'Listen, Simon, you mustn't say nothing about Donovan at home. You mustn't tell Mum we went to his gran's house. Promise!'

'Can I have a lolly?'

'After we get home.'

'I want a lolly n-o-o-w!'

'Well you *can't* have a lolly now. I haven't got any money to buy it with now, and neither has Cynthia. And if you say one word to our mum about we went to Donovan's gran's house I'm never going to buy you a lolly again. Nor a birthday present. Nor a Christmas present.'

'Can I have a piggy bank then?'

'Come on,' said Cynthia. 'I'll give you a piggyback to your house. . . . Amy, why mustn't Simon tell about Donovan?'

'No reason.'

'You've got a secret from me!'

'No I haven't.'

'Yes you have. And you're supposed to be my best friend.'

'I *am* your best friend.' There were some things you couldn't tell your best friend though, weren't there? Some things you couldn't tell your best friend but you

183

could tell your mum and dad. And some things you couldn't tell your mum and dad but could tell your best friend. And some things you couldn't tell anybody at all. 'I'll tell you one day,' said Amy to Cynthia. 'When we're both very, very old.'

'It's raining again,' Simon complained.

'Nearly there,' said Cynthia.

'There's somebody on our wall,' Simon shouted.

'It's *Donovan*,' said Cynthia.

'Make him go away, make him go away,' said Amy. 'I don't want my mum to see.'

'Your mum won't see, she's at the dentist,' said Cynthia.

'Hello Donovan,' said Simon.

Donovan looked lonely, almost pathetic, sitting on the wall. His shirt was wet from previous rain, and his bare arms had bruises on them. His feet were resting on a bulging nylon holdall. 'Do you want to do something for me then?' he said to Amy, not looking at her.

'Yes. I don't know. What?'

Donovan looked embarrassed. 'You said you worry about me, right?'

'Did I?'

'Yesterday. You said you worry about me, right?' So now, do you want to do something for me?'

'Your mum's coming, Amy,' said Cynthia. 'I see her coming down the road.'

'What must I do?' said Amy, to Donovan.

'Let me come in your house.'

'What?'

'Your *mum's* coming,' said Cynthia. 'And I know your mum must not see Donovan, because of the thing you won't tell me till we are old ladies. Which is a very long time to wait!' she added reproachfully.

'You aren't allowed to come in our house, Donovan, you know that,' said Amy. 'I would like to let you but I can't.'

'Go and hide round the corner, Donovan,' said Cynthia.

'Keep out of it, Parrot,' said Donovan. 'I'm not talking to you.'

'Go and hide round the corner, quick!' said Cynthia.

'Don't have to, if I don't want to.'

'If you don't go in a minute, it's going to be too late,' said Cynthia. 'Go on! You can trust me. I'm your friend now, and you ought to know that without being told.' Resentful and unsure, Donovan climbed off the wall. 'And take your luggage with you! . . . Run!'

Donovan ran.

'Where has Donovan gone?' said Simon.

'It wasn't Donovan, it was somebody else,' said Cynthia.

'Can I have my lolly now?'

'In a minute,' said Cynthia. 'Hello, Mrs Baker. Did you have a nice time at the dentist?'

'My face feels funny,' said Mum. 'Can't feel anything at all one side. Is it that Donald I see, running down the road? No? Looks like him. . . . My face feels funny. . . . Well come on inside the lot of you, going to be cats and dogs in a minute!'

'Cynthia's going to get me a lolly,' said Simon.

'That's kind of Cynthia,' said Mum. 'Hope you said thank you.'

'Even if it's raining, she's going to get me a lolly, aren't you Cynthia? It's so I don't tell.'

'*Simon*!' said Amy.

'Oh *secrets* is it?' said Mum, in great good humour now she had been to the dentist and it was all over. '*Secrets*, eh? Oh all right, I don't want to know anybody's secrets, I got plenty of my own, so there! . . . What do you want for your tea then? Cynthia staying?'

'I expect so,' said Amy.

'What's the matter with you?' said Mum, suddenly noticing. 'You're as white as a sheet again. You did have too much sun yesterday didn't you!'

'The miserable old cow sicked in the bowl,' said Simon.

'Don't be disgusting, Simon,' said Mum, disappearing into the kitchen.

'When can I have my lolly?' said Simon.

'In a minute,' said Cynthia. She pulled Amy into a corner of the room, and whispered in her ear. 'One of us got to go out and find Donovan. Go away, Simon. Amy and me's talking big people's things. . . . All right, the longer you stand there listening, the longer it's going to be before you get your lolly! . . . I think Donovan's in more trouble, and we got to find out what it is.'

'*You* go,' said Amy.

'Can I? Are you sure? You don't mind? All right then, I'll go.' Cynthia was enjoying herself enormously. 'All right Simon, I'm going to get your lolly now, if Amy can lend me some money. And if you tell anything you're not supposed to, while I'm gone, I shall eat it all myself.'

'Hurry, hurry, hurry!' said Simon.

'She will probably be a long time,' said Amy. 'She will probably have to go to three different shops, four

186

different shops, *six* different shops. They probably all run out of lollies, so you be a good boy and watch telly till she comes. . . . And don't forget, if you say Donovan's name to our mum, the most terrible things are going to happen to you!'

'What?'

'I'll make a spell, and turn you into a spider. And you know what Mum does to spiders!'

'Put them down the plughole!' Simon rolled over and over on the carpet, chuckling with glee. 'Mum's going to put me down the plughole! Down the plughole! . . . Turn on the telly, Amy,' he said, losing interest in the joke.

After about ten thousand years, or so it seemed, Cynthia returned. Her eyes were round and gleaming, and little drops of rain glistened in all the braids. Excitement flowed from her in waves; she was bursting with something to tell. 'Let's go in your bedroom,' she said. 'Here you are Simon, fill up your gob with that.'

'Tell me before I die,' said Amy, closing the bedroom door behind them.

'I got it out of him,' said Cynthia.

'Well?'

'He wasn't very nice to me. He didn't want me, he wanted you. So he was all grumpy. But I got it out of him. In the end.'

'CYNTHIA!'

'All right, it's like this. Donovan's mum throw him out of the house!

'I know that bit,' said Amy. 'His gran told us that bit.'

'But again,' said Cynthia. 'Donovan went back to his mum's last night, and she was not pleased because his gran send him back, and Donovan was cheeky to his mum, and they started rowing, and his mum hit him, and I think Donovan hit his mum too, but he didn't say that bit, and in the morning she throw him out of the house again, and say he must go to his gran's.'

'And . . .?'

'And he was scared to go to his gran's because he knows his gran won't have him.'

'But *somebody* got to have him,' said Amy. 'What will happen if his mum won't have him, and his gran won't have him?'

'Well that's it, that's it,' said Cynthia. 'That's what the trouble is all about. . . . Donovan says, if nobody won't have him, he will have to go IN CARE.'

'What's that?' said Amy.

'I don't know really,' said Cynthia, 'but I think it's like prison. It's for really bad children, and it's like prison, and Donovan's really frightened. . . . Only he's got a idea.'

'What idea?'

'You won't like it.'

'What is it?'

'You won't like it, though.'

'CYNTHIA.'

'All right, this is Donovan's idea. Donovan's gran is sick, right? And she is cross-tempered because she's sick. . . . I mean, she's more cross-tempered than she usually is. She's always cross-tempered, but Donovan says she's better than his mum really. He says she will get over being cross-tempered when she is not sick any more, and she will be sorry for him and have him back. But not if he's IN CARE. If he's IN CARE

188

they won't let him out of IN CARE, and he will have to stay there for always.'

'How does he know that?'

'His mum told him.'

'So what is the idea that I won't like?' Said Amy.

'Well—'

'Come on!'

'Well it's raining, and he hasn't got anywhere to go. And he is very sorrowful, Amy.'

'I know *that*.'

'He wants to hide in your loft.'

'What!'

'Only for a few days.'

'A few *days*?'

'Till his gran is better, and got over her cross temper. I think it's quite a good idea. . . . I wish *I* thought of it.'

'But I *can't*,' said Amy.

'Why can't you?'

'Lots of things. . . . I will have to tell all lies, and my mum says I'm not good at it.'

'*Aren't* you not good at it?'

'I'm better at it than my mum thinks,' Amy admitted.

'There you are then!'

'But it's bad to my mum and dad. I can't do such bad things to my mum and dad, I like my mum and dad.'

'So you rather be bad to Donovan!'

'I don't know, I don't know.'

'Poor Donovan!' said Cynthia. 'Out there in all the rain, and he got nowhere to go. And it isn't his fault he's bad you know. I feel so sorry for poor Donovan.'

'Why don't you hide him in your loft then?' said Amy weakly.

'There isn't a camp in my loft, only yours. With a floor, and cushions and things. . . . I think you are being selfish, Amy. We all got to make a sacrifice some time, our minister said. And stand by our friends in their hour of need.'

'I can't do it, Cynthia, I *can't*. . . . All right, what will he eat? Tell me, what will he eat?'

'We can sneak food up to him,' said Cynthia. 'I'll help, it will be fun! . . . No, I don't mean that, I don't mean that. Poor Donovan!'

'What about when they're looking for him?'

'They won't be.'

'How do you know?' said Amy.

'They won't be looking for him, because they won't know he's missing. His mum thinks he's at his gran's, and his gran thinks he's at his mum's.'

'They'll tell each other.'

'They won't,' said Cynthia.

'How do you know they won't?'

'They've fell out. They're not speaking.'

Amy climbed on her bunk, and took up her favourite position – curled up into a tight little ball. 'I can't, I can't, I *can't*.'

'You're a coward, Amy, that's what you are.'

'I know. I can't help it.'

'I'll go and tell him then, shall I?' said Cynthia, in a cold and distant voice.

Silence.

'Shall I, Amy? Shall I tell Donovan you're too scared to stand by him in his hour of need? Poor Donovan. All alone. And cold. And *wet*!'

Silence.

'I'm going Amy, I'm going now. To tell Donovan. All right?'

Silence.

'I'm *nearly* going then. . . . All right?'

'. . . No,' said Amy.

'I might as well, seeing you're too scared.'

'Wait a minute,' said Amy. 'Wait a minute, Cynthia.' She sat up slowly. 'You'll have to help me mind. I can't do it all by myself.'

13

The great adventure

Amy was terrified at what she had agreed to do. It was crazy, was she really going to do it? 'Don't forget I'm here too,' said Cynthia.

'But I don't know how to start even,' said Amy.

'I'll tell you how. I'm clever at thinking, remember?'

'All right then, think.'

'First,' said Cynthia, 'first somebody got to go and get Donovan. And second, somebody got to keep your mum busy in the kitchen, so she don't see him coming in. . . . And third, third, somebody got to do something about Downstairs. We don't want *her* to see Donovan coming in.'

'It's too hard,' said Amy.

'No it's not. The hardest is Downstairs. I'll do that bit.'

'What about the steps?' said Amy.

'What about them?'

'I mean getting them out, and putting them back. . . . And Simon. Simon's going to see you know, Cynthia. And tell.'

'Make him promise.'

'He won't remember. He's too little. He nearly give it away just now! He didn't mean to, he's just too little.'

'He's a nuisance,' said Cynthia crossly. 'What do you want to have a little nuisance brother for? *I* haven't got one. . . . You'll have to make him be in the kitchen as well.'

'I can't. It's too hard.'

'It's for *Donovan*. Remember?'

'All right, what about the steps?'

'You keep on about those steps,' said Cynthia. 'Do you think I'm stupid or something? *I* know where the steps are. *I* know how to use them, and so does Donovan. Leave it to me.'

'All right. What about Downstairs?'

'Yeah,' Cynthia admitted. 'That is the problem.'

'She'll see,' said Amy. 'She sees everybody comes into the house. She hides behind the door, and she spies.'

'She might not tell your mum though. They don't speak much do they, her and your mum? Only to row with each other sometimes.'

'We can't risk it,' said Amy. 'We can't risk it, Cynthia, we can't!'

'All right, all right we can't risk it,' said Cynthia. 'Wait a minute, there must be a way. . . . Amy, what is out the back?'

'I dunno. It's hers. We never go there.'

'Can you see out the back from here?'

'Yeah. There's nothing there. Only some old pots and things, I think. I never noticed.'

Cynthia went to the bedroom window and looked down. 'I shall say to Downstairs, Amy told me there's lovely flowers in the pots, and she looks at them every day, and please can I go out and see them close.'

'They aren't lovely,' said Amy. 'They look as if they're dying, mostly. Anyway, she won't let you.'

'Leave it to me,' said Cynthia. 'And while me and Downstairs are out the back, Donovan can sneak up

193

the stairs, and get the steps, and get in the loft, and I can come up after I been out the back with Downstairs, and put the steps away. You see Amy, it's all quite easy really. What about your dad, is he going to come in, in a minute?'

'Not till late tonight,' said Amy.

'There you are!'

Amy went into the front room. Simon was watching the television and seemed totally absorbed. She thought he would hardly be distracted if the house fell down; it seemed silly to disturb him. 'Can you hear all right?' she asked.

Simon did not answer her. Amy turned the television up loud. 'You don't want to strain your ears,' she said.

She was blocking his view. Simon leaned forward and pushed at her impatiently, craning sideways not to miss anything. Amy left him and went into the kitchen, closing the front room door very firmly. 'Simon's got the telly on too loud,' said Mum.

'He asked me to turn it up,' said Amy.

'I hope he's not getting deaf,' said Mum.

'Oh I don't think so, I don't think so,' said Amy. 'Listen Mum, lisen . . .'

'All right, I'm listening.' Mum was peeling the potatoes, and cutting them up for chips.

'Listen,' said Amy, desperately trying to think of something. She didn't know how long it was going to take Cynthia to fetch Donovan. He might be coming up the stairs at this very moment. 'Listen . . .' she said again.

'If I listen any harder my ears going to drop off,' said Mum. 'But I haven't heard anything up to yet.

Are you trying to tell me something bad? You been in trouble at school, something like that?'

'No,' said Amy, 'nothing like that. Nothing bad. Something good. I want to tell you. . . . I want to tell you about this story I wrote, and Miss Elliot said it was the best I ever done. It was about . . .'

'Go on,' said Mum, pleased, 'I'm listening.'

'It was about . . . a boy who was always throwing stones at trains, and climbing on the bridge, and getting in trouble.'

'That don't sound like your sort of story,' said Mum. 'Your stories are all about witches, aren't they? And people from other planets, with more arms and legs than they supposed to have.' She shrieked with laughter, attacking the potatoes with renewed vigour.

'No, they supposed to have them if they're from other planets,' said Amy. 'They come from planets where people are supposed to have a lot of arms.'

'I can't think what for,' said Mum. 'Two was always enough for me. Go on, what happened to this boy?'

'Well that's it,' said Amy. 'He was a alien from another planet really, but nobody knew it because he was found when he was a baby. In a dustbin.'

'Poor little thing. How did he get in the dustbin though, if he was from another planet and he was only a baby?'

'A lady alien laid a egg. In the dustbin.'

'The telephone's ringing,' said Mum. 'Go and answer it, there's a good girl.'

'But I'm telling you about my story.'

'Amy! . . . And don't close the door like that, I want to hear who it is.'

The phone was on the landing at the top of the stairs. 'Is that Amy? Is Cynthia there?'

'Oh hello, Mrs Garrett. Yes, yes, she's here, she's staying to tea. She must have forgot to ring you. . . . Mum, Mum,' Amy called. 'It's all right, it's Cynthia's mum. You can close the door now.'

'Why you so anxious about the kitchen door all of a sudden?' said Mum.

'Not let the cooking smells out,' said Amy.

'I'm not cooking, I'm peeling potatoes,' said Mum, coming out into the passage. 'What is this? Is something going on? . . . No, don't tell me, don't tell me, you get back to the telephone. How rude of you Amy, go fussing about doors, when you're supposed to be talking to Cynthia's mum. Really, I don't know what got into you! Touch of the sun it must be still! Here, give me the phone . . . Hello there, long time no see! Nice weather, eh? If you happen to be a duck! We had our summer of course, so we mustn't grumble. Yesterday was our summer. . . . Did you? . . . Oh really? . . . She never! Well, that's a turnup, innit!'

Standing in the passage, expecting Donovan to come bounding up the stairs at any minute, Amy thought she would die. Would Cynthia's mum and her mum never end their everlasting chatter?

'Yes, yes,' Mum was saying. 'Cynthia's here all right. Large as life, and not to worry . . . No, we won't let her stay late . . . Yes well, you know she's always welcome. . . . No, no, Amy *often* has her tea at your place. Works out about even I should say, anyway who's counting? . . . You want a word with her? Amy, go and get Cynthia to the phone, there's a good girl!'

Now what was she supposed to do? Amy opened the door to the front room, and pretended to look inside. 'And turn the telly down,' said Mum. 'Enough to make anybody deaf!'

'She's not here,' said Amy.

'Well that's funny, where's she got to?'

'Perhaps she went out for another lolly,' said Amy.

'She's not here for the minute,' said Mum, into the telephone. 'Gone out to buy a lolly or something. . . . Yes they *do* eat too many sweets. . . . Yes, I agree with you, and I just been to the dentist myself, this afternoon. And I wish I never ate so many sweets myself, but it's too late now. . . .'

'*Mum*,' called Amy desperately, from the kitchen. '*Mum*, I think Downstairs got a visitor!'

'What! . . . So I'll get her to ring you back when she comes in, shall I? . . . What did you say, Amy? A visitor? Downstairs? She never had a visitor in her life.'

'She's talking to somebody,' said Amy. 'I can hear her, out the back.'

'Out the back? It's raining.'

'Only a little bit,' said Amy.

'Let's have a nose,' said Mum. She went to the kitchen window, and peeped from behind the curtain. 'It's Cynthia,' she said in astonishment.

'Did you say Cynthia?' said Amy, pretending to be just as surprised as Mum.

'She's talking to Downstairs!' said Mum. 'Nineteen to the dozen. She must be mad, who in their right mind would want to talk to Downstairs?'

'What is she talking about?'

'I dunno. Something to do with them weeds in the flower-pots. Look at her, Amy – she's gone barmy, for definite!'

'She's very, very kind you know,' said Amy. 'She's probably doing her good deed for the day.'

'I didn't know she was in the Guides.'

'I think she's practising to be.'

'What you shutting that door again for, Amy? You got a thing about doors today.'

'It's a bit cold with it open.'

'Go and get a thicker cardigan then, if you're cold.'

'That's a good idea,' said Amy.

He was coming! He was coming up the stairs. Amy put a finger to her lips to tell him he must come quieter, but he was quiet enough anyway, bounding along on his toes. He gave her a little thump as he passed, which was a funny thing to do in a way, but left her feeling oddly pleased. It was a thump which said, me and you are in something together, aren't we?

Deftly, Donovan whipped the steps from their place in the cupboard, and his feet flew upwards. The last bit was the trickiest, and in his anxiety Donovan was just a bit too clumsy. His foot knocked against one of the bottles on the shelf, and down it came, clatter clatter against the steps.

'What's going on *now*?'

Mum was in the passage, staring at Amy, who was halfway up the step ladder. The trapdoor was shut, but not properly. Fortunately Mum was looking at Amy, not the partly open trapdoor. 'Whatever are you doing?'

'I thought I'd go up in the loft. See if our camp's still there.'

'By *yourself*?'

'With Cynthia. I was getting it ready, for when Cynthia comes.'

Simon was in the passage as well now. His television programme was over, and he was looking for fresh amusement. '*I* wanna come, *I* wanna come!'

'Well you can't,' said Amy. 'It's not for you, it's for us. So we can talk our secret things without you hearing all the time.'

'In the loft, though?' said Mum. The damaged ceiling had been mended a long time ago, but there was a permanent scar in Mum's mind.

'The hole's a bit open,' said Simon.

'I know,' said Amy. 'I tried to push it, but I couldn't properly. It's too heavy for me.'

'Wait for Cynthia,' said Mum. 'She's bigger than you.'

'Mind your head, Amy,' shrieked Cynthia loudly, for Mum's benefit. '*Mind*, silly! Mind your foot going through the ceiling like last time. It's good up here Amy, innit! Without that silly gang! I'm glad we come Amy, aren't you? It's good just the two of us innit? Just you and me!'

Donovan had switched on the light Dad had fixed. Cynthia slammed down the trapdoor so the light wouldn't show below.

'You forgot about the steps,' said Amy. 'You forgot about putting them away.'

'No I didn't, I didn't *forget*. I just didn't have time.'

'You said "Leave it to me,"' said Amy. 'And *I* had to do it, after all.'

'Well I can't be in two places at once, can I? I was out the back, wasn't I? I can't be in two places at once. Tell me how I'm supposed to do that. Be in two places at once?'

'Are you two going to do something else besides quarrel?' said Donovan sullenly. Amy put a finger to her lips, to warn him to keep his voice to a whisper.

199

'Have you two come up here just to have a quarrel?' he hissed.

He was soaking wet, and shivering. He sat on the cushions, on the floor of the camp, hugging himself and rocking. The nylon holdall was beside him. 'Why don't you put on some dry clothes?' said Cynthia. 'You got them in the bag I suppose, why don't you put them on?'

'When I get some privacy,' said Donovan.

'Oh *we* won't look, will we, Amy?' said Cynthia. The girls turned their backs, and Cynthia went on talking about Donovan as though he were not there. 'We will have to think about how to feed him.'

There were going to be other problems too. 'We can save some of our tea,' said Amy.

'That will be fun,' said Cynthia.

'But what about – you know!'

'What?'

'*You* know,' said Amy. 'Toilet.'

'He'll have to hold it,' said Cynthia.

'I heard that,' said Donovan. 'You can turn round now, if you like. . . . Can't I come down to the bathroom, when your mum is not here? And in the night?'

'Someone will catch you,' said Amy. 'It's too risky. Do you want to meet my dad one time, when you come down to the toilet?'

'No,' said Donovan.

'Anyway, how can you get down, without the steps?'

'I can think up a plan,' said Donovan.

'I will have to let you down each night,' said Amy. 'And you will have to wait till then.'

'It's a long time,' said Donovan miserably.

200

'I think you will have to have a bucket,' said Amy, not looking at him.

'That's not very nice,' said Donovan, his face hot with shame.

'You're just making a fuss, Donovan,' said Cynthia. 'You shouldn't make such a fuss, when we're trying to help you.'

'Who asked you, Parrot?' said Donovan.

'Don't call me Parrot,' said Cynthia. 'You didn't ought to call me that, now I'm your friend. And you will have to put up with the bucket, and not make such a fuss about such a little thing.'

'We don't want to talk any more about the bucket,' said Amy. 'The bucket is boring, and we don't have to talk about it any more, excepting I shall have to find one for you, Donovan, and bring it to you in the night.'

She was deeply embarrassed, and she didn't know where the thought of the bucket had come from. Saving the tea was easy. People in adventure stories were always saving their tea to give to their friends in hiding, but she couldn't remember ever reading anything about buckets. Somehow, out of this great necessity, the idea had emerged all by itself. 'I think we ought to talk about making a bed for you, Donovan,' she said.

'The cushions are good to sleep on. I can lay them out, look!' said Donovan.

'You want something to cover you though.'

'There's still some old curtains. We didn't use them all.'

'They're *dirty*,' said Amy.

'Get him a blanket,' said Cynthia.

'Where from?' said Amy.

201

'I dunno. Off of your bed. We all got to make sacrifices, remember.'

'I think there's two blankets on my bed,' said Amy.

'I can have one of them then,' said Donovan. 'Right?'

'You should say thank you to Amy,' said Cynthia. 'For giving you the blanket off her bed.'

'I don't need you to tell me when to say thank you, Parrot.'

'I don't mind if Donovan doesn't say thank you,' said Amy.

'Well you *ought* to mind,' said Cynthia.

'Why don't you mind your own business?' said Donovan.

'It *is* my business if I'm helping you,' said Cynthia. 'And you ought to say thank you to Amy, and you ought to say thank you to me, when I took so much trouble to get you in here. You don't know how much trouble I took, and you don't care do you, because you're selfish, and you don't never care about other people do you, only yourself!'

'Am I supposed to care about *you* then?'

'You care about me a bit, if I'm your friend.'

'I didn't ask you to be my friend.'

'I wish I never wasted my time then,' said Cynthia.

'Oh stop it, stop it,' said Amy.

'I wish I never wasted my time,' said Cynthia again. 'And you want to know something? I don't like you at all, Donovan Grant! And I'm not going to help you no more. And I hope you get cold. And I hope you get hungry. And I hope you get put IN CARE. And that's all I got to say.'

'She doesn't mean it,' said Amy, terrified that perhaps she did.

202

'Yes I do.'

'Cynthia!' said Amy. 'And Donovan! Please try to be friends with each other. *Please!*'

They wouldn't look at her, either of them. The atmosphere was tense, hostile, explosive.

'*Please!*' said Amy.

'All right,' said Cynthia. 'I will if he will.'

'Donovan?'

'. . . Long as she stop getting on my nerves!'

'You didn't use to close that trap over,' said Mum, 'when you went up before.'

'We got very private things to talk about,' said Amy.

'Sound like you was having words,' said Mum.

'We made it up,' said Amy.

'What did you put those chips under the table for, Cynthia?' said Simon.

'Chips? What chips?' said Cynthia. 'I didn't put no chips under the table, Simon. Eat your tea, and stop imagining things.'

'Better pick them up if they went on the floor,' said Mum. 'They get tramped in the carpet else.'

'They didn't go on the floor,' said Cynthia. 'Simon *thought* they went on the floor but they didn't. You got too much imagination, Simon. You are always imagining things that don't happen. Like going to houses, where you didn't really go. And people in the road, that you thought it was one person, but it was really somebody else. Things like that.'

'I didn't say on the floor,' said Simon. 'I said under the table. And Amy. She put a fishfinger, I saw her. What did you do that for, Amy?'

'What's going on?' said Mum.

'Nothing,' said Amy. 'Shut up, Simon, making trouble.'

'Let me see,' said Mum, pulling up the cloth to look in Amy's lap. 'You got something there! What you got there?'

'Told you,' said Simon.

'It's nothing,' said Amy. She had hidden a plastic bag in her lap, and she tried now, unsuccessfully, to push it between her knees.

'What's this then?' said Mum. 'What's all this nothing I found in your lap? All this squashed-up greasy nothing? What is it Amy?'

Amy's mind went blank.

'It's for the cat,' said Cynthia.

'What cat?' said Mum. 'We haven't got a cat.'

'It's a stray,' said Cynthia. 'It's hungry, so we saved it some food.'

'Oh did you?' said Mum. 'And who gave you permission to feed best fishfingers from Sainsbury's to some mangy stray cat? Hopping with fleas, most likely. Next thing, we'll be having all the stray cats in the neighbourhood round our house begging. All yarling, and squalling, and messing up the front. What's Downstairs going to say?'

'It's not her house,' said Amy.

'That's beside the point,' said Mum. 'She *thinks* it is.'

'Where's the cat?' said Simon. 'I wanna see the cat.'

'Put all that stuff in the bin,' said Mum firmly. 'And you, Cynthia. Go on, I want to see you do it. And wash your hands the both of you, and come and finish your tea.'

'I wanna see the cat,' said Simon.

'Cat's gone to see the Queen,' said Mum. 'Gone to Buckingham Palace after *her* fishfingers.'

This was the worst bit, the bit that was coming next. This was the bit she had to do all by herself. Amy thrashed about in the bunk above Simon, then worried she might be waking him, and made herself lie still. It was hard lying still, when she wanted to thrash about. Her thoughts were racing, round and round like the engines in Simon's train set, and they wouldn't stop, and they were thoughts in a way, but it wasn't proper thinking because the thoughts weren't going anywhere.

Donovan, Cynthia, Mum and Dad – Donovan, Cynthia, Mum and Dad – Donovan . . . the train set in Amy's head went faster and faster, and she was all alone now, and it was all up to her. And she was frightened. She had done something too big, and too wicked, and it was frightening her. And she couldn't go on with it because it was too wicked, tricking Mum and Dad who trusted her. And she couldn't *not* go on with it, because Donovan trusted her too. And 'he didn't want me, he wanted you,' Cynthia had said.

When would it be safe to get up, and do all the unthinkably frightening things she had to do? Mum was already in bed, she knew. Mum had a television all to herself in her bedroom, and she always went to bed when Dad was on late shift, like now, to watch television till he came home. Come on, Dad, come on! Finish driving your train and come home, and go to bed, and go to sleep so I can get up, and do my things I have to do. And I don't believe I can do them really, but anyway I want to get it over! And Donovan doesn't want Cynthia, he wants *me*.

At last! The front door banging, and Downstairs grumbling because Dad banged the door, and Dad coming up the stairs. And soon Dad's snores, ferocious and nerve-shattering, and reassuring, vibrating through the house.

Now! Now she must do it. Amy sat up in bed, and manoeuvred herself on to the little ladder. Simon snuffled a bit in his sleep, and Amy held her breath so as not to wake him. The beds creaked as she came down, and Simon muttered and turned over, but didn't wake. Amy's legs felt weak and shaky, and there was a funny feeling in her head. She pulled the top blanket off her bed, and rolled it up and left it on the floor just outside the bedroom door, while she went to look for a bucket.

She *ought* to know where the buckets were kept, she *ought* to. She had lived in this house for eleven years, so she really ought to know where the buckets were kept. She knew where the plates and cups were, of course, and the pans, and the food, but she didn't remember ever needing a bucket before, so she wasn't quite sure where to look.

Under the sink? Had she seen Mum taking a bucket from under the sink? She was almost sure she had. It was necessary to look in the dark, because she dared not switch the kitchen light on, and when she opened the cupboard under the sink, something fell out, and rolled across the floor, and made a noise. Amy waited for someone to think it was burglars, and if they did that she would have to say she had a nightmare, which she very occasionally did, and she was coming for a drink of water. . . . Why was she in the dark though? She would have to pretend to be sleepwalking, and she tried to remember how they did it, in the stories she had read.

The house slept on.

There were no buckets under the sink. Where then, where? Cynthia would know where they were. Cynthia wasn't like her, Cynthia *noticed* things. Cynthia was brave too, not like her. And Cynthia was scornful, sometimes, about people who weren't as brave as she was, or as clever. And she's gone home, Amy thought, and left me all alone. And I got to look after Donovan all by myself, and I can't find a bucket, and it's not fair. And where is there a bucket? And I'm scared what I'm doing and I don't want to do it, and I *can't* do it because I can't find a bucket, and you made me do it, Cynthia, you made me and I hate you! And we're all going to get in trouble now and it's your fault because you made me do it.

And my mum and dad don't know what I'm doing, and they're going to be so upset if they find out. And they trust me, and they think I don't tell lies and I do. Sometimes. And Donovan is up there all cold and hungry, and he trusts me too, and I don't know where there is a bucket, and I have to go to the toilet, and Donovan wants to go to the toilet too, and Donovan *relies* on me. Anyway, he doesn't want Cynthia, he wants *me*.

In the bathroom was a bucket, full of dirty clothes. Shaking with relief, Amy tipped the dirty clothes into the bath. Mum would think it was funny in the morning, finding the dirty clothes in the bath, when she had left them in the bucket, but perhaps she wouldn't remember. She didn't always remember where she put things, and she left things soaking in the bath too, sometimes.

207

Now she had found the bucket, Amy felt a little bit calmer. The whirling thoughts in her head slowed, and her heart stopped its wild fluttering. What else? There was something else she had to find, what was it? *Food*! Donovan had had nothing to eat all day, because he was walking round all day with his luggage, and he didn't have any money. And Mum made them throw away the fishfingers, so she would have to take something from the fridge. She would have to, she would have to! Donovan couldn't starve, and he couldn't go IN CARE. So Amy would have to take some food for him, out of the kitchen. There was no choice, she would have to do it.

She found a cut loaf in the bread bin, only just started, and she took six slices. She wasn't sure if that would be enough, so she took two more. She found a plastic bag – there were always plenty of *them* around – and put the bread at the bottom of it. Funny how her eyes were getting used to the dark. They must be opening wide, like a cat's, she thought. There was a light in the fridge anyway, that came on when you opened the door. The light showed bacon and eggs, and some stewed fruit in a bowl. And – the remains of the chicken from Sunday's roast! Would Mum miss the chicken? She might forget, she might forget! Or she might think Dad took it. Anyway Donovan needed it. Amy wrapped the chicken in the foil it was already covered with, and put it in the plastic bag with the bread.

That was enough; she was frightened again. She wouldn't take any more, not this time. She would get the steps now, and let Donovan down to go to the bathroom, and give him the blanket, and the bucket,

208

and the plastic bag with the food in it, and go back to bed herself, and cover herself up, warm and safe.

How lovely, to be warm and safe in bed.

How lovely it was going to be, when things were back to ordinary again.

14

Snags and snares

Amy took the steps from the cupboard. She held her breath as she did that, because it made a surprising lot of noise, taking them out in the night. It was lucky Dad snored so loudly. Even if Mum woke up, or Simon, they would not hear the sound of the steps coming out, because those horrendous snores were covering up all the other sounds, she thought.

Amy climbed the steps. She stood on the little platform at the top, and pushed at the trapdoor. It was heavy, and too high for her; and she could only move it a little bit. The fib she had made up earlier was coming true. She tapped gently, then held her breath again, because someone might hear the tap in spite of the snores. Amy tapped again.

No response, nothing. Was Donovan asleep? She dared not tap any louder, or call his name. She reached up again, and pushed at the trapdoor. Her heart thumped with panic, and she pushed and pushed. She took a deep breath, and strained. The trapdoor moved. She reached, and pushed, and nearly toppled off the steps. She grabbed at the cupboard shelves to steady herself, and tried again. The trapdoor moved up, up, a little bit more and – *across*. Amy climbed into the loft.

It was pitch dark up here, her cat's eyes were no good at all. She sat on the edge of the opening and trembled. 'Donovan!' she called, as loudly as she dared, but he didn't answer. Amy worked out her bearings; the camp was *that* way – no, *that* way. In the dark, she began to crawl across the joists; terrified, feeling her way, expecting her foot to slip at any minute, and go through the ceiling, like Cynthia's foot that other time. 'Donovan!' she called, in a harsh whisper – but there was no reply.

There was no sound coming from the camp at all. Nothing, not even breathing. Was he still there? He must be, he must be, he couldn't have climbed out and gone away without anyone knowing. Was he all right then? Was he ill? Hurt? *Dead*? If he was just asleep, why couldn't she hear him breathing? You could always hear Simon, when *he* was asleep. She groped her way across the joists, in the sooty dark, and it was like a nightmare. Worse than before, when she couldn't find the bucket.

She was there! She was feeling the jagged edge of the floor they made, pushing back the curtains which still smelled of damp and disuse. Her heart was beating so wildly, she thought it would jump out of her chest as her hand touched something warm and alive, at last. 'Donovan!' she whispered, but still he did not wake.

Amy tried to remember just where the switch was, for the light Dad made them. She stood up, and felt above her head. Here? No, *here*! Amy clicked the switch, and blinked in the sudden brightness.

For a few moments Donovan slept on. Very still, very quiet, his body curled under yet another damp and smelly curtain. His face was pale, and somehow innocent, with the tensions and the craftiness wiped away. He lay with both hands under his cheek, and he had been crying.

211

He woke suddenly, and sat up with a jerk. 'What? . . . What? . . . What you put the light on for?'

'Hush!' said Amy. 'I brought you the things. . . . I mean, I didn't bring them, I got them for you downstairs.'

'What you wake me up for?'

'You want to go down to the toilet don't you?'

'I was having a good kip. . . . What you wake me up for?'

'I said. So you can go to the toilet.'

'Oh yeah, that's right. . . . Mind out the way then!' He pushed back the curtain, and clambered to his feet. 'It's cold,' he complained.

'I got you a blanket,' said Amy, and smiled at him to encourage him to be nicer to her since, after all, it was her he wanted, and not Cynthia. 'It's blue,' she said 'with orange squares.' But he wouldn't look at her, and the smile died on her face.

'Come on then,' was all he said. 'Let's get on with it, right?'

Donovan climbed down the steps deftly enough, and Amy climbed after him. 'What's that racket I can hear? That terrible noise?'

'That's my dad, snoring,' said Amy, with dignity.

'Sounds like the pighouse.' Donovan smiled his not-very-nice smile then, but Amy did not smile back. '. . . All right, I been in the bathroom, I done that, thank goodness. Where's the things you got me? Here? . . . Isn't there nothing to drink then? Didn't you get me nothing to drink?

'I forgot,' Amy faltered.

'How'm I supposed to manage without nothing to drink?'

212

'I forgot, I told you. I remembered everything else. I did Donovan, I remembered *everything* else.'

'Is there some Coke then?'

'Couldn't you manage with water, if I find a empty bottle to put it in?'

'I rather Coke.'

'There's a bottle in the kitchen, I think.'

'Hurry up and get it then. . . . Well, go on, hurry up and get it! . . . When you coming up again?'

'Tomorrow after school I suppose.' Amy's heart was like a lead weight. She had tried so hard, and she had been so frightened, and he *did* want her, not Cynthia. And still he couldn't be bothered to say one nice thing!

'Do you have to bring that Parrot with you?'

'If you mean Cynthia, yes I *do*,' said Amy. 'She's my best friend, and I *do* need to bring her.'

'She gets on my nerves, right?'

'Yes, well *you* get on people's nerves sometimes, Donovan Grant.'

He was silent, climbing the steps and into the loft, and reaching to take the things as she handed them to him from below. 'Don't forget to put the trap over,' she said in a small, disappointed voice.

'All right . . . er . . . anyway . . . thanks what you done Amy.'

Amy put the steps away and climbed on to her bunk. 'Is it morning?' said Simon, fretful and sleepy.

'No. Go back to sleep.'

It's all right for you, she thought. You don't have hard things to do like me, and hard things to choose. She envied Simon his simplicity – but Donovan had said thank you! He had said thank you!

Full of love, and confusion, Amy fell asleep.

'What's all this gubbage in the bath?' said Mum. 'All this wet clothes? What's it doing here?'

Amy was suddenly very busy, dressing herself. Mum would answer her own questions, most likely, sooner or later.

'I left them in a bucket,' Mum clattered on, talking to herself in a puzzled voice. 'The brown one, not the yellow one. *He* took the yellow one for his car, and I never saw it since. Where *is* the bucket anyway? Who's had my brown bucket? Before I went to the dentist, I remember! I remember thinking, they're too filthy to go in the machine, I'll put them in to soak first, else they'll come out black as they went in. So I thought I'll put 'em in to soak first. But I never put 'em in the bath, I do know that. Anyway, Simon had a bath since, so I couldn't have. Somebody must have shifted them. I said somebody must have shifted them clothes.'

'Oh ah!' muttered Dad, who was trying to have a lie-in after his late night shift.

'Who then?'

'Not me. Amy?'

'Amy! When did you ever know Amy touch such a thing as dirty washing? Don't make me laugh!'

In the front room, Simon was munching corn-flakes. 'Who's been at the bread then?' Mum's voice floated up from the kitchen. 'There was a whole loaf here yesterday, now it's half gone!'

'You must have forgot how much was left,' said Amy, sitting down with Simon. She yawned, trying not to.

Mum came in with some toast. 'You're looking peeky again,' she said to Amy. 'What's the matter? Didn't you sleep all right?'

214

'I'm fine,' said Amy.

'Well you don't look it. You haven't looked right since Sunday. If you don't perk up soon, I'm taking you round the doctor's.'

'No, don't do that,' said Amy, alarmed. 'There's nothing wrong with me, honestly.'

'Well if you don't get some colour back in your cheeks soon, I shall want to know why,' said Mum.

Amy put on her mac quickly, and collected her things for school before Mum should discover about the missing chicken.

At school, Cynthia was in great spirits. She had a large, mysterious parcel in her school bag, which she couldn't wait to show Amy. 'What's that?' said Lorraine.

'Mind your own business,' said Cynthia.

'It's all *food*,' said Lorraine, pushing to see anyway. 'Did you bring a pack lunch to school today then?'

'That's right,' said Cynthia, nodding and winking at Amy. 'I brought a pack lunch.'

She nodded and winked at Amy, on and off, all the morning, patting her parcel knowingly. 'If you keep doing that, Lorraine's going to guess,' said Amy. 'Or Andrea.'

'*They* won't guess,' said Cynthia. 'They haven't got the brains.'

She was not at all disconcerted when Lorraine challenged her, at dinnertime. 'You supposed to have a pack lunch,' she said. 'So how come you're having school dinner, with us?'

'I changed my mind,' said Cynthia, nodding and winking at Amy again.'

'I think you got a secret,' said Lorraine.

'No!' said Cynthia, delighted to be the centre of

215

mystery and speculation. 'We haven't got a secret, have we, Amy? What we want to have a secret for? Of course, if you want to think we got a secret, there's nothing to stop you. You can think we got a secret if it makes you happy. Can't she, Amy?'

'We don't care about their secrets, do we, Lorraine?' asked Andrea.

'That's right,' said Maxine.

'I think we got a poltergeist,' said Mum.

'What's a polgerteist?' said Cynthia.

'A ghost,' said Mum, 'that moves things about. I think this is a haunted house all of a sudden. I can't think of no other explanation. Clothes in the bath, and I had to buy a new bucket. Half a loaf gone, and the chicken disappeared I don't know where. *And* nearly a full bottle of Coke we had yesterday, and Simon swears he didn't drink it, and anyway I can't see the empty.'

'Oh I *see*,' said Cynthia.

'See what?' said Mum.

'About the polgerteist,' said Cynthia. 'I mean I understand what you said. I didn't mean anything else. Just I understand about the polgerteist. I didn't mean anything else.'

'All right Cynthia,' said Mum. 'I think you made that clear.'

'I didn't mean anything *else*,' said Cynthia.

'We're going up to our secret place now, Mum,' said Amy, before Cynthia could say it again.

'Oh ah – well make the most of it,' said Mum, with a little secret chuckle of her own. 'And if you see the ghost up there, you could ask it very nicely, if it doesn't mind, if it's finished playing silly beggars, to

216

bring my piece of chicken back, because I was going to have it for my lunch today, and I could still have it tomorrow, if it hasn't gone off.'

He was up in the beams, swinging by his knees like a monkey. 'What you doing up there?' said Cynthia.

'What do you think, Parrot?' said Donovan. 'Exercise of course. It's getting on my nerves being still all day.'

They sat in the camp, and really it was quite cosy with the curtains all round, and the light bulb shining down, and the bouncy cushions from someone's old sofa to sprawl on. 'I'm starving,' said Donovan.

'Look what I brought then,' said Cynthia proudly. 'Manners!' she reproved him, as he grabbed. She had thought of everything. Cheese, a tin of corned beef with a key to open it, bread, biscuits, an apple, and a small bottle of lemonade. She must have ransacked her mother's larder. 'Is that all your mum's stuff?' said Amy uneasily.

'Not the drink,' said Cynthia. 'I bought the drink with *my own money*.' She beamed at Donovan, confident of appreciation at last.

'It's not enough,' he said. 'And anyway I rather Coke.'

'Is that all you got to say?' said Cynthia.

'What am I supposed to say?'

'You know, a little word beginning with "T".'

Donovan shrugged, and looked away.

'It's all right,' said Cynthia kindly. 'I'll let you off this time because I know it's not your fault. It's not your fault that you aren't very nice, and you do bad things, so I am going to be very patient with you. Because it's not your fault.'

217

'Stop keep on saying it's not my fault,' said Donovan. 'You get on my nerves keep saying it's not my fault. It can be my fault if I want it to be, right? Anyway, it's boring up here. How would you like it if you were stuck up here, right? With nothing to do all day, right? You don't think of that, do you?'

'I could bring you a book,' said Amy. 'I've got lots of books.'

'Don't like books,' said Donovan peevishly.

'A jigsaw puzzle?'

'Don't like jigsaw puzzles.'

'Some paper to draw, and some felt-tips?'

'Don't like drawing.'

'Except rude pictures,' said Cynthia under her breath.

'I heard that!' said Donovan.

'I don't think you like anything, Donovan,' said Cynthia. 'I don't think you even like yourself.'

'Yes I do then,' said Donovan, stung. 'I like myself very well. I like myself *perfectly*, right? I like doing maths.'

'What?'

'You heard . . . I like doing maths. I like doing maths at school and getting them right. I like that. Any objections?'

'We'll bring your maths book tomorrow,' said Amy, overjoyed to find there was something good that Donovan liked.

'What are we going to do for now though?' said Cynthia. 'To pass the time. That is the problem.' She gazed around her, looking for inspiration. '*I* know . . . I spy with my little eye, something beginning with "R".'

Amy looked at Donovan anxiously. She thought

Donovan was going to be angry that Cynthia wanted to play I-Spy. He turned his head, and thumped the cushion with his fist. 'Rubbish,' he said, in a half-shamed voice.

'Don't be like that,' said Amy. 'Cynthia's trying to be nice to you.

'Well I'm playing, aren't I?' said Donovan. 'What more do you want? I'm asking if that's the answer. *Rubbish*. Is that it?'

Amy woke with a start. She did not know what had wakened her, and for a moment she lay, confused, trying to remember why it was she wanted to be awake anyway. Of course – Donovan! She was supposed to get up, and let Donovan down to the bathroom, and she hadn't meant to go to sleep at all, but she was tired, so tired, and her lids had fallen over and shut themselves, before she could stop them.

And now there was a noise. Dad's snores, of course, reassuring in their awfulness – but something else as well. Right outside her bedroom door. A soft bumping, thudding noise. Shaking, because she had woken too abruptly, and because she was frightened of what she might find outside, Amy went to see.

It was Donovan, coming down by himself. Not by the steps, of course; there was no way he could have got the steps. He had made a rope. He had torn old curtains and knotted them together, and tied one end over the beam above the trapdoor, and let himself down, hand over hand, neatly and quietly, waking no one but Amy. There was another home-made rope as well, this one was lying on the floor with its end tied to the handle of the bucket. Donovan had let his bucket down, all by himself. Angry and shamefaced, he

219

picked it up now, and padded off towards the bathroom. Amy heard water running, and the flush being pulled. She was anxious for a moment, realising she had heard these sounds over and above the trumpeting of Dad's snores, but if anyone else heard them they didn't seem to be bothered.

Donovan came back, carrying his bucket, and leaned against the wall in the passage, kicking his feet on the skirting opposite, and looking at Amy sideways, through narrowed eyes.

'You should have waited for me,' she said.

'Didn't have to,' said Donovan.

'I wouldn't have *looked*.'

'I'll wait for you next time, right?'

'Did you get something to drink?'

'I filled the Coke bottle.' He had it tucked into his trousers, ready for the climb back.

'Can you get *up* by yourself?'

'Easy peasy.' He made no move though, but went on kicking the skirting, his eyes slithering round and over and beyond her.

'Aren't you going then?' said Amy.

'In a minute.'

'Why not now?'

'Come up with me a bit, right?'

'What?'

'It's lonely up there. I got nobody to talk to.'

'You're supposed to be sleeping,' said Amy.

'I slept enough, right? I got nothing to do excepting sleep. It's boring. I want to talk to somebody, right?'

'We can't go on talking to each other here,' said Amy. 'It will wake Simon.'

'I know. Come up in the camp and talk to me there. Right? Right, Amy?'

'Just for a little while then. . . . Only for a little while.' She yawned, longing to get back to bed.

'I'll get the steps for you, right? I'll help you get up. I don't like that Parrot, you know. I rather you. . . . Careful you don't hurt yourself, going up in the dark!'

They sat in the camp, side by side, not touching. 'You start then,' said Amy.

'Start what?'

'Talking. Having a conversation.'

'No *you*. Ladies first.'

Amy could not think of a thing to say. But suddenly there *was* something. A question. Something she wanted to know. 'Donovan, how come you know how to drive a car?'

'My dad learned me.'

'My dad never learned *me* how to drive.'

'That's because you haven't got such a good dad as I have.'

'Is your dad good then, Donovan?'

'Yes he is,' said Donovan fiercely. 'And he didn't ought to be in prison because he never done it, what they said. And when he comes out, we're going to have a good time, me and my dad.'

'Oh.'

'Don't you believe me?'

'Yes of course.'

'Why don't you tell me one of your stories now?'

'All right,' said Amy, 'which one?'

'The one about the alien, with four arms, I like that one.'

'You heard it before though. Would you like the one about the baby alien, the one that was found in a dustbin?'

'Yes I would. I would like that. . . . Go on then, go on, Amy, I'm waiting. . . . I'm listening, right?'

She was shy. It wasn't like telling stories to Simon, who was too little to criticize if they weren't all that good. But after a while she forgot to be shy. The ideas tumbled out, helter skelter. The boy and girl sat together, absorbed, almost happy.

'There *is* something wrong with you,' said Mum. 'And don't tell me otherwise because I've got eyes in my head to see. You look knocked out Amy, I never see you looking so washed-out in my life. You got great dark circles under your eyes. Didn't you sleep all right?'

'Course I did.'

'I heard you get up. I heard you in the bathroom. . . . You weren't sick again, were you?'

'Course not.'

'You seem – I dunno, you don't seem yourself the past few days. Jumpy. . . . You wouldn't hide anything else from me, would you Amy? Like that car thing?'

'Course not.'

'Or if you had a pain or something. You would *tell* me?'

'There's nothing to tell,' said Amy.

'What's that funny noise?' said Mum.

'What noise?' said Amy.

'Up in the loft. A funny noise. I heard it before, I wonder if we got rats!'

'Oh I don't *think* so.'

'You'd have had the screaming hab-dabs at the very mention of the word one time!'

'Well, *I* never heard any funny noise,' said Amy. 'I think you imagined it.'

'Very likely,' said Mum. 'Go on to school then.'

Amy left Simon in his own playground, under the eye of someone's mum as usual. At least she always remembered to do that, when they were early. Cynthia was waiting for her, hopping with impatience for her to come. She left Lorraine, who was in mid-sentence about something, and ran to wrap her arm heavily round Amy's neck. Lorraine's reproachful gaze followed her.

'My mum found out about the things I took,' said Cynthia cheerfully.

'Oh Cynthia!'

'I don't mean she found out it was me. I told her we must have got a polgerteist.'

'What did she say?'

'She *believed* it. Now every time she can't find anything she says the polgerteist has got it. She calls it George. I think she's quite happy about it really. It's good excuse so my dad can't blame her when something goes missing. . . . I got some more food for Donovan, look!'

'Cynthia. Your *mum*.'

'It's all right, she'll just think it's George.'

'My mum thinks I'm ill,' said Amy.

Cynthia regarded her. 'You do look a bit pale.'

'I'm afraid she's going to take me to the doctor.'

'Put some lipstick on your cheeks.'

'You *know* I haven't got any lipstick,' said Amy.

'Something else then. . . . Red chalk will do. *I'll* fix it for you, I'm good at fixing things. Leave it to me. . . . And don't forget we got to get Donovan's maths book for him, don't forget that, Amy!'

'Miss Elliot,' said Andrew, 'Parrot's going in Donovan's desk.'

'No I'm not.'

'Yes you are, I saw you. She is, Miss Elliot, she took something out.'

'Please come back to your place, Cynthia,' said Miss Elliot. 'I mean, please stop fussing about at the back of the room and come and do some work. I mean, you didn't really take anything from Donovan's desk, did you?'

'Oh Miss Elliot, *of* course not.'

'What are you hiding behind your back?'

'Nothing.'

'*Cynthia!*'

'All right,' said Cynthia, 'I borrowed it. I lost mine, so I borrowed Donovan's. Donovan doesn't need it because he's away. I'll give it to him when he comes back. Come on, Miss Elliot, you're my *best* teacher!'

'But this is Book Five, and you're only on Book Four.'

'I mean, Amy lost hers, it's for Amy.'

'Try another one, Cynthia, you know very well Amy's only on Book Three.'

'Well we wanted to have a look of Book Five. To see what the maths is going to be like when we get to it. Can we, Miss Elliot? Can we keep Book Five till hometime? Just to have a look?'

'You never *will* get to Book Five if you don't get on with Book Four,' said Miss Elliot, not believing this extremely thin story anyway.

'Miss Elliot, Miss Elliot, I'm stuck!' said Bharat. 'Come and help me Miss Elliot, please!'

'She'll have forgot by hometime,' whispered Cynthia to Amy.

'Whispering again!' said Lorraine jealously. 'Miss Elliot, I think Cynthia's up to something!'

'Get on with your work, Lorraine,' said Miss Elliot. 'I don't want to hear another sound out of any of you until playtime. I mean, not another word!'

'But you ought to know what Cynthia's up to,' said Lorraine. 'She's brought all food to school again.' It was not like Lorraine to be spiteful and tell tales, but she was feeling quite lonely and left out just now, with Gloria away, and Cynthia keeping her out of the secret.

'How do *you* know what I brought to school?' said Cynthia.

'I looked in your bag, when you was going to Donovan's desk.'

'You're not supposed to look in my bag,' said Cynthia. 'You keep your nose out of my bag!'

'All right,' said Miss Elliot. 'If there's something going on, please tell me what it is, then perhaps we can, sort of, get on with what we came to school for.'

'Well what *could* be going on then?' said Cynthia. 'You see, you can't think of anything it could be, can you? Any of you? So it can't be anything, can it? There's nothing going on at all, so everybody can mind their own business and get on with their work. Like me!'

'That little speech was quite rude, Cynthia,' said Miss Elliot coldly.

'There *is* something,' Lorraine whispered, to Andrea.

'I know there is,' whispered Andrea.

'That's right,' whispered Maxine.

'QUIET!' said Miss Elliot.

'We shall need the answer book as well,' said Amy.

225

'If we don't have the answer book Donovan won't know if his maths are right. He likes getting them right.'

'The answer book is in Miss Elliot's desk,' said Cynthia.

'She'll think it's funny if we ask for it.'

'I know. And she's getting quite a bit ratty these days.'

'We shall have to take it,' said Amy, sinking to new depths of wickedness.

'Dinnertime?' said Cynthia.

'All right,' said Amy.

'We can get the chalk at the same time.'

'Don't you know it's *rude* to whisper?' said Lorraine.

Miss Elliot burst out laughing. She had come back unexpectedly, and caught Cynthia and Amy in the classroom, where they had no business to be, but instead of being cross, which she ought to have been, she could only laugh. Peals and peals of Miss Elliot's rusty-saw laughter washed over the untidy class-room.

'Is there a joke?' said Cynthia.

'Only Amy's face,' said Miss Elliot. 'I mean, I don't want to be unkind but really, what *has* she put on her cheeks?'

'Nothing,' said Cynthia. 'That's her natural colour, isn't it, Amy?'

'Well if you take my advice,' said Miss Elliot. 'I mean, if you'll just go and look in the mirror, what I mean is, I don't honestly think Amy, you'll want the other girls to see you looking quite so feverish.'

'Do I look feverish?' said Amy. 'I don't want to look feverish, I just want to look well.'

226

'You look in the last stage of consumption,' said Miss Elliot. 'I mean, as the Victorians would say. I should go and wash if off if I were you, before someone thinks you've got something infectious. Go on, both of you. I mean, I've got piles to do. Simply piles and piles.' Miss Elliot looked ruefully at the littered desk. 'And I need some peace to do it.'

'What's she talking about, last stages of combustion?' said Cynthia indignantly, on the way to the washroom. 'Anyway we got the answer book, and that's the main thing.'

15

The net closes

'Cynthia staying to tea again?' said Mum. 'She might as well move in and have done with it! No, I'm only joking, only joking. . . . Amy, you didn't come back here dinnertime, did you?'

'No, why?'

'Well *somebody* was here that didn't ought to have been. Frightened Downstairs half to death. She saw you and Simon go to school, and she saw me and your dad go out, 'cos we went to look at. . . . Never mind what we went to look at, I nearly give it away then!'

'Give what away?' said Amy.

'Ask no questions, you'll be told no lies,' said Mum. But she was dressed smartly, in a tight black skirt, and her best flowered blouse, as though she had been somewhere special. 'Anyway, the thing is, Downstairs saw us all go out, and the next thing, somebody thumping about, up here. *Thump thump*, she said, and like steps running. Frightened her half to death.'

'She imagined it,' said Amy. 'She must have.'

'I don't think so,' said Mum. 'She said she banged her stick, and somebody went and banged back! Frightened her half to death, poor old soul.'

'It's probably the polgerteist,' said Cynthia.

'Oh yeah,' said Mum. 'I forgot about him.'

'We've got a polgerteist as well you know,' said Cynthia. 'Our one is called George.'

'Well I never!' said Mum. 'They must be breeding.'

'It could have been a burglar,' said Amy.

'But there's nothing missing', said Mum. 'Nothing at all, I looked. The money for the Pools man even, it's all here. Nothing been touched. . . . Hang about, hang about, I think there *is* something. . . . I don't think I saw. . . . No, I didn't, it's gone! Your dad's watch, it's supposed to be in the bathroom! He found out when we were in the tube. Going down to the *West End* if you must know, only I'm not telling you what for, and there wasn't time to come back for it, 'cos he had to go to work after. "Botheration," he said, I forgot to put my watch on! Well I tell a lie, he didn't say "botheration", exactly, but that's near enough for your young ears.'

'And now it's gone,' said Amy, feeling sick. 'Are you sure, Mum? Are you sure?'

'Well it's not in the bathroom,' said Mum. 'Everybody help to look for it, come on! Because if it doesn't turn up I reckon we *have* had a burglar.' Her face had gone quite pale. 'We've had a burglar!'

'You didn't ought to have come down, Donovan,' Cynthia scolded him. 'Serve you right if you met Amy's dad.'

'Well I didn't, did I? So what you worrying about, Parrot?'

'And you didn't ought to have thumped back at Downstairs. You frightened her half to death poor old soul!'

'Good.'

'Where's my dad's watch?' said Amy.

'I don't know nothing about your dad's watch.'

229

'Yes you do,' said Amy. 'You went to the bathroom and you saw my dad's watch and you took it. What did you do with it?'

'I went to the bathroom for you know what,' said Donovan. 'It's not nice bringing it down in the night, with you seeing.'

'*And* you took my dad's watch,' said Amy. She looked at the rumpled blanket, still more or less spread over the cushions which were Donovan's bed, and wondered if the watch was somewhere underneath. She looked at the open holdall, its contents spilling over the camp floor. He had dug out a few pathetic toys – a pair of plastic handcuffs, a water pistol, a little puzzle game. Apart from his clothes, these were the only possessions he seemed to have.

'I bet he put it in his bag,' said Cynthia. 'I bet that's what he done with it.'

'No I didn't then,' said Donovan. 'You can look if you like. Go on – look!'

That meant it wasn't there. Donovan was sitting on the rumpled up blue blanket with the orange squares. Pretending to move towards the bag, Cynthia grabbed the blanket instead, and yanked it up. Taken by surprise, Donovan toppled sideways, and Cynthia's hand burrowed under the cushion where he had been sitting. 'What's this then? What's this I found?' She held it aloft in triumph. Donovan turned his head, and began kicking backwards at the cushions. 'Satisfied?' he said.

'No use getting up your temper now, now you got found out,' said Cynthia.

'Why though?' said Amy, deeply hurt. '*Why*?'

'You don't have to make a big thing of it,' said Donovan. 'It's only a watch. It's no big deal.'

230

'But it's my *dad's* watch!'

'Your dad got plenty of things,' said Donovan. 'And you.'

'There's something else,' said Cynthia, burrowing again. 'Look what I found now! Look, Amy, look!'

It was a small, cuddly doll, all pink frills and bows, which had sat on Amy's pillow for years. Cynthia laughed. 'What you take this for Donovan? What you want this for?'

'Shut up, Parrot!' He lunged at Cynthia and tried to snatch the doll, but she held it away from him, teasing. 'Come on then, come and get your dolly!'

'You can have it if you like, Donovan,' said Amy, not understanding but wanting to keep the peace.

'Catch then,' said Cynthia, throwing it into his lap.

Shamefaced and angry, Donovan threw the doll at the roof, and it lodged in an angle of the rafters. 'I don't want it,' he shouted. 'I don't want it now!'

'Hush!' said Amy in alarm. 'You mustn't shout like that, Donovan. My mum's going to notice a different voice. . . . Let's all talk about something else, eh? Let's all talk about something else. *I* know what we can talk about, we can talk about Donovan's maths we brought for him. And some paper and pencil, look Donovan. And the answer book. So tomorrow, Donovan, you will have plently to do, and you will not need to take other people's things to pass the time. And me and Cynthia will look what you done when we come home from school if you like. And we will give you a star if you done well. And *no cheating!*'

'Here's Dad's watch,' said Amy. 'Look – he never left it in the bathroom at all, it was here behind this cushion all the time!'

'It wasn't there before,' said Simon.

'Course it was Simon,' said Amy. 'You don't know everything. It must have been there.'

'It wasn't,' said Simon.

'Must have been the poltergeist then,' said Mum. 'Took it away and brought it back. And thumped at Downstairs, dinnertime.' She laughed, a slightly uncomfortable laugh, as though she had begun to think the poltergeist might be real after all, and not just a family joke.

'It better not take my new car!' said Simon.

'You put the car under your pillow and keep it safe,' said Mum. 'Now! Because it's past your bedtime.'

'Is Amy coming to tell me my story?'

'You go on to bed too, Amy,' said Mum. 'Do you good to have a nice long sleep. Put the roses back, perhaps.'

'Amy moves about, in the night,' said Simon.

'No I don't,' said Amy.

'Well she won't be disturbing you much longer perhaps,' said Mum.

'What do you mean?' said Amy.

'It's a secret,' said Mum.

'*What* is?' said Amy. 'It's not fair keep on saying there's a secret, and you don't tell what it is.'

'Don't let on to your dad then.'

'I won't.'

'Because we won't be sure till the men been to have a look.'

'Won't be sure about what?' said Amy.

'Go and put your car under the pillow like I said, Simon,' said Mum. 'And all the other things you don't want the poltergeist to take. Make sure you don't forget anything. Have a good look round.'

'*Mum*,' said Amy.

'It's something exciting,' said Mum, whispering behind her hand. 'Something really good!'

'It's all right,' said Amy, 'Simon's not listening.'

'This is it then,' said Mum. 'Me and your dad thought, seeing you're getting a big girl now, and Simon's getting a big boy, we thought, well we got all the space over our heads going to waste, so we thought, why not make a proper bedroom up there? So you can have a room to yourself, Amy, and Simon can have one, and it will save all the bother of moving house. There! I knew you'd be pleased.'

'When is it going to be?' said Amy faintly.

'Oh not for a long time yet, not for a long time. Got to get planning permission and all sorts. . . . We went to look at furniture though, that's where your dad and me went today so now you know. It's all backwards, he said, we got to get the room first, but you know me, once I got an idea I'm all excited and I can't wait to start making the plans. . . . All right, Amy, don't look like that! We didn't *buy* nothing. You'll have your say later on. You'll help choose, of course you will.'

'You did say it won't be for a long time,' said Amy. 'You did say that, didn't you?'

'You're same as me, aren't you?' said Mum. 'When you want something you want it now. And like I said, it's not for definite till the builders been to have a look, so I didn't ought to have told you really, but that's me innit! Big-mouth! They're coming tomorrow, anyway.'

'*Who's* coming tomorrow?'

'I told you. The builders. To have a look at the loft.'

'Tell them not to,' said Amy.

'*What*?'

'Tell them not to,' said Amy frantically. 'I don't *want* a new bedroom, I don't *want* one!'

'Yes you do,' said Mum, puzzled. 'You kept on about it.'

'I changed my mind. I don't want a bedroom to myself. I want things to be the same. I want them always to be the same, and not change.'

'Don't be silly, Amy,' said Mum sharply. 'You can't always share a bedroom with Simon, you know that. You're growing up!'

'Well I don't want it yet. I don't have to have it yet. I want the loft to be our camp. Like it is now.'

'Well it can be. I told you. Be ages before the building part. Months.'

'But they're coming to look tomorrow?'

'Yes.'

'And they're going up? Right up in the loft?'

'No no, they're bringing a X-ray machine. . . . Don't be silly, Amy, of course they're going in the loft.'

'I don't want them to go in our camp. I don't want them to disturb anything. I don't want them to! I don't want them to!'

'Amy, is there something in the camp you don't want anybody to see?'

'No.'

'I think there is,' said Mum. 'I think you're hiding something. All this funny behaviour and looking so poorly. I should have thought before, might be something to do with the camp.'

'You thought wrong now. There's nothing up there, there *isn't*.'

'Well,' said Mum, 'there's one way to find out!'

She took the steps out of the cupboard. She climbed the steps and opened the top part of the cupboard where the shelves were. She pushed the trapdoor, and Amy watched it go up, up, and *across*. She put one foot on the lower shelf, and grasped the edge of the opening with her hand. Awkwardly, she hauled herself up so her head was through the opening, and both feet were on the lower shelf. '*Now* we'll see what guilty secrets you and Cynthia been having up here!'

Mum's skirt was too tight for climbing, and her heels were too high, but she made it that far. And she didn't even have to go all the way. She only had to turn her head in the right direction and she would see! Amy waited for the shout of astonishment and outrage – that was going to come in a moment.

Mum looked down, and swayed. She looked up again quickly, but went on swaying. She put one foot on the next shelf, made a shaky attempt to pull herself higher – and put the foot back again. 'Hold the steps, Amy,' she said, in a different sort of voice. 'Hold them, I said! Hold them still!'

'Are you coming down then?'

'How did you guess?'

Mum stood on firm ground once more, and shuddered. 'Not my scene, as they say. Best climber in the class I was one time, and you better believe it, Amy. Too giddy now though, must be getting old! Your dad can go instead. First thing in the morning, I'm sending him up to have a looksee, and don't think I'll forget, because I won't!'

The morning, the morning! Nothing was going to

happen until the morning! The relief was so great that, for the moment, she was almost joyful.

'By the way, you left the light on up there,' said Mum. 'You and Cynthia, you left the light on.'

'I'll go up now,' said Amy. 'I don't mind. I'll go up and switch it off.'

'No you won't,' said Mum. 'You don't catch me like that! My head for heights might not be so good's it was, but there's nothing wrong with my brains. I let you go up there, you're going to shift something, aren't you? You're not going up there again, Miss Madam, till your dad been up there first!'

'The trapdoor's still open,' said Amy. 'Don't you want it shut?'

'You mean *you* do I suppose,' said Mum. 'You got doors on the brain haven't you, lately? Open doors and shut doors. Go on and shut it then, but that's all. I'm watching you mind!'

Truth to tell, Mum was glad enough to have the trapdoor closed. The sight of that gaping hole, so far above, recently so uncomfortably near, was making her feel giddy still.

Amy picked up a book. 'What time are the builders coming tomorrow?' she asked, turning the pages of the book so Mum wouldn't think she was all that much interested in the builders *really*.

'I don't know. Some time. Morning I think. Or might be afternoon, anyway you dad knows. It's his rest day tomorrow, so he'll be home all day to see to them. . . . What you want to know the time for anyway? What difference does *that* make to you?'

'Nothing, nothing,' said Amy.

'Are you going *peculiar*, Amy? Is that what it is?' said Mum, in a worried voice.

He wasn't asleep when she climbed into the loft, he hadn't even switched off the light. He was sitting on his cushion, in the cosy little camp, working away at his maths. 'I done a lot,' he told her proudly. 'And I got all these right – look!'

'Didn't you see my mum come up, before?' said Amy.

'Your mum? Oh yeah, your mum! Just her head, like a jack-in-the-box! What happened to the rest of her?'

He was grinning; an ordinary sort of a grin, with ordinary little-boy mischief in it. Amy had never seen him grin like that before. 'I think you have to go, Donovan,' she said miserably.

The grin vanished. 'Why?'

'There's some men coming to look at the loft tomorrow. I mean today. To see if they can make it into a proper bedroom. And my dad's coming up before that.'

'He's not supposed to come up! He doesn't come up hardly ever, you said!'

'My mum's going to make him. To see if me and Cynthia got something naughty up here. I don't know what we're going to do.'

Donovan looked frightened. 'I better go now. While your mum and dad's asleep, I better go!' He began stuffing his belongings into the holdhall.

'In the dark?' said Amy, horrified.

'That don't matter, that's nothing to me!'

'But where will you go?'

Donovan thought. 'Hide in the park, right?'

'But you *can't*.'

'Why can't I?'

'It's dangerous. There's strangers. Bad people. I

237

won't *let* you. I'll scream if you try to go, and wake
them all up, and stop you.'

'You mean it, don't you? said Donovan, not
altogether displeased.

'Yes.'

'I better not go then, right?'

'No.'

'I better stay here for now, right?'

'Yes. I don't know. I don't know what you can do.
I wish Cynthia was here.'

'Oh *her*!' said Donovan. 'We don't need that
Parrot. . . . I know, I'll run out in the morning. When
it's light.'

'They'll see you. They'll catch you!'

'I'll run fast,' said Donovan. 'I'll push them away
and run fast, right?'

'They'll still see you,' said Amy. 'They'll *tell* of you.
And you will have to go IN CARE.'

'I'll hide then. When the builders come. And your
dad. I'll hide behind those boxes in the corner. Those
ones, over there. They won't see me.'

'Won't they?' It seemed a possibility.

'It'll be all right, don't you worry. Don't you
worry, Amy, it'll be *all right*. I won't have to go after
all. That's good, innit?'

'You'll have to move all your luggage. So my dad
doesn't see.'

'I know, I know, don't you worry.'

'And the blanket, and the bucket.'

'I know, I know. I know all the things I must move,
right? Don't you worry about it.'

'We better move them now,' said Amy. 'Before you
go to the bathroom. While I see you do it.'

'But I won't have a bed,' said Donovan.

'You will have to sleep in the corner somehow.'

'But it will be all knobbly. . . . Can't I do it in the morning? I'll do it in the morning, right?'

'I don't trust you.'

'Not trust *me*?' Donovan sounded really hurt.

'Yes, of course. I didn't mean it.' She was tired, and saying the wrong things, and it was all too much, and she was near the end of her strength, but she knew she would go on trying until she dropped. 'Will you have to be here much longer, Donovan? Now we decided for you to stay. Do you think it will be much longer?'

'Oh yes, a *long* time yet. I should think so. . . . I quite like it here now.'

'Oh.' How could she do it? She had managed to keep awake tonight, because she was so frightened. But tomorrow? And the next night, and the one after that? With the best will in the world – how long could she keep it up? 'Anyway,' she said, trying to keep the weariness out of her voice, 'anyway, Donovan, you better get Samantha down.'

'Samantha?'

'My doll.'

He was angry, suddenly. 'What you going on about that for?'

'My dad's going to think it's funny, seeing her up there.'

'It's only a *doll*.'

'I know, but my dad's going to think it's funny. . . . Why did you take her?'

'I don't know. You can't expect me to know why *everything* I do.'

'You don't play with dolls, do you?'

'Of course I don't.'

239

'Why then?'

'I dunno, I said. . . . All right, it was the quickest thing to take . . . in your room. Satisfied?'

'Why did you want to take something from my room?'

'I don't know. I just did.'

'Please don't take anything else, Donovan.'

Silence.

'If you want anything, you can just ask me and I'll give it to you.'

Silence.

'Did you hear what I said?'

More silence. 'What I said the other day, I changed my mind again.'

'What was that?'

'I said "Amy Baker's boring." I changed my mind again. Right?'

'Oh.'

Amy woke, full of black dread. They were going to go into the loft and they mustn't, mustn't! She didn't trust Donovan because she couldn't, she couldn't, because he kept changing so you never knew what he was going to do. Somehow, somehow, she must stop all these people from going into the loft at all.

She was too tired, and too confused, to have a proper plan. The main thing was, she must be *there*. 'I don't feel well,' she said, quite truthfully.

'Surprise, surprise,' said Mum.

'I don't feel well enough to go to school,' said Amy. 'I got a pain.'

'Oh? Where is this pain?' said Mum.

'Here,' said Amy, pointing vaguely to her stomach.

'That does it. I'm taking you round the doctor's.'

'It's not bad enough to go the doctor's,' said Amy. 'Just bad enough to stay home from school.'

'Don't be silly,' said Mum. 'I'll have to take Simon to school first, and we'll go to the doctor's when I get back. . . . Hurry up, Simon, I haven't got all morning.'

'Cheer up Amy,' said Dad. 'Big day today, the builders are coming. Aren't you excited? . . . Oh I forgot, you aren't! Dark secrets in the loft, or something. What is it then? You can tell *me*.'

'It's nothing,' said Amy. 'There's nothing there, you can go and look.' If she said that, perhaps he wouldn't. 'Go on and look,' she said. 'You won't find anything 'cos there's nothing to find.'

'Don't seem much point now,' said Dad. 'Your mum said you were all upset last night though.'

'I had this pain,' said Amy. 'I was upset about the pain, but Mum thought it was the loft. I don't know why she thought that. I tried to tell her.'

'She does get the wrong end of the stick sometimes, your mum. Did you tell her about the pain then?'

'Well not the *pain*,' Amy floundered. 'Not the *pain* exactly.'

'Why not?'

'I didn't want to go to the doctor.'

'Now that's silly, Amy. Doctor's there to make you better, you know she is. You just go along with your mum like a good girl when she comes back . . . eh?'

'When are the builders coming?'

'Well – I couldn't say, could I? You know what builders are like, they come when they feel like it.'

'Could I go to the doctor tomorrow? So I don't miss the builders?'

241

'You *are* excited about the new room, aren't you!'

'I'm *incredibly* pleased. That's why I don't want to miss the builders!'

'Well now,' said Dad. 'How about this? If they come before you and your mum get back from the doctor's, I'll tell them to just go away again and come back later.'

'You're tricking me!' said Amy.

'It's my best offer,' said Dad.

'Looks a bit like school-itis to me,' said the doctor cheerfully. 'I can't find anything really wrong.'

'I don't know what to make of it,' said Mum. 'I don't know if she's playing me up, or what. She hasn't *looked* well for days.'

'Something worrying you, Amy?' said the doctor.

'No,' said Amy. 'Just the pain.'

'Would you like to go to hospital, so we can find out what the pain is?'

'*No!*' said Amy.

'What do you want to do then?'

'If I just stay at home,' said Amy, 'I think the pain will go away by itself.'

'Correct diagnosis,' said the doctor.

'Have they been? Have they been?' said Amy.

'Not yet,' said Dad.

'Supposed to be something worrying her at *school* now,' said Mum. 'She got me so mixed up I don't know if I'm on my head or my heels!'

'I thought she had a pain,' said Dad.

'Doctor says she made that up, because she's in trouble at school,' said Mum. '*She* say so too. At least, I think that's the latest story!'

242

'I didn't like to tell you before,' said Amy.

'Well tell us now,' said Mum. 'I tried to get it out of her on the way home, but she wouldn't open her mouth. . . . Well?'

'I don't like to.'

'*Amy.*'

'Are you sure that doctor got it right?' said Dad. 'I suppose she was only looking at the kid five minutes.'

'She's a doctor,' said Mum. 'She ought to know.'

'They don't always,' said Dad.

'You'd better stop this nonsense Amy and tell me what's wrong,' said Mum. 'Because to tell you the truth, I'm sick to death of being messed about.'

'I can't,' said Amy.

'Why not?'

'There's other people in it. I can't tell on them.'

'Other people in *what*? ' said Dad.

'I can't tell you.'

'I'm taking you up the school,' said Mum. 'I'm taking you straight up to see the headmaster. *He'll* get to the bottom of it, *he'll* sort you out.'

Dad was looking very worried, and very unhappy. 'Whatever it is, *I* want to hear it an' all,' he said.

'Well,' said Mum, 'no time like the present.'

'Somebody got to stay in for the builders though,' said Dad.

'Bother the builders!' said Mum. '. . . All right, first thing tomorrow morning then.'

16

The end

Cynthia was worried, because Amy had not come to school. She was hardly ever away from school, and she was never late so it couldn't be that. Had they found Donovan, in the loft? Had he come down by himself again, and got caught, the silly stupid mad raving lunatic?'

'I can't find Book Five answer book,' said Miss Elliot, throwing heaps of junk around as she looked for it.

'*I'll* help you, Miss Elliot,' said Lorraine. 'You should be more tidier you know, Miss Elliot, then you wouldn't lose things.'

'I know,' said Miss Elliot humbly.

Cynthia felt a pang of guilt, for adding to Miss Elliot's problems when she had enough already. And then she went back to fretting about Amy, and wishing it would be hometime so she could go round to Amy's house and find out what was wrong.

The day dragged, and dragged. It was just before play in the afternoon that the door opened, and an uncombed head appeared. 'Not here,' said the head, blowing a puff of smoke, and disappeared. Cynthia's heart began to beat faster; the head undoubtedly belonged to Donovan's gran!

What did *she* want to come up to school for? Nosy old bag, spoiling everything! Now she'd go and tell, that Donovan wasn't in school. Tell who though? Mr

Bassett knew already, because it was in the register. Anyway it was only four days. People were often away for four days. Mr Bassett wouldn't get worried because Donovan was away for four days, would he?

Tell his mum then? Now that was the problem. If she did that it would be a nuisance because *then* everybody would find out that Donovan was actually missing. It was all right though, they weren't speaking! Nothing was going to happen. It was all right, his gran and his mum weren't speaking, so they wouldn't be telling each other *anything*.

The doorbell was ringing. It was them, it was them, it was the builders! Amy's eyes opened wide in their sunken hollows, and she jumped to her feet.

'What's the matter with *you*?' said Mum. 'You're like a flea in a fit!'

'I can't wait to see what they say,' said Amy.

'*You've* changed your tune!'

'I can't wait to get my new bedroom,' said Amy.

'That's not what you said yesterday.'

'I was all mixed up yesterday.'

'And I'm mixed up today,' said Mum. 'I don't know what to think, and that's the truth. Never mind, Mr Bassett'll sort it out tomorrow. He's a good headmaster, Mr Bassett – *he'll* find what it's all about.'

There was only one builder after all, and he had a big torch in his hand. 'There's a light up there already,' Amy told him. 'You won't need that. You needn't bother to take the torch up with you.'

'This got a good beam to go in all the corners, love,' said the builder, switching it on to show her what he meant. Amy felt faint, and sick.

The builder began to climb the steps. 'I'll come up as well,' said Dad.

A picture flashed into Amy's mind. Donovan telling a little girl to scream. 'Scream and scream,' he told her, 'then people will come to see what's wrong.' Amy began to scream.

'Stop it!' said Mum, who could see no reason for the screaming. 'Stop it this minute, Amy!'

Dad hugged her. 'Whatever is the matter? Tell me!' Staring past his shoulder, Amy continued to scream.

'I think she's going funny,' said Mum, really worried now.

'I can see it though,' said Amy. 'I can see it!'

'See what?'

'That ghost! I can see the ghost!'

'You're right,' said Dad to Mum. 'I think she is going funny.'

'On second thoughts I'm not sure,' said Mum. 'Perhaps she *can* see something. There's weird things been going on in this house lately, besides *her* silly nonsense.'

The builder had left the door open, at the foot of the stairs, so Downstairs had heard every word, as well as the screams, and she set up her own hullabaloo. 'A ghost, there's a ghost!' she shrieked. 'I'm not staying in no house with a ghost in it!'

'Good riddance then,' said Dad.

'Don't be so cruel,' said Mum.

'Are we going in the loft or what?' said the builder.

'In case you haven't noticed,' said Dad 'we're a bit concerned about a ghost just now.'

Amy screamed again.

'You don't want to worry about *them*,' said the

builder. '*They* don't do no harm. If you'd seen as many ghostses as what I have, you wouldn't worry about *them* no more.'

'Come on then,' said Dad. He didn't know if the builder was joking or not, about all the ghosts he had seen – but after all, the man did have a job to do.

Dad and the builder disappeared into the loft. It was not worth screaming again. 'Did you really see something?' said Mum.

'It was all in white,' said Amy. 'And a bony face, like a skull.' She added a few more details, but her heart was not in it.

'Wish I knew whether to believe you,' said Mum.

'It's gone now anyway,' said Amy. She was listening, numbly resigned to discovery now, for the shout of astonishment and anger, that was going to come at any moment from the loft above. The shout which did not come, after all.

There were thumping footsteps and rumbling male voices and soon, amazingly soon, the two of them coming down the steps with smiling faces. 'We'll send you an estimate,' said the builder, 'and take it from there.'

'*You* were quick,' said Amy.

'We done quite a few of these jobs round here,' said the builder. 'I didn't think there'd be any trouble. Stairs is the biggest problem. Not much room – but we'll work something out.'

'Is that all then?' said Amy.

'Did you want more?'

'I'm going to have a new bedroom!' said Amy, trying to sound thrilled.

'Perhaps we should move house after all though,' said Mum. 'If there's a ghost in this one.'

'Well I don't believe *that* for a minute,' said Dad.

'We could go up the school now if you like,' said Mum. 'Now the builder's been we could go up the school to see Mr Bassett, instead of tomorrow.'

Dad looked at his watch, and Amy held her breath. 'They'll be coming out time we get there,' he said. 'Poor bloke'll be wanting to get home to his tea. . . . Nah, best leave it till tomorrow. . . . She seems a bit calmer now, anyway.'

'I'll just fetch Simon for now then,' said Mum.

Ten minutes before hometime, Mr Bassett came into the classroom looking very serious and concerned. He said something in a low voice to Miss Elliot, and she began to look serious and concerned as well. 'Oh no!' she kept saying, jabbing the big glasses back up her nose.

Cynthia hovered at the bin, pretending to sharpen her pencil. 'It's a bizarre business,' she heard Mr Bassett saying. 'They each thought the other had the boy. . . . Cynthia, go and do that somewhere else, dear. *Right* away. Thank you.'

She had heard it though, she had heard it! Now what was going to happen? Cynthia wanted Amy badly, so they could talk together about what was going to happen. Come on bell! Come on bell!

'Put your things away,' said Miss Elliot.

Mr Bassett came back into the classroom. 'Fold your arms and sit up straight,' he said.

'The bell's gone, sir,' said Andrew.

'This is important,' said Mr Bassett. 'I want you all to think very carefully, boys and girls. Very carefully. I want to see who can remember something for me. I know some of you seem to have a forgettory

248

instead of a memory, ha, ha, ha! But this is more important than washing your hands before dinner or – er – pieces of paper in the playground. A *lot* more important. Now. Can *anyone* remember seeing Donovan Grant anywhere out of school since Monday morning?'

Silence.

'The thing is,' said Mr Bassett, 'we don't know where he is now, so anything that anyone can tell us might be helpful.'

'I saw him, I think,' said Bharat. 'In the High Street.'

'Oh, which day?' said Mr Basset.

'Tuesday,' said Bharat. 'I think.'

Silly fool, thought Cynthia. How could you see Donovan in the High Street, when he was in Amy's loft all the time?

After that quite a few people remembered seeing Donovan in various places, and at various times, and Mr Bassett seemed to weary of the recital, though he said before that it was important, so he ought to have been pleased that so many people remembered 'Oh yes,' he said, cutting the flow short, 'there is one more thing. . . . Where's Amy Baker?'

'Not here today, Mr Bassett,' said Miss Elliot.

'Ah. Mrs Bowers described a girl – white girl with red hair, I think it *must* have been Amy. . . . And a black girl with her. Cynthia, did you—?'

'No sir,' said Cynthia.

'What do you mean, "no sir?" You don't know what I'm going to say.'

Cynthia was silent, wary of falling into another trap.

'Mrs Bowers said two girls came to her house on

249

Monday afternoon, asking about Donovan. Were you one of them, Cynthia?'

'No sir.'

'Nobody's *accusing* you of anything, Cynthia. Actually I think it was rather a nice thing to do. Kind, if a little unexpected! In fact, that's what set Mrs Bowers thinking. The girls were worried, she said, and she couldn't get it out of her mind.'

'It wasn't me,' said Cynthia.

'What a pity,' said Mr Bassett. 'Anyway, girls and boys, Mrs Bowers will almost certainly be going to the police, and I think it's more than likely the police will be coming here some time tomorrow, to see if they can find anything out. Unless Donovan shows up before that, of course. We must just hope, and pray, that he is somewhere safe.'

'The bell's gone, sir,' said Andrew.

Mr Bassett sighed.

Cynthia put up her chair, and fussed about collecting her things for going home. She was not happy. They had their eye on her now. She could go on denying it of course, but she didn't at all relish the idea of being singled out by the police for questioning. She would have to be very clever, not to give it away. It suddenly occurred to her that the police would not be at all pleased with her, if they found out what she had been doing. Perhaps it was a crime. Perhaps – perhaps they would put her IN CARE, for helping to hide Donovan in Amy's loft!

It was a terrible thought. Cynthia's stricken face attracted Miss Elliot's attention, and *she* began to think, trying to remember. . . .

Outside the school gates, Cynthia asked the others. 'Lorraine, do you know anything about IN CARE?'

'No,' said Lorraine. 'What's that?'

'I heard something about it one time. Do you know what it is?'

'*I* know,' said Andrea.

'Tell me,' said Cynthia.

'I'm IN CARE,' said Andrea.

'*What*!'

'I'm IN CARE. My mum is not my real mum, she's my foster mum. And my sister is not my real sister, she's my foster sister.'

'You never said that!' said Lorraine.

'I forgot,' said Andrea.

'Is that what IN CARE is then?' said Cynthia, amazed. 'To have a foster mum, instead of a real mum? Is that what it is?'

'I was in a children's home one time as well,' said Andrea, giggling a bit as usual.

'Was *that* terrible?' said Cynthia. 'Was it like prison?'

'It was nice,' said Andrea. 'They were kind.'

'Isn't it supposed to be for bad children though?' said Cynthia.

'*I* didn't do anything bad,' said Andrea. 'My real mum went away, that's all.'

'She told a lie!' said Cynthia furiously.

'No I didn't,' said Andrea.

'Not you, somebody else.'

Cynthia was extremely upset. So it was all for nothing, was it? They wasted their time, did they? All that trouble they took, to hide Donovan and protect him, and save him, and what was it for in the end? IN CARE was supposed to be terrible, but it wasn't terrible after all, it was all right. The whole question needed reviewing, and Cynthia reviewed it frantically, as she ran all the way to Amy's house.

Donovan was in hiding, and it was great fun hiding him, and there was no doubt about *that*. And if they hid him long enough he might go back to live with his gran in the end, like before. But if he went IN CARE he might have a foster mum like Andrea's, and Andrea's foster mum was a lovely mum, and there was no doubt about that! The only thing was, perhaps Donovan wouldn't *want* a lovely foster mum. Perhaps he would rather live with his gran after all, and come and go as he pleased, and do what he liked. It was very hard to know.

And besides all that, besides all that, what about her and Amy and the police? What about that? What about the crime they did already, perhaps? It didn't seem likely, any longer, that they would have to go IN CARE for it, but they could be in a lot of trouble, when it was all found out. Cynthia ached for Amy, and she was nearly there, nearly there. One more minute and they could sort it all out together.

Mum answered the door. 'Oh it's you,' she said to Cynthia, not very warmly. Mum had only just arrived with Simon, who had been very naughty and trying, wanting to drag and step off the kerb, even though Mum was holding his hand. Simon had been smacked, and Mum was not in the best of tempers.

'Is something wrong with Amy?' said Cynthia. 'Is she ill?'

'Good question,' said Mum. 'I wish I knew the answer. First she doesn't want her new bedroom, then she got a pain in her belly, then it's something wrong with school, and last she sees a ghost. If you ask me, it's her head wants looking at. . . . Anyway, since you're here, perhaps *you* can tell me. Is there some trouble she's in at school?'

'No,' said Cynthia.

'Yes I am,' said Amy, who had followed Mum down the stairs. 'You *know* I am.'

'I mean yes,' said Cynthia. 'Well – she is a *little* bit.'

'What, for instance?' said Mum.

'We can't say can we, Cynthia?' said Amy.

'That's right,' said Cynthia. 'We can't say. Sorry Mrs Baker.'

'In that case,' said Mum, 'I think you'd better go home, Cynthia. We're all a bit busy here today, and Amy's – er – not very well. So you go home for your tea today, and you can come again when we've sorted it all out, perhaps. When we've been to see the headmaster. Which we are going to do tomorrow morning, and then everybody's sins will find them out. *Everybody's.*'

'Can't I stay for just a little while?' said Cynthia.

'Not today,' said Mum.

Miss Elliot sat alone in her classroom, filling in the report forms, which were still not done. She was worried about Donovan Grant, of course, but she was also worried about the report forms, because she was going to get into a lot of trouble if they were not finished soon. And besides that, the report forms were undoubtedly her responsibility, whereas the Donovan Grant business, as far as anyone could tell, was not really anything to do with school at all.

All the same, there was a nagging question at the back of Miss Elliot's mind. Something to do with Cynthia Garrett. And Amy Baker. And Donovan Grant. Besides that funny business about going to

253

Donovan's grandmother's house. There was a book. *What* book? Miss Elliot shook her head to clear the cobwebs, but the answer did not come. She glanced down at the report forms again. *Andrew.* Now what could she say about Andrew that would be truthful, but at the same time not damage him at his new school? Miss Elliot chewed her biro, and inked her teeth, and messed up her hair, and spilled her coffee all down the front of her dress.

'You didn't have to snub Cynthia off like that,' said Dad.

'I reckon she's at the bottom of it,' said Mum. 'She always was the strongest willed out of them two. I'm not sure I want her in the house any more, if she's going to lead Amy in bad ways.'

'If you'd let her stay, we might have got something out of her,' said Dad.'

'Or a lot more lies,' said Mum. 'Which I'm sick of listening to, which is not like Amy at all, which I reckon that Cynthia is at the bottom of.'

'Anybody says anything against Cynthia got *me* to answer to,' said Dad.

'You said that before, and what I say is, none so blind as those who won't see!'

'What *is* there to see?'

'I dunno, you wouldn't go and look, would you? Up in the loft. Where they got their secrets. I told you last night. Do it in the morning, I said, but oh no, you knew better. "No need," you said, just because she tried it on and you fell for it.'

'I *have* been up, with the builder.'

'For five minutes!' said Mum. 'What good's that?'

'Don't mind me,' said Amy. 'I'm not here.'

'Don't be cheeky,' said Mum. 'On top of everything else.'

Amy supposed she would have to see the ghost again, and scream. She had no real hope that they would believe her, but she was too tired to think of a different plan. She yawned, trying to keep awake.

'So when are you going?' said Mum, to Dad.

'Going where?' said Dad.

'Up in the loft of course,' said Mum. 'Don't make out.'

'After I finished this wiring job you wanted me to do.'

'*Then* it'll be after you had your tea, and after you done the pools, next week's, and after you seen something special on telly, and after you read the paper.'

'I still don't see the point,' said Dad. 'All this mystery trouble, it's all about something at school, isn't it? I thought we got that decided.'

'Could be to do with both,' said Mum.

It could indeed, and why couldn't *he* have thought of that? Dad began to have a nasty suspicion he hadn't been all that clever, this morning. Mum was scatty, and she got things wrong sometimes – why had he been so quick to assume this was one of them? . . . The screaming, too. Could that have been . . .? But no, not *Amy*! Amy just wasn't capable of that much cunning . . . was she?

The more Dad thought about it the more he thought he hadn't, perhaps, been clever at all.

'So when are you going?' said Mum again.

'Presently,' said Dad, in no great hurry to discover exactly how clever he had not been. Especially with Mum nagging him to do it.

The evening dragged on. Amy yawned incessantly. 'Go to bed, Amy,' said Mum. That made it even more difficult; she would have to lie awake and listen.

And lying in bed, Amy suddenly thought of something else. *Food*. And *drink*. When did Donovan last have something to eat? Yesterday? *Yesterday*. Yesterday Cynthia brought food. So Donovan had food today. But tomorrow? Would Cynthia bring food for Donovan for tomorrow? But Cynthia had been already, and Mum wouldn't let her stay, so she took the food away with her, didn't she, if she had any in the first place. *Food*. Amy tried to think, but she was so tired, so tired! She must take food to Donovan tonight, and she must get it from somewhere, but she was so tired, and they were suspicious now, and watching her for certain, and she was so tired, and Dad was going up in the loft soon, to search, because Mum would make him, and she must stay awake to scream, but she was so *tired*; and they wouldn't let her go up to feed Donovan, she wasn't going to be able to get up there, and he would be hungry, and he would starve, and she wouldn't be able to find any food for him, and she wouldn't be able to get to him, and he would get thinner, and thinner, and he was waiting for her to come, and hungry, and getting thinner like a skeleton, and she was so tired . . .

She was dreaming, and it was a nightmare, and there was a ghost all in white, with hollow cheeks and narrowed eyes that wouldn't look her in the face, and she tried to make it look at her and it wouldn't. 'Why didn't you come?' it reproached her. And it was *Donovan*. 'He's a ghost,' she screamed. 'He's turned into a ghost!'

256

And she was *really* screaming it, not just in a dream. And there were other voices shouting, not just hers. And the bedroom door was opening, and Dad was pushing Donovan in, and Dad was very, very angry. 'Here's your ghost!' he shouted. And Dad was so angry his face was on fire nearly, and Donovan was looking more frightened than she had ever seen him look before. 'Here he is, you naughty girl!' shouted Dad. 'Naughty, stupid, disobedient little girl! This is your ghost, isn't it!'

Simon woke, and was sleepily delighted. 'It's *Donovan!*' he said, starting to climb out of bed.

'You get back in!' said Dad. 'I forgot about you. Amy, you put on your dressing gown, and come in the front room!'

Mum was in the front room, collapsed on the sofa with legs straight and stiff in front of her, her head twisting from side to side. 'I don't *believe* it,' she chanted, over and over. 'I don't *believe* it.' Her head went faster and faster, and only stopped for a moment to peep at Donovan to reassure herself that he was real. 'That Donald!' she said, changing the words of the chant. 'That Donald up there, all the time!'

'How long?' Dad shouted, shaking Donovan by the shoulder. Donovan shrugged away from Dad, looking at the ground.

'Answer me!'

Donovan swallowed, and bit his lips.

'How long Amy?' said Dad.

Amy counted on her fingers. 'Three days,' she said. 'And a bit more.' Her voice seemed to be coming from far away, as though her voice was in the room, but she wasn't. The far away room was coming and going a bit, as well, and she felt cold, inside the fleecy dressing gown.

'I've a good mind to get the police!' Dad bellowed.

Donovan found his voice. 'It wasn't my fault, *she* made me!'

'What!'

'She made me, right?' said Donovan. 'And that Parrot. They made me do it.

'You see!' thundered Dad. 'You see, Amy? Remember what I said? Remember what I told you? Here he is! Your charmer! Your hero!'

'Well what do you expect?' said Mum. 'Driving him into a corner, poor little perisher! Frightening him half to death! Course he's going to try and throw the blame! Blame the lamp-post if he could, I daresay!'

Dad stared at her. 'I shall never understand women,' he said, marvelling.

'And don't shout at Amy neither,' said Mum. 'She's had enough.'

'She's *done* enough,' said Dad.

'Yeah,' said Mum. 'Never thought she had it in her, did you?' In a way, she sounded quite pleased.

'Never thought she'd be so daft!' said Dad.

'I'm not saying she done *right*.' said Mum. 'I'm not saying *that*.'

'I should hope not!' said Dad.

'She must have had her reasons,' said Mum.

'They must have been daft ones then,' said Dad. 'I'll listen to Amy's daft reasons later. First thing, get shot of – THIS! . . . Where do you live? I mean, where did you live before you lived in our loft?'

'I'm not telling you,' said Donovan.

'He hasn't got a home,' said Amy.

'There you are!' said Mum. 'Poor little perisher!'

'His mum won't have him, and his gran won't have him,' said Amy. 'And he might have to go IN CARE.'

'Best place for him, I should think,' said Dad. 'Police station then. Come on. Now!'

'No!' said Donovan. 'No, don't make me! No! No!' He flung away and turned his back on all of them, his shoulders heaving.

'They won't kill you, you know,' said Dad.

'They'll put me IN CARE.'

'That's not my problem,' said Dad.

'Don't be cruel,' said Mum.

'*Now* what's the matter?' said Dad.

'Turning a homeless child out of the house this time of night?' said Mum. 'No hot food for days? What you got in place of a heart?'

'Give me strength!' said Dad. 'All right, what do *you* think we should do with him? Send him back up in the loft perhaps! Is that your idea? Have some sense, woman!'

'Just till morning,' said Mum.

'She means it!' said Dad.

'And then,' said Mum, 'we can take him to Mr Bassett. *He'll* sort it out. He's a good headmaster, Mr Bassett is, *he'll* know what to do.'

'I give up,' said Dad.

'I'll just go and cook Donald some supper,' said Mum.

Amy had gone quite dead inside. She had felt so much the past few days, and now she couldn't seem to feel anything at all. And she didn't want to.

Miss Elliot twisted and turned in bed. The reports were finished at last. She had stayed up until midnight, working at them, and now she could not get to sleep. She was thinking about Donovan Grant, and wondering where he was, and trying to put together the nagging thoughts that were floating around in the muddle of her mind. There were connections somewhere, if only she could see what they were. Cynthia Garrett, Amy Baker, and Donovan Grant – now why did she want to link those three? Something very recent. Something to do with a book. What book? A *maths* book. Out of Donovan Grant's desk! What did they really want it for?

Miss Elliot's thinking floundered on. The *answer* book was missing. Book Five answer book, she never did find it. And Amy Baker in the classroom that time, with red chalk on her face, and looking poorly for days, and yawning all the time in class. And Amy Baker had a thing about Donovan Grant, everyone knew *that*.

Miss Elliot was getting excited. Could it be, could it be, that she was really *on* to something? Steady now, calm down, what else? 'Cynthia Garrett's up to something. She's brought all food to school.' But Cynthia Garrett had hot school dinners, always, so the food must be for someone else. And she should have listened, she should have thought, but there was always so much to be done, and there was never enough time for thinking. Now though, now there was time . . . Could it be, could it be, that somewhere, somehow . . .?

Step by step, and much too late, Miss Elliot worked it out.

'Is Donovan living with us now?' said Simon, beaming.

260

'No,' said Dad.

'Why isn't Amy saying anything?' said Simon.

'She's thinking how naughty she's been,' said Dad. 'And how silly.'

'Eat up your breakfast,' said Mum. 'We're all going to school in a minute.'

'Will Donovan give me a piggy bank?' said Simon.

'*No!*' said Dad. 'Anyway we're going in the car. You can leave your stuff,' he told Donovan, ''till we see where it's supposed to go.'

Donovan wouldn't look at Amy at all, not even to glance in her direction. Amy thought he might actually be ashamed about trying to blame everything on her last night. But she didn't really care if he was ashamed or not. She was too tired to care.

They trooped down to the hall, and Dad glared at Downstairs to discourage her from spying, but it was too late, of course, she had seen.

Dad opened the bonnet of the car, and fiddled about inside. 'The radiator's leaking,' said Donovan, interested.

'Mind your own business,' said Dad.

They all piled in. The engine started all right, but something was wrong; Dad said a bad word. 'Clutch is gone! I knew it was dicky!'

'My dad can drive without a clutch,' said Donovan.

Dad said a few more bad words.

'I don't like the language in this car,' said Mum. 'Anyway, looks like we got to walk.'

They all piled out. '*Now* can Donovan give me a piggy bank?' said Simon.

'No,' said Dad.

'It's all right you know,' said Donovan, hurt. 'I haven't got anything catching.'

'You walk with your mum,' said Dad to Simon. 'And *you*,' he said to Donovan, 'you keep there, just in front of me, where I can see you.'

Dad and Donovan were in front, and Mum and Simon behind. Amy trailed last; they seemed to have forgotten all about her.

Simon was dragging at Mum's hand, trying to catch up with Donovan. 'I wanna *piggy bank*,' he whined.

'Why can't I give him one?' said Donovan. 'I like little kids.'

'We're not here to play games,' said Dad.

Simon pulled on Mum's hand again, and she gave his arm a sharp jerk. Simon stood mulishly, refusing to go any further. 'Come on, or I'll clip you one,' said Mum.

Simon went on standing still, and a group of big girls, on their way to the High School, passed Mum and Simon on the pavement. They spread across, and Mum was losing sight of Dad and Donovan. Amy stood still behind Mum and Simon, waiting listlessly for Simon to give in. She didn't care much whether they went or stayed; her life was more or less finished anyway.

Mum tried to smack Simon, reaching round her with her free hand to do it, but Simon dodged behind her back. Exasperated, Mum dropped Simon's hand, intending a good smart wallop on the legs – and Simon moved! Free at last, he darted on nimble legs to get to his beloved Donovan. The big girls were in the way, and he couldn't push through them so, in the path of the morning traffic, Simon ran in a big curve; off the pavement, round the girls, and on to the road!

After that, everything happened very quickly. Mum screamed, and Amy screamed too. And Donovan turned round, to see what the screaming was about. And there was a car coming, fast, and much too near the kerb. And then Simon was on the pavement again, where Donovan had thrown him, but Donovan was lying half on the pavement and half in the road, because his foot had slipped when he grabbed Simon, and the car had gone right over it.

Simon bawled loudly. Mum caught up with them about then, and began slapping Simon so hard his shrieks pierced the sky. Amy stood by Donovan, while the world shimmered, and blurred.

The driver of the car stopped. 'What happened?' he said.

'What's it look like, you fool!' said Dad furiously. 'Some people shouldn't be allowed behind a wheel! Go on then, what you waiting for? Get an ambulance can't you, for my boy!'

'Simon's all right,' said Amy, her voice sounding strange and distraught. 'He's only shouting 'cos Mum was belting him.'

'I mean *this* boy,' said Dad. 'Whatsisname. Should have a medal what he did! . . . How is it then, son?'

'It's all right,' said Donovan. Slyly, and hopefully, he peered round at Dad. 'Have you stopped being angry with me? Couldn't you let me off, now I saved Simon?'

'You'll have to go to hospital,' said Dad.

'I don't want to go to hospital,' said Donovan. 'Will the hospital put me IN CARE? I don't want to go. I don't want to go, right? . . . My foot's not bad anyway,' he said, trying to get up. 'It don't hurt much.'

'It will!' said Dad, wincing.

'I wish I never done it,' said Donovan. 'I wish I never saved him, I changed my mind.'

'Shut up,' said Dad. 'Don't you know you're a hero?'

'Let me off then,' said Donovan. 'Let me off, right? I don't want to go IN CARE.'

'It's not up to me,' said Dad. 'I think you're getting it all a bit mixed up. I know one thing though. Anybody says anything about you got *me* to answer to. From now on!'

The world clicked into focus suddenly, and Amy's spirits soared heavenward. A crowd had gathered, to offer praise and sympathy and Amy, who hardly ever cried, found her eyes brimming over. 'He's *my friend*,' she told them all. 'And he's *good*.'

Other great reads ⌇from **Red Fox**

Further Red Fox titles that you might enjoy reading are listed on the following pages. They are available in bookshops or they can be ordered directly from us.

If you would like to order books, please send this form and the money due to:

ARROW BOOKS, BOOKSERVICE BY POST, PO BOX 29, DOUGLAS, ISLE OF MAN, BRITISH ISLES. Please enclose a cheque or postal order made out to Arrow Books Ltd for the amount due, plus 75p per book for postage and packing to a maximum of £7.50, both for orders within the UK. For customers outside the UK, please allow £1.00 per book.

NAME _____

ADDRESS _____

_____

Please print clearly.

Whilst every effort is made to keep prices low, it is sometimes necessary to increase cover prices at short notice. If you are ordering books by post, to save delay it is advisable to phone to confirm the correct price. The number to ring is THE SALES DEPARTMENT 0171 (if outside London) 840 8400.

Other great reads from **Red Fox**

Gripping reads by Ruth Thomas

Guilty

Kate is thrilled by the local burglary until playground gossip points the finger at her friend Desmond's father who has recently come out of prison. Kate and Desmond set out together to discover who really is . . . GUILTY!

ISBN 0 09 918519 1   £2.99

The Runaways
Winner of the Guardian Fiction Award

Teachers and parents are suspicious when Julia and Nathan start flashing around the stash of money they found in a deserted house. There's only one way out – to run away . . .

ISBN 0 09 959660 1   £2.99

The New Boy

Donovan is the new boy in the class – secretive, brooding and mysterious. At first Amy is flattered that he wants her to be his friend – until he pushes the limit of her loyalty to the extreme.

ISBN 0 09 973410 9   £2.99

The Secret

When Mum fails to return from her weekend away, Nicky and Roy resolve not to let on to anyone that their mother has abandoned them.

ISBN 0 09 984000 6   £2.99

The Class that Went Wild

Ever since Mrs Lloyd left to have a baby, Class 4L has been impossible! Sean and the gang just get rowdier and rowdier, and even Gillian's twin brother Joseph joins in. Gillian tries to save the situation, but then Joseph goes missing . . .

ISBN 0 09 963210 1   £2.99